A Seasons Novel

KATE SMOAK

DEDICATION

To every girl who's had their heart broken,
had their feelings dismissed by friends and family,
only to find their true love in the end.

– Kate Smoak

CONTENT WARNING

Scenes of graphic sexual content
Consumption of alcohol
Getting date-rape drugged.

PROLOGUE

LEXI

I'm nervous.

I'm meeting Brandt's friends tonight.

This is a big thing for us. I feel like he's hidden me for the last couple of weeks.

I'm not sure what tonight means, but it must be good. Right?

I shake off the nerves as I stand wrapped in a soft grey towel twisted around my thin frame, facing my wardrobe options for tonight. *What should I wear?* There's barely any thing nice enough for tonight's occasion. I know we're just going to a pub, but all my clothes are leggings and sports bras—minus a few items that are too fancy for a pub. I pull out a pair of black lululemon leggings that fit me like a second skin; they're a little shimmery, so they're my fancy pair. I find a flowing long sleeve tee that has a deep V-neck line that shows off just a smidge of cleavage.

I fluff my platinum-blonde hair with the darker roots starting to show, and it falls around my shoulders. I grab my perfume and dab some on the back of my neck so that every time I move my head, my hair will gently breeze my scent, intoxicating Brandt.

Nerves strangle me as I pull on my clothes, feeling woefully underdressed.

Fuck it, he likes you just the way you are. Any man would be lucky to be seen with you, sports leggings and all. And I even have the classy ones on. So, there.

The ding from my phone breaks my thoughts.

Brandt: *I'll be there in a few seconds.*

My inner voice's argument falls flat against the crashing waves of anxiety inside me. It doesn't take Brandt long to get to my apartment. My hands tremble as I smooth down my top when there's a knock at the door. We share the same building. I'm a few floors lower than him, as he's in one of the penthouse levels.

My shiny black heels clack against the hardwood as I make my way to the front door, my heart racing in my chest. When I reach the door, I clasp my hand over my pounding heart and take a cleansing, steadying breath. I'm so excited but so nervous. I hope they like me. Hell, I hope I like them because friends can make or break a relationship, and I've waited for Brandt for the last two years.

My small hands wrap around the brass door handle, and I tug on the door, and there he is. Golden-brown hair swooped to the side, so nice and neat that it makes my fingers ache to dig into the perfect mould and break it. His frame is imposing and towers over me from his six feet, one inch to my five feet, four inches, with his broad shoulders expertly defined even underneath his jacket, which hangs open. My eyes glide over his body and see the black form-fitting tee underneath that clings to his torso, and I can picture his delicious washboard abs perfectly, just like how I've seen them before in the building's gym.

His emerald eyes lock on to mine, and I melt on the spot. Heat coils in my stomach, and my clit throbs. I want this man so badly, I'm almost tempted to delay our plans to fit a quickie in, but this is a huge step for us. Me meeting his friends. It says "commitment," no? Or am I just fooling myself? I've been head over heels for this guy since I moved into the building three years ago, just after a long relationship ended. But I've been panting after Brandt for the last two years, trying to convince him to go out with me. I don't know what changed, but he finally relented.

"Hey. You look beautiful." His voice is a low, gentle tone that wraps me up in a warm blanket. I fight the urge to roll my eyes into the back of my head at the sound. He's truly perfect.

"You're not looking too bad yourself," I quip. He steps forward slightly, placing a firm hand on the small of my back, pulling me in to place a gentle kiss on my temple. My heart flutters in my chest, and a breath catches in my throat. I roll my shoulders back and flick my hair over my shoulder as I step out of his embrace and grab a jacket hanging by the door. "Are you ready to go?"

He nods, and as I step through the threshold of the door, his hand closes my door behind me, taking my keys from my hands and locking the door, just like the gentleman he is. Brandt's hand finds my lower back again and guides me down the long hallway towards the elevator. *God, this man is swoon worthy.* Ripples of anticipation grip my heart as we near the elevator.

• • •

When we arrive at the pub, the anxiety that had a hold on me earlier increases tenfold. When we step inside, his friends flag us down from across the room. A tall man with dark-black hair stands as he waves us over, a stupid grin on his face.

My skin prickles as we near, and I feel a suffocating heat seep into me. Piercing grey eyes level on me, and something resembling fear grapples at me, squeezing my heart. I can't look away; he's like a predator with me caught in his trap. His lips curve into a faint smirk, and my heart skips a beat. *What's going on?* All the tiny hairs on my body stand at attention as a wave of uneasiness settles into me. If I thought I was scared before, I'm petrified now.

Mr. Grey Eyes doesn't break his gaze from mine until Brandt whispers something in my ear and I'm able to tear my eyes away. Not hearing what he said, I smile at him and play coy. My eyes dart to the side and his eyes are still on me. I lose my senses and forget how to breathe. This behemoth of a man is all solid muscle, broad shoulders, smouldering features, and a strong, sharp jaw. His caramel hair is shorn at the sides and just enough on the top that you could tangle your fingers into and pull. *Woah, where did that come from?* I feel the heat rise to my cheeks, and I nervously bite the inside of my cheek.

Brandt tugs me into his side, breaking my thoughts, and I smile up at him innocently. Our eyes connect, and I'm set at ease when his lips smile back at me. When I look into his eyes, I feel calm. One of his friends clears his throat, and I turn my attention to see who it was.

The one standing with dark hair stretches out a hand, and his voice is deep but loud as it carries across the crowded, noisy pub.

"The name's Rhys Kessler. It's nice to finally meet you, Lexi." I offer up a small smile and slip my hand in his, shaking it firmly.

"It's nice to meet you as well," I chime. And it is. I know from my conversations with Brandt that Rhys is his best friend. Which would make the other guy...

"Liam." His voice reverberates to my core, setting everything inside me alight. Everything drowns out the minute he speaks. I can't even hear one of my favourite songs that was playing when we entered: *Nonsense* by Sabrina Carpenter. Everything hushes, and for a minute, it's only Liam's voice I hear. My pulse races, and a twist in my stomach makes me feel like I'm going to be sick. This feeling towards him is visceral, and it scares me. He stands, and he's not nearly as tall as the other two. If I had to guess, he'd be about six feet, so he still towers over me. *Where the hell do these guys grow?*

Comparing Rhys and Liam to Brandt, they're all fairly similar in stature, each one an inch taller than the other. But the muscles on these guys are thick and bulky. Like they're all linebackers for the University of Toronto, and that's when I notice a class ring from UOT on Liam's outstretched hand, waiting for mine. I pause a moment longer than necessary before placing my hand in his, and before we touch, I swear a spark flickers between us, sending electricity shooting up my arm and down my spine. His warmth eclipses my hand, and it takes everything I have to stifle the audible gasp.

A knowing smirk paints his face, and I'm left wondering what the hell is so amusing. When he releases my hand, it shoots to my side and I rub it against my hip, effectively rubbing him off of me. Rhys and Liam sit back down, and Brandt pulls a chair out for me. Taking my seat, I glance up at him and say a soft "thank you," and I feel Liam's grey eyes still on me, leaving me feeling unsettled. A creeping, burning-hot flush crosses my chest and up to my ears as I shrug off my jacket, trying to make myself comfortable. *I have a feeling this is going to be a long night...*

CHAPTER

ONE

A Year and a half later…

LEXI

It's been almost a year and a half since Brandt broke up with me to go back to Elissa, but it still hurts.

I haven't been able to move on. I fell hard for that man and ended up with my heart shattered on the floor of my apartment. I truly thought he'd be the one. Hell, I still think he is; he's just someone else's *one.* The hardest thing about this? I'm happy for him. I'm glad he's happy and in love and things are working out well for him. It just sucks because it's not with me. I've gone on plenty of dates since then, but nothing or no one holds my attention. They're all fuckboys and good for one thing: fucking.

I think back to the last time I had hope. It was when I met Brandt's friends for the first time. Overall, the entire night went well. I got along with his friends, and at the end of the night, when we had some wild sex, I thought it meant something. Thought that we were headed somewhere because you don't just let anyone meet your close relations like best friends and family. At least, I wouldn't.

"Lex." My friend Abby's voice pulls me from my thoughts. I shake it off, and the crowd of the pub comes rushing in. The same pub I met his friends. There's a small dance section in the centre of the room near the bar area where people are making out and swaying to the music. My friends and I are crowded around a table, resisting the urge to move because there's no other tables left. We all take turns going to the bar and ordering rounds of drinks.

Abby elbows a sharp blow to my ribs, and I turn and shoot her a death glare. "What the fuck was that for?" I ask, wishing my words had venom in them.

"Girl, you keep going in and out. We're trying to have fun here. Fucking lighten up." She's the only one who talks like this to me, or anyone. There's something about her that is unapologetically rude, but I love it. There's no sugar-coating things, and she calls you out on your bullshit. "You were thinking of *him* again, weren't you?"

I squirm, avoiding another blow from her elbow, and I feel the tinge of pink on my cheeks.

"I can't help it, Abby. I fucking love him. And it doesn't help that I had him make plans at this pub where we go all the time. I was fucking stupid."

Lillian snorts. I turn my glare on her next. Her hand runs through her blonde pixie cut. Her bright blue eyes level with mine, and she shrugs when I ask her what the snort meant.

"Nothing, okay. I just mean, you couldn't have loved him after that short time together."

Anger rolls off my skin like steam. "Oh, I couldn't, could I? Coming from the haughty bitch who can't stand a guy longer than ten minutes or as long as it takes to orgasm? So, yes. Please tell me how love works." Fuck, I know that was rude, but I'm sick of her holier-than-thou attitude. I love her, but she can be a major bitch. Her face is cold, and her eyes are void of any emotion. She's like an automaton; nothing affects her. A second later, and a twitch of her lips means I need to tread carefully these next words. We stare at each other from across the table, both of us in a silent stare off, and the tension is palpable. I can feel the nerves vibrating between Abby and Henry, and it grates on my nerves.

"Guys, *please*," Abby pleads with us, her eyes darting between the two of us, and her voice instantly breaks the tension. Lillian whips her invisible hair and transitions it into a neck roll, stretching out her fire. Henry is looking at Abby gratefully and with a side of something else in his eyes. Pride? Admiration? No, it's something more…

"*Anyway,*" I say. "Tell me about your weeks…I feel like we haven't talked in such a long time." Lillian scoffs and rolls her eyes but stays silent.

"We literally talk every day in our group chat, dork," Abby retorts. I roll my eyes at her.

"Yeah, but that's just memes and shit. We hardly get together anymore and talk over a good beer. So let's go. I want to hear aaaaall about your week. Starting with you, Abs."

Her cheeks tinge violet-red, and her eyes shuffle slightly to the side towards Henry, and he seems tense but doesn't react. *Okay?*

"Oh, n-nothing much. Just work and stuff. Boring stuff. Like supes boring." She tries to dismiss the question. Something is definitely off.

"Oooohkay. So how is work then? How did the trial go?" I ask. Her demeanour instantly changes. Her shoulders square up, she's rigid, and a cold front rolls off of her. Abby's brows crease and her face hardens. Abby is a business and employment lawyer. She's one of the top ones in Toronto, but still has yet to make partner at her firm.

"It went well. As well as it could have gone, I suppose. I'm representing a client that's fired an employee for embezzlement, but the employee is claiming wrongful dismissal, and they have a bunch of documentation that proves some of their claims, but it doesn't negate the embezzlement. It's just a gigantic clusterfuck. We're only in discovery and it's just...ugh. I need another drink," she says, sliding her ass off the chair and stomping over to the bar to order another round.

Henry's head turns and his eyes follow her, his eyes swimming with worry. His reaction to her piques my interest. *Is something going on between them? Typically, they can't stand each other.* Something has changed between

Henry and Abby in the last few weeks. There's been less bickering, and now, seeing the way he looks at her, I'd say there's definitely something going on between the two. Henry's head turns back to face me, and his cheeks drain of colour as my eyebrows raise in question. He glances away quickly, bringing his beer up to his mouth, tipping it back, and draining the rest of its contents.

"I, uh…I'm going to help Abby with those drinks," he says, his voice raising an octave. He slides from the booth side of the table and takes after Abby, walking a little too fast. *Oh yeah, something is definitely going on between them.* Lillian is oblivious to what's going on around us as she makes googly eyes at a guy from across the room. Her body stretches a little straighter as she tugs the hem of her shirt down, revealing a bit more of her cleavage. I notice the guy nodding his head to her, and she places a hand on my shoulder and talks close to my ear.

"I'll be back. *Maybe.*" Lillian grabs her drink and saunters over to the guy. He's hard to make out, but he seems tall from how his feet touch the floor from the barstool. He has spiked dark hair, and stubble peppering his face. The guy's definitely good looking, I'll give him that. I keep my eyes trained on them because, hell, I'm all alone at this moment. His hand caresses her thigh and slides up slowly until it's on her ass, and his giant hand squeezes her cheek. Her hand draws loopy patterns on his muscular arms, and she leans in close, just enough for her chest to dip, and I watch his eyes dart downward.

I scoff to myself and change my focus to Henry and Abby at the bar. They still haven't come back over, but

Abby looks pissed off, and they're arguing over something. I'm trying to read lips from over five feet away, and I feel like Henry just mouthed "tell them," but I could totally be wrong. I'm fully engrossed in their actions and trying to read their lips from here when someone plops into the seat across from me and breaks my attention.

"Hey there," his low, rumbly voice says. I turn to look at him, and heat pools in my core. This man is handsome in a way that he knows it as well. He's perfectly groomed: neat hair, perfect teeth, flawless eyebrows, respectably trimmed beard. His hands dwarf the tumbler in his grip that's filled with amber liquid. My eyes skate over his expansive build, shoulders, chest, and I can imagine the ripples of muscles on his torso. His lips curl at the corners as I check him out, he's no doubt checking me out as well as I feel his eyes roam my body in return. *He would make an excellent distraction for the night.*

"Lexi," I say, tipping my bottle towards him in a salute. He mimics my gesture, beaming a one hundred-watt smile at me, and my centre below warms.

"Kyle." His voice settles between us, leaving a small pregnant pause, seeing who will break first.

I win.

"I saw you here with your friends. Glad they decided to vanish, so I'd get a chance to talk to you. I didn't want to leave a beautiful woman like yourself all alone." I choke back a laugh as I sip my beer. What a line.

"Oh?" I say, playing coy. "Well, what a knight in shining armour you are. Rescuing little ol' me from the conundrum of sitting all alone." His smirk grows into a shit-eating grin as he takes a pull of his whisky with a dark chuckle.

"Kitty's got claws. I like claws. Especially digging into my back." My clit throbs at the insinuation, and visions of what he might be able to do to me with me on my back excites me in a way that I haven't felt in a while. The fact that he's so direct makes it even better. There's no guessing what this is. A plain and simple hookup, and I could use one.

I down the rest of my beer, and his eyes settle on my throat as I drink. My tongue flicks against my lips, and his blue eyes darken with lust. The corners of my mouth curl into a seductive smile.

"Want me to show you what these claws can do?" I place my bottle on the table and loop my purse over my shoulder, and Kyle's eyes widen slightly in shock, probably that I'm so direct as well. I stand and start to sway my hips as I walk a few steps before I throw my head over my shoulder and raise an eyebrow. "You coming?" He leans, taking his phone out of his pocket, tapping a quick message to someone who I assume is one of his buddies at the bar with him. He stands, struts over to me, wrapping his corded arms around my waist, and leads me out the door of the pub.

CHAPTER
TWO

LEXI

A loud, rumbling snore rips through the room, and I startle awake. Sitting up, I squint as I look around the room and notice Kyle beside me, mouth open and drooling on the pillow. I go to move and realize his heavy arm is draped across my waist, holding me down and making it hard for me to escape.

I blink the sleep from my eyes and look around the plain, but messy room. It definitely screams bachelor, and I guess I overlooked it a bit too much when we got back to his place. Clothes are piled in the corner of the room as well as on top of the dresser, and that's when I notice the gym-like musk of his room. There are random half-empty water bottles littered around the room, and a cracked alarm clock sits on the bedside table.

I shift my weight on the bed carefully as I slip from under Kyle's arm. A snort breaks the silence in the room, and he stirs, withdrawing his arm from my waist. I freeze and let go of the breath I'm holding when he settles and continues snoring softly. I slide off the bed and tiptoe around his room, collecting my clothes and gathering them in a heap in my arms and sneak out his bedroom door without trying to creak the hardwood floor.

I tug my shirt over my head and slip into my pants as quickly as I can before he wakes. I never intended to crash here, but I guess slipping out in the morning undetected is better than the awkward *thanks again for the fuck* and leaving right after. I'm so out of practice with this walk of shame. It's been a while since I've done it.

My heart sinks in my chest at the thought of Brandt. I really thought there was something there between us. I'd been chasing after him since I moved into his apartment complex. I truly thought he could have been the one, but how could he be when his heart already belonged to someone else? My constant struggle to be happy for him sometimes clashes with the broken heart I'm still recovering from. Knowing that his love for Elissa outshines anything we could've had makes it a bitter pill to swallow, but I'm happy he's found his happily ever after. Even if it wasn't with me.

I shake the depressing thoughts away as I escape from Kyle's apartment and down the long stretch of hallway to the elevator. The glow of the button gives me anxiety as I wait for the doors to crank open. I toss my hair and look over my shoulder towards his apartment and pray the elevator hurries. I don't think he's the type of guy to make things awkward and look for me after I sneak out. But who knows? Lately, it seems like these days I'm wrong about all sorts of things.

• • •

It's about a half-hour subway ride back to my apartment, and my stomach growls at me. My face heats as I look around the car and wonder if anyone else heard the loud rumble. But no one flinches or looks my way. The train is already packed with commuters, and it's only 6 AM. Most of them lost in their own digital worlds or reading the *Toronto Star*. I relax into my seat a little, allowing my nerves and anxiety to wash away with each swift motion of the car. My eyes slowly drift, and it seems like no time has passed as I'm waking up to the electronic bell dinging and a robotic woman's voice over the speaker, letting me know we've reached my stop. I hustle off the car with a handful of other people, pushing through the small crowd that gathers to get into the subway car. Muttering my *excuse me*'s, I continue past them and rush up the stairs into the terminal.

When I finally make it to my apartment building, I stand in front of the doors, staring up at the tall skyscraper, and a small bit of sadness washes over me. I'm only here for a few more weeks. I decided to move out when I heard Elissa was moving in with Brandt. I know I shouldn't have to leave, but it's too hard on me to stay. Not that Brandt and I were soulmates, or that we dated very long, but my feelings were so strong for him and it tore me apart. I need to move on, and it's hard to do that when I bump into them every so often. I really loved this place, but my new apartment has charm.

I'm ripped from my thoughts as my phone bleeps, playing the most annoying ringtone that I set as my alarm. I sigh. I only have an hour to get ready and head to the studio. I shuffle into the building and head towards the elevator to make my way to my apartment. Once there, I hop into the shower, taking a quick one so that I have time to get to work. If the subway was any indication, this morning is going to be busy on the train, and it's a Saturday.

Most people probably think I'm nuts. I own my own business, and I make sure my studio is open at 7:30 AM on a Saturday and Sunday. But you know what? I'm not the only crazy one. My classes are full every weekend with people in them, ready to work out and sweat. And 7:30 AM is late for us fitness fanatics. My Monday to Friday classes all start at 6 AM, so today is really a treat for us to sleep in. My stomach growls again, and I quickly toss some workout clothes on before heading to the kitchen and blending up a quick smoothie.

As I'm pouring my green blend into the cup, my phone dings and I see the group chat notification. It's Abby wondering how my night went with Kyle. I roll my eyes and shoot a message back.

Me: *It was alright. He was nice enough.*

And I mean it. He at least made sure I came before he did. So that was…refreshing?

Abby: *Think you'll see him again?*

As I go to type my reply, a snarky comment from Lillian comes in, and I can practically hear her snorting her response.

Lill: *She said he was "nice enough," Abs. No, she won't see him again.*

I roll my eyes at her response, but she's not wrong.

Me: *Besides, I practically ghosted him. I just left this morning while he was sleeping and didn't leave my number. So I doubt I'll be seeing him again.*

I can't help but feel a twinge of guilt over how I just slipped out this morning. If it were me, I'd be a little self-conscious. But then again, he's probably not going to lose any sleep over it. But there's a part of me that's proud of myself for getting out there again and trying to move on. It's been a year and a half, and I've been celibate for far too long.

The chat dings a bunch more times and I turn off my ringer as I finish getting ready for work. I'm back in the bathroom, and my phone buzzes on the granite bathroom counter as I swipe some mascara over my lashes. I don't put too much effort into my makeup on the days I work, which is practically every day, but I need a smidge of mascara to make me feel complete. It's like putting on a shield or a temporary mask, something like putting on a brave face, strengthening myself. Fuck it, it just makes me feel better about myself. I stop in front of the mirror in my hallway before leaving, taking one last look at myself, ruffling my hair before heading out the door. Making sure my phone is in my leggings pocket, I grab my mini duffle bag, my smoothie, and head out the door.

• • •

I finally reach the studio with about five minutes to spare. There's a handful of people gathered outside the door waiting for me to open up. I give each one a *hello* and make my way to the door, unlocking it for all of us to get in and get ready for this morning's spin class. I head inside first and turn on all the lights and put my stuff away so I can go around the studio and water the plants. My studio has a very earthy, holistic vibe to it. I wanted it to be calm and serene—an escape for people or a place they can go to relax while staying fit and healthy.

I wasn't always into fitness, but it slowly became an addiction of sorts. When I was growing up, I was always on the heavier side. I wasn't terribly overweight per se, but I wasn't exactly healthy either. In college, I found my love of fitness—yoga and spinning to be more exact—and it became like this high I needed to seek. The adrenaline I had coursing through my body after working out helped ease the tension in my mind and felt like it put my soul to rest. So I changed my major from accounting (boring) to kinesiology, and my passion for it kind of just spiralled from there. Now, five years after graduation, I have a thriving studio where I can share and engage in my passion with the community.

As everyone gets settled and chooses a stationary bike, I make my way to the front of the class, connecting my phone through Bluetooth to the speaker system, selecting a playlist that gets my blood pumping. As I mount my bike and get ready to start the class's warm-up, a straggler hurries through the door, dropping his bag in the corner of the room, and rushes over to the last available bike in the back. He looks up at me, and when our eyes lock, my heart starts racing. There's something familiar about him, and I freeze, trying to place him from somewhere. *I swear I know this man.* A shiver runs down my spine, and I break the contact, grab the microphone headset off my bike, place it around my head, and start the class. But before I even start pedalling, my Apple Watch tells me my heart rate is already racing, and I feel a slight panic rising through my body. I hazard a glance at the gorgeous man who just walked in, and his eyes are still locked on me, and my stomach flips.

CHAPTER

THREE

LEXI

The rest of the class I spent avoiding this man's gaze. I know his eyes were on me the whole time, but I tell myself that's the point. I'm the instructor. Where else is he supposed to look?

But there's something different about the way I feel up on the bike leading the class today. Like something is burning under my skin, setting me on fire. The sensation is distracting and making me feel like I've forgotten how to run the damn class. One of my regulars, Rachel, who sits up at the front of every class, whispers to me each time when we need to switch gears.

I feel like a complete idiot, a fraud. It's like someone snatched my body today and left a brainless moron inside. I try to brush it off. Try to blame last night for this awful class I'm running, but my head and conscience just aren't agreeing. There's something nagging at me about the guy in the back row, his intense stare and focus, how his eyes never leave me, the strange humidity suddenly clogging the air.

"Everything okay, Lexi?" Rachel says as she approaches me on my bike in the front of the class. Small droplets of sweat trickle down from her hairline as she grabs the towel from her shoulder and swipes it away. The room feels stifling and thick as I breathe. Catching my breath, I nod my head.

"Yeah, yeah. Just a long…night."

She gives me a knowing look, and the corners of her mouth curl. "Ohhh, juicy. I want to hear all the deets," she says, but then her watch dings, and she looks down and frowns. "Unfortunately, it's going to have to wait…" her voice fades from my focus as my eyes drift off to the spot where the man is still on his bike, absentmindedly pedalling while he taps on his phone and takes a swig of his water bottle. The roll of his Adam's apple as he swallows slows down, and my mouth runs dry. The hairs prickle on the back of my neck, and suddenly a hand waves in front of my face, pulling me out of my trance. I shake it off and tear my eyes away to look back at Rachel.

"Earth to Lexi!" she jokes and tosses a glance over her shoulder to where I was looking. A heat rises to my cheeks, and a salacious grin spreads across her face. "Oh. Yummy. I forgive you for your…distraction." She chuckles, turning her attention back to me, and wiggles her fingers, saying that she'll see me tomorrow for the yoga class. As Rachel walks away, I spin on my heel before he catches me staring, and I wipe down my bike. Moments later, when the room quiets down and I think everyone is finally gone, footsteps make their way towards me, and I feel every muscle in my body tense.

A deep rumble comes from behind me, like someone clearing their throat. "Erm, Lexi?" The deep voice is melodic and slips against my skin like silk. Goosebumps pepper my skin, although I feel like I'm boiling from the inside out. I suck in a deep breath and turn around, plastering a nervous smile on my face, hoping that it doesn't look like it. Up close, he seems taller than I thought he'd be. He's maybe a foot taller than me, and when our eyes connect, I am met with stormy grey eyes.

"Uh…Yes, that's me. Lexi," I stammer, like an absolute idiot. My eyes drop to his lips briefly as I see them twitch.

"I didn't know you worked here?" *I'm sorry, but who is this guy? I know he looks familiar, but he's acting like he knows me.* He must see the confusion on my face because he says, "I'm sorry. You probably don't remember me. I'm Liam West, a friend of Brandt's." And for the second time this hour, my mouth runs dry.

I'm staring at Liam like a wide-eyed idiot. My lips part slightly as I struggle with the words to say. He shifts his weight, waiting for me to say something—anything—but furrows his brows when I come up silent. His hand runs through his damp caramel hair, and he shakes his head, scoffing.

"Well, it was nice seeing you again too." His words drip with sarcasm, and I still struggle to say something. He turns and stalks away, grabbing his bag from the floor and walks out of the classroom. When I hear the front entrance bell ring, I wince and release a shaky breath.

It can't be just a coincidence that he showed up here. This is some sick, twisted game, right? There's no way that Liam would come here just to…what? Remind me of Brandt? I mean, it's been a year and a half, it's got to be a coincidence.

I hear Lillian's voice swirling through my head: "*You need to get over yourself and move on. There's no way you loved him after a few weeks.*" Yeah, I know this. But it's not that easy. I pined after that man for two years, and I finally had him, and he slipped through my grasp. And maybe that's what hurts the most. Maybe I didn't really love him, who knows? But it sure hurts like I did.

CHAPTER

FOUR

Liam

It was a complete coincidence that I signed up for some spin classes at Yoga and Cycle. It's right around the corner from my firm on Dundas and Bay Street, so I figured it was an easy way to get some exercise in the mornings and in between meetings. Never did I expect to run into Lexi. I knew she did something with fitness, but I didn't know it was that particular one. Honestly, the thought of walking into her studio makes me chuckle. Like out of all the places in downtown Toronto, I pick hers. Brandt's ex.

I've only met her once, and she was nice enough. Gorgeous, funny, and all that. But when I walked into the class and saw her, something in the room changed, like all the air had evaporated from the room. When my eyes settled on her, I couldn't help but notice how gorgeous she really is, and she wasn't even trying. The subtle hints of makeup, her blonde hair twisted into a bun on the top of her head… It was hard to tear my eyes away from her. One, because she is so damn gorgeous. And two, because I still couldn't believe the fact that I stumbled upon her gym.

As I make my way over to her to say hi, something underneath my skin hums. She spins on her heel, and it feels like she's deliberately ignoring me. Like I've done something to cause this tension. She's got a wipe and is furiously scrubbing her bike, and when I clear my throat to get her attention, I swear I see her pause briefly but continue cleaning as if she didn't hear me. Slightly irritated by being ignored, my voice comes out a little harsher than I'd have liked.

"Erm, Lexi?"

When she spins around, it seems like it's in slow motion. My heart beat slows, and my breathing stalls as our eyes connect. I knew she was gorgeous, but being so close to her? It's…I don't know. The last time I saw her was in a dim pub, so seeing her in all this light is…different. I see the flecks of amber and brown around her pupils to the hazy green.

"Uh…Yes, that's me. Lexi." Her tongue stumbles over her words. But her voice is sweet, like strawberries dipped in chocolate, and my eyes drift to her lips as she speaks, and my brain wanders off wondering if they taste like fucking strawberries too. I snap out of these thoughts quickly, re-composing myself. *She's Brandt's ex. Fuck off.*

"I didn't know you worked here?" Her brows pinch together, and her eyes are unsure as they study me, as if she doesn't know who I am. "I'm sorry. You probably don't remember me. I'm Liam West, a friend of Brandt's." All the confusion is washed away from her face at the mention of Brandt. Her hazel eyes widen in surprise, or is it distrust? I'm not sure, but I don't like the feeling that slithers under my skin when she looks at me like that.

She leaves the air silent between us, not offering anything in return. My irritation grows. *I thought she was nice and sweet? That's what Brandt always said about her.* But all I get is the silent treatment. I quickly glance around the room, finally noticing all the plants that live here, giving her another moment to collect whatever the hell is running through her head. When I look back at her and she's still just staring at me like I'm some sort of fucking ghost, my irritation is now a simmering anger. I run my hands through my hair, trying to calm myself down for a moment before I say something rude.

"Well, it was nice seeing you again too." Shocking myself with those words because I wasn't expecting it to be so pleasant. Without another glance at her, I stomp away, gather my things, and leave. I burst out of the studio, accidentally letting my control slip and taking my anger out on her door. *Why the fuck am I so irrational right now?*

Usually I'm pretty level-headed, or most of the time. I have to be, especially when I manage investment portfolios. I have to be able to keep my cool because one wrong emotional crack leads to a mistake or a poorly made decision. But there's something about Lexi right now that just has me boiling over. There's something suffocating about the one-sided exchange, and I had to get out of there.

As I walk down Dundas back towards my office where I plan on taking a shower and washing off this horrible start to my morning, I resolve to try to not let this get to me any longer. Which, why would it get to me? It's not like I really know her. I feel like a bobblehead as I walk down the road, my head shaking the anger away. With my bag slung over my shoulder, I navigate past the walking commuters, twisting my body, trying to avoid bumping into them with my bag.

When I get to my office building, I take the elevator up to the thirtieth floor and head straight to the washroom, which is complete with a locker room and showers. A lot of the staff work around the clock here, so when they renovated the floor a few years ago, the owner of the firm decided to add locker rooms. A nice convenience for us, and selfish for them. Russell Jade and Daniel Moores, the firm's owners and principal partners, have ensured the utmost comfort for their employees. Almost making it so none of us ever need to leave the office for anything. The common area is equipped with a food buffet every day, complete with fresh coffee and tea, locker rooms for staying fresh, and every office is equipped with a couch that is comfier than most beds. My office is no exception.

I've been with the company since before graduation, when I worked as an intern with no pay, from sunrise to sunset most days. I worked my ass off to get this office. It's a giant corner office with floor-to-ceiling windows on the two walls, and I get an incredible panoramic view of downtown Toronto. I feel like a God from up here. The space is complete with a sturdy mahogany desk that sits in the centre of the room, making me the sole focus, with some leather chairs opposite of where I sit. Beside the door, the comfiest leather couch stands against the wall; it reclines and everything. It's amazing. I've slept countless nights on that thing, thus fulfilling my bosses' evil-genius plan.

I grab the shower bag and a spare suit from the closet in my office, and I head towards the locker room to shower and get ready for the day. But something in the back of my mind nags at me because of the interaction with Lexi. I'm not sure why it's bugging me this much. If I were a smarter, more frivolous man, I'd never go back to her classes again. But I've paid for twelve weeks of classes, and fuck if I'm going to let good money go down the drain. I invest for a living, and I don't enjoy wasting cash. A small part of me enjoys seeing the abundance of zeroes in my account. Growing up in a small town with a family that lived pay cheque to pay cheque, I've made a habit of saving everything I have and spending wisely. Sure, I splurge on things I don't need. Who doesn't?

My fingers dig into my scalp as the scalding water plinks off my body, and I try to think of anything that doesn't bring my mind back to Lexi. I just don't understand why she stared at me like that. Like I was the one who did something terrible to her, like dumping her. Yeah, so I'm friends with Brandt. But she didn't have to act like it was such a terrible thing that I was there. Frustration bubbles inside me as I try to work out why her attitude is bugging me so much. Clearly my mind fails my attempts to think of other things.

I finish washing up, step out of the shower, and wrap a plush white towel around my waist and walk over to the sink and mirror. I push my hands through my hair like a comb, pushing it off to the one side, then grab my extra toothbrush and quickly scrub my teeth before getting dressed and heading back to my office.

As I walk down the hallway, I try to focus on my upcoming meetings for the day, but my mind keeps wandering back to the obnoxious blonde from this morning. Ugh. My mind tosses back and forth the idea of never stepping foot in that place again, but there's a small part of me that wants to go back now just to bother her. To see if I can make her squirm.

I just might do that.

CHAPTER
FIVE

Liam

It's a few days before I decide to return to the gym. Not for anything other than a few early morning meetings, but the perk that she might think that I won't show up again kind of makes me giddy. Because she would be wrong.

I sneak into the back of the class a minute before it's about to start, and she's climbing onto the platform, mounting her bike. Her shoulders raise as she draws in a breath and plasters a wide smile on her face as she looks around the room and greets everyone. As her eyes slide across the murmuring room, her eyes find mine, and her whole body stiffens, and the tension radiates over here.

Her eyes widen, and her smile tightens and drops a little. I feel a smirk tug at my lips, and just because I can, I wink at her.

A few beats later, she shakes off the shock. She presses something on her watch, and music pours out of the speakers mounted on the wall. She composes herself, locks her feet into the pedals, and her knuckles turn white from gripping the handles. Rosy splashes of colour tint her skin, radiating from her face down to the hem of her tank top, to where her cleavage just peaks out. My eyes linger on the swell of her breasts, and my mouth salivates as my mind wonders if her nipples match the pink that tinges her, or are they more of a dusty rose? My cock twitches against my thigh as I lock my feet into the pedals. I release a measured breath, an attempt to calm my libido.

"Morning everyone." Lexi's dulcet voice dances across the room, and something inside me stirs. Like waking me up from a long nap. Her eyes crinkle softly as she takes another look around the room, but her gaze never lands on mine. *Is she avoiding me?* Over the next forty-five minutes, every time her eyes flit around the room, it never once stops on me. My jaw is pulsing and aching from how hard I'm grinding down. The beads of sweat that roll down my skin, the blood pumping in my veins, the stifling heat of the room does nothing to help my rising level of irritation. My feet spin faster, trying to outpace the flurry of negativity and angry thoughts swirling around in my head.

Why. The. Fuck. Is. This. Bothering. Me.

With every harsh breath, I repeat these words in my head over and over.

Nearing the end of class, during the cooldown, she slips up. Her golden eyes lock on to mine, and I swear I see her pupils dilate and her breath catching. *Victory.* But my celebration is cut short when she suddenly jumps off her bike, mutters a quick goodbye, and dashes out of the class. A ripple of chatter follows her exit, and no one seems to notice anything off about her departure. I flick my wrist and look at my Patek Philippe watch making sure I have time before I need to head into the office, because if she thinks she can escape me that easily, she's mistaken.

It takes a torturous twenty minutes for the room to clear out, and I look and feel like a loser hanging by myself in the back of the room, but close to the door. Mindlessly scrolling through stocks while waiting for everyone to fucking leave. I know she has to come back in here before her next class and disinfect all the bikes, so I just have to wait long enough until she thinks everyone is gone and then she'll come back in. Unless…Shit. *Is there a camera in here?* My eyes dart around the corners of the room to make sure there are none. I let out a sigh of relief.

It's not much longer of a wait. My mouth quirks when I hear footsteps and humming approaching. I straighten my posture and let the smirk sprawl across my face. She enters the room, distracted. Her fingers pounding into the screen, typing furiously.

"I'd hate to be your phone the way you're pounding on it," I say. She halts. Fumbling her phone, a high-pitched shriek cuts me off. Her chest is heaving, and she's clutching her phone for dear life. Chuckling, I continue, "Well, I might like it. Just a little bit." I flash her a sly grin and crimson rises from her core and spreads over her face until it reaches the burning tips of her ears. Watching the colour seep sends a jolt to my crotch. I bite back a grin fighting to come through. Her vibrant hazel eyes are wide, but they narrow as they settle on mine.

"What the fuck?" she hisses. "You can't just lurk in a corner of a room and spring yourself on some unsuspecting person." Her words earn a small chuckle from me, tilting up the corners of my lips. "Wipe that look off your face," she bites, crossing her hands across her chest, locking them into place. I raise my hands and turn my gaze from her, showing submission.

"That wasn't my intention, I assure you. I just wanted to talk, and the only way it seemed it was going to happen was if I waited around until everyone left. The way you bolted from the room after class made me think you don't want to talk to me."

She huffs, rolling her eyes. "Well, if you knew that I didn't want to talk, why did you stick around? Clearly I'm avoiding you."

A sliver of shock ripples on my face, but I quickly compose myself. "Okay...So, you *are* avoiding me. Why?"

Lexi's eyes pinch together as her head tilts ever so slightly. I can hear the gears grinding in her head like she's trying to figure out what to say, or she's somehow confused. Her eyes flit between mine as her arms relax from the rigid fold until her hands find purchase on her hips. Her mouth parts as she gasps, and squeezes her eyes shut tight. She clicks her tongue before her eyes spring open and lock onto mine. "Because...You're friends with *him.*"

"Yeah, and so? I don't understand."

She grits her teeth, sucking a breath between them. Her cheeks darken as she breaks our eye contact. "I don't want to be reminded of Brandt. Okay?" Her eyes find mine again, full of fire and hurt. I feel the sadness radiating off of her, and a nicer guy would be considerate. Let this conversation drop. Walk away. But not me. Something inside makes me dig my heels in.

"Wow. So because Brandt hurt you, I'm lumped in with him, and you're going to ignore and avoid me?" I wave my hands at her, and her breath catches. My eyes zero in on the shallow of her throat, and my lips burn to taste her. "You two were barely together, and you had to have known his heart was always with Elissa. Every-fucking-one knew it. Either you're blind or dumb." Her face falls, and her body looks like a tidal wave of defeat hit her.

Sadness, embarrassment, or both bubble in her eyes, and I instantly feel like an asshole. Her lip trembles as she struggles to hold back the tears, and I inwardly kick myself in the ass. I sigh, my shoulders droop, and I scrub my face.

"I'm sorry, Lexi. I didn't mean that. I'm just pissed, and I'm not sure why. Something about how you're acting is pissing me off, and I snapped." I try to find her eyes, but her head's turned away, looking off into the distance. Her head nods gently, as if only pretending to accept my half-assed apology so I'll leave. "Can we start over? I've got like a month's worth of classes left, and I plan on using them all. It'd be nice if we could be cordial," I say softly.

Her eyes peek at me from the corners as she rolls her bottom lip between her teeth, and every fibre inside of me screams to be the one biting into her lip. I groan inwardly as I try to keep my composure. *What the fuck is wrong with me?* I'm so confused as to this constant surge of need when I'm around her. My body reacts to her all of its own accord, and it takes all of my restraint to keep myself in check.

She finally sighs in resignation, and the tension from her body melts away. Her head turns my way, and our eyes connect, and when they do, I see the acceptance in them. Her blonde hair swishes as she nods, and her voice is fragile and soft as she says, "Okay."

A gentle smile wriggles onto my face, and her lips quirk up as well. I stick out my hand, and her purple polish shines as she slips her tiny hand into mine. Electricity courses through my body when her soft, warm skin grazes mine and sends the current straight to my dick. A bead of sweat rolls down my neck and trickles down my back from the restraint I'm holding back, trying to make sure I don't pitch a tent in my gym shorts.

I clear my throat and rip my hand away from hers as if I've been burned—it feels like it. Her wondering eyes burrow into me, and all I can do is give her a curt nod.

"I'll see you tomorrow, then," I say before I move quickly out of the room, and I don't stop until I reach my office.

CHAPTER SIX

LEXI

It sort of surprised me the way Liam called me out like that. It's been sitting with me for days. I never expected him to care about how I acted towards him. I know I was kind of a bitch to him, punishing him for something he didn't do, but what else was I going to do when he's a constant reminder of Brandt?

It honestly bothers me that everyone thinks because Brandt and I weren't together very long that I couldn't have had feelings for him—not real ones anyway. But that's besides the point. Even if they weren't *true* feelings, it doesn't make rejection any less hurtful. It fucking sucks.

Maybe that's what my problem is. My pride is wounded. But it's okay to feel what you feel. It's okay to be sad, hurt, and angry. So what if he wasn't the great love of my life? It can still hurt.

Still, I shouldn't have acted like I did and treated someone who hasn't wronged me in that way. Liam didn't deserve it, and he seems nice. He honestly seemed pissed about how I acted, like he was truly hurt. For the first time in a while, I've felt something I haven't. I feel…noticed.

I drape a few garment bags over my arms and then load up with two small boxes and trudge my way out of my apartment and onto the elevator, trying to press buttons with a finger that's pried away from the stack. Balancing everything in my arms, I'm able to *just* reach the button, and it lights up. I back away from the buttons and slump against the wall with everything still in my arms.

Slowly, I've been moving things into my new apartment a little each day. The new apartment I rented is even closer to my studio, which is nice and convenient since I can gradually take my things over. I was lucky enough to get the place a month before I had to be out of my current one, so I've been taking my time, a few boxes here and there and unpacking them right away. Not the most efficient, but I'm struggling with leaving my apartment. I know it's my choice to leave, but I feel like there wasn't really a choice. It's either I stay at this place and run into Elissa and Brandt all the time, or I can really move on and leave all of this behind me.

God, listen to me. No wonder why my friends are so done with hearing about this. I really *do* sound like a pathetic and mopey loser. But that's why I'm doing this. To move on.

The elevator door dings, and the metal doors grind open, and I navigate my way through the lobby to the building's entrance. I push the door open with my hip and burst out onto the street, and Abby is leaning against her parents' van, attention laser focused on her phone.

"Uh, little help here, please." Abby rolls her eyes before looking at me and sticking her tongue out and popping her phone back into her pocket. She takes her time pushing off the van, meeting me only a foot away from the trunk, and grabs a single box. Walking it around the corner to the back and placing it on top of the few boxes I brought down and stuffing them into the trunk. I roll my eyes and follow her to put the rest of the stuff in the back. "You know, you came here to help...I'm sure no one is going to want to steal my shit. And lucky us because your parents' van...you know...locks."

"Ugh, fiiiiine. Let's go," Abby says, exasperated, as if at this point, she's actually helped at all. "I figured since I borrowed the van, my job could be supervisor." The metal keys clink together as she pulls them out of her purse and beeps the car. "Let's get this over with. I need a fucking drink; moving is stressful."

A sarcastic chuckle rolls in my throat. I love Abby to death, I really do. She's an amazing person and totally reliable, unless it requires anything to do with physical strength. "Yeah, it is. And you wonder why I asked for help..."

"Oh, Lex..." Abby walks over to me, links her arm through mine, and rests her head on my shoulder. Her chestnut hair rustles in my face, and the smell of strawberries and lemon tickles my nose as we pass through the lobby and make our way to the elevator for another trip. "You know I'm here for you, no matter what. Even if it requires me to use my muscles, and you *know* I only use my muscles for one thing. And I better be getting an 'O' at the end."

Another few trips and the van is bursting with about thirty boxes. The sliding door slams shut on the side of the van as I wipe the beads of sweat off my brow.

"Let's gooooooo," Abby shouts out the window. I slide into the passenger seat up front and buckle in. "Girl, you so totally are getting me drunk tonight. And I already invited Henry and Lillian to meet us afterwards."

• • •

After we finish bringing everything up to my new apartment, we both run home to get ready to meet our other friends at the bar.

I'm hit with a pungent cloud of beer, wings, and fries as I walk in and can barely hear myself think over the loud atmosphere of people chatting and the live band playing in the corner of the bar. My eyes scan the crowded tables and room until they settle on my friends sitting in a booth a few feet opposite of the bar. Henry catches my stare, his smooth ebony arm waving me over. My lips curl, and I nod to him and make my way over. I slide into the booth beside Abby, and she nudges me with her shoulder as a *hello* as I drop my clutch between the two of us.

"Glad you finally made it." Abby chuckles.

"Yeah, well some of us actually broke a sweat when moving things today. So I needed a shower," I tease, sticking my tongue out at her. Her brown eyes flutter as she smirks, shrugging her shoulders. The table is already cluttered with a couple of empty glasses each while they're enjoying their third drink.

"What? No one thought to grab me a round? Rude," I jest. "Fine, I guess I'll just go grab my own." Grabbing a twenty from my clutch, I slide out of the booth and saunter over to the bar. I lean up against the hard, worn mahogany where my finger swirls around a knot in the grain, while my foot rests on the brass bar at the base.

The bartender nods my way as I look towards him, tossing a rag over his shoulder, and comes my way.

"What can I get you?" His voice is rough and marbled like he smokes a pack a day.

"Vodka cranberry, please. And make it a double."

The bartender smirks, nodding his head as he mixes my drink. When he slides it in front of me, a giant hand smacks and slides a red fifty towards him.

"I'll pay for that, and I'll take another two beers, please." The rich, deep voice vibrates in my ear and sends shivers down my spine. His creamy tone flows over my skin, sending heat to my core. My bottom lip rolls in, biting back a grin in the familiarity of who is beside me. I slowly turn to face him.

"Well, long time no see, Liam. And thanks for the drink." A smirk twitches on his face.

"I'm surprised you're not arguing over me paying for it like most women." His tone is dusted with surprise.

"One, I'm not like most women, and two, I never turn down a free drink."

Liam's grey eyes shine, a twinkle of intrigue and a smirk tugging at the corner of his lips. Heat strikes my core and burns the longer he looks at me. His eyes are on mine, never wavering, and only break when the bartender interrupts us, setting the two bottles of beer in front of Liam. He briefly nods at the bartender before his gaze is back on me, and I nibble on my lip.

"Well...Thank you for the drink. I better get back to my friends." I try to dismiss myself pleasantly, but as I walk away, I feel the heat from him as he follows close behind me. *Is he actually following me?* My friends are all staring wide-eyed at the hunk of a man trailing behind. Lillian shifts in her spot, rolling her shoulders back to press her tits out, and practically salivates at the mouth.

Venom pulses through my body at her reaction to Liam. A green-eyed gremlin inside of me wants to claw out her eyes for looking at him like that. A strange hum pumps through my veins as her eyes darken as we close in on the table. He must have noticed Lillian as well, since he followed me. The gremlin roars its ugly head at the thought of them together.

CHAPTER

SEVEN

LIAM

A few of the guys from the office and I went to the bar after work. It's a weekly ritual that we've developed over the years to break free from the stress of the week, Friday night happy hour at the place around the corner. But tonight, we followed Richie to a new place he came across. "Want to change up the options," he says, as if he didn't leave the bar every Friday night with a different woman on his arm.

Richie leads me, Gavin, and Kane into the bar, and I'm slightly surprised at how relaxed this place is, and it's packed. The places we typically frequent are the swankiest ones in the Entertainment District. I'm honestly shocked that Richie found this place and is willing to come here. He usually likes his drinks and women as expensive as they come.

I glance around the dim room, and there isn't a shortage of beautiful women here in tight, expensive clothes. The room is all dark, sleek surroundings with accents of mahogany. The bar went minimalist in the decor, clean and simple. There's a house band playing some nondescript melodies of the top 100 charts, all instrumental that flows through the speakers. Beautiful people mush their bodies together as they grind and dance on the space in front of the small platform where the band plays.

There are people crowding around the bar, waiting for one of three bartenders to take their order or flirting with the person next to them. Almost all the standing tables are taken by groups of the opposite sex, eyes wandering to find someone to spend the night with. There are a handful of booths scattered around, and all are occupied. Gavin nudges my ribs and nods to a table in the far corner near the bar that's open, and we all follow his lead. I'm a little thrown off by how nice this place is for being laid back, but the floor is still as sticky as any other normal bar as we head towards the table.

When we snag the table, Gavin and Richie offer to grab us all a round at the bar, and disappear into the crowd.

"So how's things going with the Furlan merger?" Kane asks. His voice slightly shouting over the noise. I run a hand through my thick hair, a smug smile tugging at my lips.

"Got it in the fucking bag. Just waiting on the final contract from legal, then all that's left is to sign this fucker." After a beat, my eyes darken, and my hand wraps on the table. "Then Jade and Moores had better fucking give me partner."

"I still can't believe you haven't gotten it yet. Out of the four of us, you've been here the longest, and have the biggest portfolio out of almost all the staff. And not just a long list of clients, some of the highest paying ones," Kane says.

Don't I fucking know it? Irritation's sharp claws dig into my chest, only growing the fury brewing inside of me. The fact Jade and Moores have had me on the hook for partner for the last four years is fucking bullshit. Sure, I get nice bonuses at the end of the year, they don't micromanage me, and I get one of the better offices in the building, but would be fucking nice if I could get off the partner track and just be a partner. Something they promised years ago.

"Son," Jade grumbles fondly, resting his hand on my shoulder before walking around Moores's desk and standing beside him. "We knew taking you on as an intern during your time at UOT was a bit of a risk. Letting some unproven fool handle a few minor accounts. But I recognized something behind your eyes—a spark. Desperate for something more."

"These last few years after your graduation have been extraordinary. Both Moores and I see great potential in you. We've taken you under our wing and crafted you into this behemoth of a businessman. Hell, I might even go as far as saying you're almost better than us." He turns to face the big window behind them, rummaging with something.

The sound of a wooden box clasping shut. Turning back around, his hands are curled around three thick Cubans. Jade passes one to Moores, his golden pinky ring glinting in the fluorescents. Moores nods his head, accepting the cigar, and stuffs it between his lips, his thick jaw securing it in place. Jade passes one to me, which I accept. Hubris flushing through my veins, knowing that very few have shared a moment like this with two of the biggest investment titans in Toronto.

We take turns passing the cutter, and then with the flick of the lighter, we all light our cigars. The puffs of smoke plume in the air, swirling the earthy, rich smell with it. After a few silent moments of appreciation of the fine stogies, Jade continues speaking.

"This is it, kid. One day, you'll be living large like us. In just a few years, your name will be on that sign. Jade, Moores, and West Investments."

I grit my teeth as the once hopeful memories now play with a sour tune in my head.

Fucking asshats.

I crack my knuckles. "Let's just say that I'm done playing their fucking bitch. Every year, for the past four, I've been waiting for them to announce partner. And every year, nothing. If I don't get it this year, I'm fucking out."

Kane's eyes search for my bluff, shock written all over his face. He's probably never thought in a million years I'd consider walking away from the firm. But before I can say any more, Richie and Gavin come back, eight Stellas in hand. The bottles chink together as they set two down in front of each of us. A tall, leggy brunette walks by, her eyes laser focused on our table. Richie nods to her, a sly grin on his face. She tosses her hair, winks at him, and her pace slows. No doubt for the benefit of Richie, so he can check out her *assets*, which is voluptuous and plump.

Richie grabs his drink and raises it into the air. "To another week being kings."

We all lift our bottles, clink them together, and rest them on our lips, taking long pulls of the beer. Richie drains the rest of his bottle in one go, then grabs the other. "See ya later, fuckers." He buttons his sport coat before he stalks off towards the brunette without another word, but a sleazy grin on his face.

The three of us have finished our first two drinks plus two more, when I notice a familiar blonde with toned legs to die for and an ass you just want to bite into brush past and anchor herself at the bar. There's an uptick in my heart rate as I stare at her from behind. I've never seen her out of leggings and tank tops before, and my dick twitches at the sight of her in dark denim jeans and turquoise pumps.

My eyes glide up her body, taking in her defined shoulders and the rivet down her back that's exposed by the deep scoop. A few bold freckles decorate her creamy skin, each one begging for my teeth to nip them. I try to tear my eyes away from her, but it's almost impossible.

She's your buddy's ex…You shouldn't be looking at her this way. Trying to remind myself that she should be off-limits, but a horny little fucker in my head says, "Go for it." *Besides, you had no problem when he made a move on Elissa, even though you had her first.*

Good point.

I down the rest of my drink, tipping the bottle, silently letting my buddies know I'm going to grab another round. I weave through the tables of people and sidle up beside her at the bar. Images of strawberries floating in coconut milk flash in my mind as I breathe the air in around her. It's overwhelming, and I want to drown in the smell. Nothing in the world has ever smelled as good.

The way she's bent over the bar, waiting for her drink, makes her ass look fantastic and juicy, and is giving my second head some dirty thoughts of how I want to sink my hands into her hips and take her from behind right where she is. See how much I can get her ass to jiggle as I pound into her. Fuck it, I don't care if we have an audience.

As the heavy tumbler of red slides across the grain of the bar top, I grab a fifty from my wallet and slam it down, ordering myself another drink, and paying for hers. Her body stiffens with a slight jolt at the noise.

"I'll pay for that, and I'll take another two beers, please." A tiny smile tugs at her mouth, those perfect, fuckable lips, and the tension slowly leaks from her body as she recognizes my voice. Our eyes lock as she faces me, and I'm trapped in the muddy flecks of her hazel eyes. There's a little banter going back and forth between us, but I get lost in what she says.

My eyes keep dipping to watch her full lips. The shapes they make as she speaks, how her lips pucker seductively as it curls around the *o*'s in her words. How her pink, sultry tongue pokes between her teeth and I wonder how it would feel sliding along my fat shaft.

The bartender breaks whatever hold she had on me as he hands me the beer. I briefly look away from her, thanking the bartender. But when I look back, her brows pull together and she nibbles the inside of her cheek, like she's feeling awkward.

"Well...Thank you for the drink. I better get back to my friends."

Lexi pushes herself off the bar and saunters away, and I feel my body being magnetized, pulling me to follow her. I can't stop my feet from moving. She throws a cautious glance over her shoulder, and her eyes widen by a fraction in surprise that I'm following her. Lexi stops at the end of the only available spot in the booth but doesn't slide in. Her friends fix their curious gazes on me. The friend she was sitting beside is undressing me with her eyes, full of lust, and like I'm an Hermès handbag.

I feel like a giant piece of meat.

Fuck, is this what women feel like all the time?

I shudder.

"Lexi," the blonde vixen purrs, dragging Lexi's name out. "Are you going to introduce me, I mean *us*, to your friend?"

Lexi's breath catches in her throat as she rolls her lip between her teeth, side-eyeing me. A clear internal debate going on to decide whether we are in fact friends or not. With a small sigh, she tips her hand out.

"Everyone, this is Liam."

CHAPTER EIGHT

Lexi

All of my friends gush over Liam, especially Lillian. She's like a cat in heat, making me switch her places so she can rub up against him. Her French manicured fingers run up and down his muscular forearm that's resting on the table with a firm grip on his beer. His thick fingers slide against the bottle, swiping at the condensation.

Liam politely chats with everyone, but it seems like he is particularly avoiding Lillian's gaze. And every so often, his eyes flit over to me and linger, which causes heat to spread throughout my body like wildfire. Every time our eyes lock, I feel an ache down below, something I haven't felt in a while. A furious itch I need to scratch.

My friends have no problem talking to Liam as if he's been a part of our group this entire time. Part of me is a little miffed at him for just following me over, but there's another part of me that's immensely giddy that he seems to fit in with my friends. It puts me at ease for some strange reason, something I can't explain.

"So what do you do?" Lillian purrs, stroking his forearm. He passes his bottle to the other hand and pulls his hand back and rests it in his lap. Lillian's body deflates at the withdrawal.

"I'm one of the investment portfolio managers for Jade and Moores Investments. I oversee about ten other people, as well as managing my own extensive portfolio."

"Oooh. So you're in charge? I like a man in charge," Lillian says, her voice laced with sugar. My careful eyes take in Liam's response, and something in my heart flutters. His one brow shoots up, and lack of interest contorts on his face, but a gentle, platonic smile tugs at his lips. He expertly continues talking, ignoring Lillian's comment.

"It's not difficult, but leaves me little time to do things outside of work. I'm a workaholic and only need a bit of downtime to tend to my"— Liam pauses as his eyes glide over to mine and lock. —"needs." My skin pebbles as a shiver runs down my spine, and I feel the heat spreading from my core, pooling in my panties. I break our eye contact before anyone at the table notices and glance down at the drink in my hands; the ice clinks on the glass as I swirl it. But that doesn't stop the heat radiating over me because I know his eyes are still on me. I shift in my seat, clenching my thighs together to suppress the need that's throbbing.

My friends rapid fire a bunch of questions at him for the next hour, and I spend that entire time avoiding his stare and guzzling back three more drinks. I ask nothing and make small conjectures here and there to seem like I am still engaged in the conversation. I hold on to everything he says, just like my friends. Liam is incredibly charming, warm, and vibrant. He doesn't waver under my friends' scrutiny.

I excuse myself once I finish my fourth drink and make my way to the bar on slightly unsteady feet. Finally, I feel like I can breathe and allow myself to relax without Liam's watchful eye on me. Maybe it was just me, but the tension was so strong it was like wading through cresting waves. His steely eyes pull me in and captivate me. I'm so drawn to this man it scares me.

I flag the bartender down and order another drink, and as I wait, I lean against the bar, and I blow my bangs out of my eyes. My fingers tap lightly on the counter, and I take a few steadying breaths. Maybe it's *just* all in my head, and the alcohol definitely doesn't help. *Fuck. I need to get it under control.*

As I try to shake these thoughts out of my head, someone steps up beside me, and I feel the heat rolling off their body. My hair prickles and my heart races. "Lexi..." Liam's deep voice slides over my body like a silk sheet. My eyes flutter shut as I take a moment to revel in his voice and the way my name sounds on his lips before I turn to face him.

"Thaaat's me."

Nice one, idiot.

My smile is weak as I look this gorgeous man in the eyes. His lips tug at the corners, no doubt holding back his smile.

"You really think another drink is a good idea?" My lips part slightly, and I stare at him vacantly. I'm not quite sure what to say. Normally, I'd find offence with someone calling me out on how many drinks and tell them just where to shove it, but with Liam, I see the storm of concern brewing behind his eyes. But I force the snark to come out.

"I don't really think it's any of your concern." I flip my hair over my shoulder and grab the drink and drain it once the bartender puts it in front of me. "Another," I say to the bartender, slamming my glass on the counter and sliding it back towards him.

A low grumble vibrates in Liam's throat as his eyes narrow at me. He shakes his head to the bartender.

"She's done."

My mouth drops open, and my eyes feel like they're going to bulge out of my head.

"Um, *excuse* me? Who the fuck do you think you are?" I lean over the bar top, my breasts squishing against the surface with my one hand flailing around, trying to get the bartender's attention again before my body deflates in defeat. "Are you fucking serious?" I whisper.

I turn my attention to Liam, fire burning behind my eyes. "Who the hell are you to cut me off? You're not my father or boyfriend." My arms cross against my chest, and my fingernails dig into my biceps with a bite.

"Be a fucking good girl, grab your friends, and go home. You could barely walk over here to order another drink. Some fucking asshole is going to take advantage of you in this state, and you're not in the right mind to think clearly. Go home and get some sleep."

The fucking balls on this dude.

"Maybe I *want* to go home with someone tonight. Ever think of that?" My words are icy and slip off my tongue with ease. My eyes fall to his lips briefly, taking in the fullness of his bottom lip and the perfectly sculpted cupid's bow. When I look at his eyes again, they're even darker, and something dangerous lurks behind them. I don't realize I've sucked my lip into my mouth until I bite down hard on it, making me jump a little. Out of the corner of my eye, I see Liam's hand curl tightly on the bar top until his knuckles turn white.

"Go home, Lexi." Liam's jaw ticks. His words are definitive and commanding. An overwhelming sense of needing to obey him slithers inside my body, making me weak at the knees. But I force myself to resist because he doesn't own me.

"No, I don't think I will." I push myself off the bar, straighten my clothes, and saunter back over to the table with my friends. And just to spite him, when a server walks by with a tray of shots, I scoop one up and toss a five-dollar bill on the tray. I turn to face Liam, and his eyes are burning with anger. With a small, victorious smile, I raise the shot glass into the air, salute him, and toss it back. The tequila burns as it goes down, but fuck it. I whip my hair over my shoulders as I turn away and continue my way back to the table.

I plop into the booth beside Lillian, and I can still feel Liam's eyes on me, staring me down, but I refuse to look his way. A sharp nudge lands into my ribs, and I whip my head to face Lillian.

"What the fuck was that for?" I hiss. Her tongue flicks along her bottom lip and runs across her teeth. Her eyes are glued in the direction I just came from, obviously still looking at Liam.

"Are you guys, ya know, together?"

"What?" My eyebrows shoot into my hairline, and my heart stutters in my chest.

"So he's fair game?" My brows furrow and eyes narrow at her in confusion. But a small prickle of anxiety washes over my body.

"Uh, yeah… I suppose he is."

CHAPTER NINE

LIAM

Acid burns in my veins as Lexi walks away from me, her perfect round ass and wide hips swaying. My jaw pulses, holding back every fucking angry word I want to shout. I roll my neck, and it pops a few times as I grab my beer off the bar and walk over to the table where my boys from work stand.

"Who was the hottie you disappeared with for a little there?" Kane asks. My blood runs cold at his question as my eyes are still focused on Lexi from across the bar.

"None of your fucking business," I growl. A low rumble of laughter comes from Kane.

"Little possessive there, bud?" I shoot him a glare out of the corner of my eyes. Fury rolls hot throughout my body at the thought of Kane or Gavin hitting on Lexi. I bring the brown bottle to my lips and take a long pull, ignoring his prodding question. *Fuck, what's wrong with me?* She's not mine. She can do whomever she wants, whenever she wants. But the thought sends spikes of jealousy poking at every organ in my body.

Gavin and Kane chuckle, clinking their drinks together, as though it was a job well done pissing me off. A waitress comes over, collecting the empty bottles on our table, and I reach into my pocket, extract my wallet, and pluck out a crisp green twenty. I hand it over to her, asking for another round.

The next hour is spent sulking like a little bitch, gulping down beer, and staring over to where Lexi sits. I'm half invested in the conversation happening with Gavin and Kane, offering little tidbits of *uh-huh*s and *okay*s. I will myself to stop looking in her direction or stop giving a fuck, but I can't.

She's swaying in her seat, cackling to what her friends are saying. She's absolutely blotted drunk at this point, and urgency to take care of her takes hold of my conscience. It takes everything inside of me not to snap and march over there and scold her fucking friends for letting her get this wasted, but it looks like they're just as fucking drunk as her.

My phone vibrates in my pocket, and I look away for one minute to pull it out to see Rhys messaged me about a basketball game tomorrow. Before I can respond, Gavin and Kane snicker beside me, and my eyes snap in the direction of theirs. A low growl escapes me as I see Richie pulling up a chair and sitting at the end of the table, fully focused on Lexi. Something inside me breaks, and I ditch my friends at the table, leaving behind my beer and stalking over there.

My vision tunnels in on Richie and Lexi, and she's basking in the attention he's giving her, like she's some neglected little child. Her lashes flutter, and she flicks her hair over her shoulder as she leans into him, her tank top tugging lower, exposing a bit more cleavage than necessary. Red-hot anger sears inside me as I get closer.

I stop abruptly, and everyone at the table but Lexi and Richie seem to notice me. Lillian sits taller, pushing her breasts out and making sex eyes at me. I ignore her and laser focus on these two idiots sitting in front of me.

I clear my throat and wrap my hand around Lexi's smooth, silky bicep and yank her to her feet.

"Time to go," I whisper low and deep into her ear. Fine hairs raise like a domino effect over her arms, and a small shiver rolls down her spine. When her eyes find mine, there's a moment of desire clouding inside them, and it sends thoughts straight to my dick that I shouldn't be thinking, but she's so goddamn exquisite that my mind just wanders there.

I turn to her friend Henry and let him know that she's leaving, and he gives me an approving wink. My hand tightens slightly on her arm, and I feel her muscle pulse, trying to resist me.

"Come," I demand. Walking away, I pull her along behind me, pushing through the crowd, parting it like the red sea.

The longer that my hand stays on her, the more my fingers tingle to touch other places. To see if her skin is silky everywhere. To see if my voice can make her skin pebble anywhere else on her body.

I glance behind me, and she's got this fucking adorable annoyed scowl on her face as she trails me. Lexi's clearly given up defying me, and something settles inside me. So much so that I finally relax my grip on her as we near the door. I actually let go as I open the door for her, allowing her to exit the building first.

"Ladies first."

She sneers at me, flicking her hair as she walks past. The ends of her ice-blonde hair flip up and smack me in the face. Strawberries in sweet cream fill my senses, and I take a moment to breathe it in, committing it to memory. She smells so fucking delicious. My mouth dries up, and my cock throbs against my zipper. I curl my fingers into fists, digging my nails deep into my palms to replace lust with pain.

"Brandt's building, yeah?" I walk to the edge of the sidewalk and hail a cab. When she doesn't answer me, I glare at her over my shoulder.

Lexi's hazel eyes roll like marbles in her head as she crosses her arms and kicks out a leg, widening her stance. She tips her head and nods in the opposite direction we're facing.

"It's not far," she breathes. "We can just walk there."

I lower my arm as my brows pinch together. "You moved?"

"Mm-hmm." Lexi swivels on her heel and starts walking, leading the way, offering no other explanation. I move quickly to fall in step beside her. Her toned arms hug tight against her torso, almost like a defensive mechanism. My hand twitches, and the need to pull her arms apart to allow herself to be vulnerable to me is overwhelming. I want to see the carefree woman that was laughing wholeheartedly with her friends across the bar from me. The weight of whatever I'm feeling as she ignores me and puts up her walls is crushing me.

"You know it's not a good idea to drink as much as you did back there," I say. My voice is low and gravelly as the words come pouring out of my mouth.

Lexi scoffs.

"I didn't drink as much as you think I did. Besides, I can handle my liquor, and I've never needed a *saviour* before."

"I wasn't trying to be a saviour."

Her chuckle is hollow. "Yeah, okay. The fact that you went all caveman in there." Her voice drops a few octaves, attempting to mock me. "Time to go, come with me if you want to live."

"I'm pretty sure I didn't say that. I would never quote *The Terminator*," I say, flatly. Lexi snickers, and she must not notice I'm watching her, but her arms relax, and her shoulders give.

"Pretty sure you did, bud." Her teeth bite into her lip, wrestling to keep herself from smiling. "So why does it seem like you're stalking me? I mean, first the classes I teach, now going to the same bar?"

"I'm not stalking you, trust me," I deadpan. Her head whips to face me; she looks offended, her lips part, making the most seductive circle, which I shouldn't be thinking about, but can't stop wondering how perfectly my cock would fit into her mouth. Knowing just how well I'd fill it until her throat spasms around my length and gags.

"What? Am I not worthy of being stalked? Pfft. I'll have you know that I'm *plenty* stalker worthy," she rambles on.

"Lexi. That is not what I meant, and you know it. Quit twisting my words."

A light breeze ruffles some leaves on the lonesome trees we pass by, and out of the corner of my eye Lexi's body delicately shivers. Without giving it another thought, my body responds automatically and shrugs off my suit jacket and drapes it over her shoulders. She turns to face me with wrinkled brows and a thousand unsaid questions in her eyes.

"Thank you," she breathes. Her words are barely a whisper, but I hear them all the same. The snarky, brazen girl from just a moment ago is replaced with a quiet, softer version of herself.

"But don't think just because you lent me your jacket that I forgive you for acting like a barbarian back at the bar." And the snarky girl is back.

Lexi stops abruptly in front of a building that looks to be about ten storeys tall. The dull, murky grey of the exterior has splotches of water damage and dirt from years of going uncleaned. The windows are old wooden ones that make you feel the draft they let in just by looking at them. The building is sandwiched between two skyscrapers, making this one cower in the shadows of the opulence of the other two.

My gut drops out from under me, and my heart isn't too far behind. This place isn't nearly as secure or nice as her last place. *Why in the world would she move here?*

"It's not much, but it's okay for now." Her voice is small as she speaks, but it's like she can read my mind. "It's actually pretty inside. It's got a lot of that old-school charm to it. There's beautiful original hardwood floors that creak as you walk, the arched doorways…" Lexi prattles on about her apartment and why it actually is a good place, but I can't focus on any of the things she's saying.

I'm just staring at her, completely oblivious to any argument she's making in favour of the place. I'm having the hardest time fathoming why she moved from such a beautiful, luxurious place. I thought she owned the apartment in the building she was living at.

Then it clicks.

She lived in the same building as Brandt, and Elissa moved in. It was probably hard for her to see them around the complex. My rough edges inside seem to soften as I realize this, and I suddenly feel like an ass for judging.

"Show me your place." The demand slips out of my mouth and lands between us. Lexi's head shakes as though she can't believe what she heard.

"Uh…Sure?" Confusion is in her voice and on her face as she pushes the key into the door and unlocks it for us. Silence follows us as we walk to the elevator and take it up to her floor. I risk a glance at Lexi, and she seems tense. Her shoulders tuck close to her ears while her arms are crossed tight across her chest, and her teeth rake her full bottom lip.

The elevator dings and the mechanical woman calls out, "Level ten."

CHAPTER

TEN

LEXI

Deep breath in…and out…

Why the fuck am I so nervous? It's gotta be the alcohol. But why do I suddenly feel completely sober?

I glance up at Liam, and realize just how tall this man is. He towers over me. His big, imposing body eclipses mine like the moon does the sun. My eyes zero in on his strong, sharp jaw that's peppered with rough caramel hair that's just long enough to hook my fingers into it.

"Level ten." The elevator dings once, and the heavy metal doors glide open. My teeth finally release my lip, and I can feel the jagged, rough skin from the nervous biting.

My tongue flicks out and swipes at it; a temporary remedy. I step outside of the elevator and into the dimly lit hallway. I take careful steps as I suddenly feel self-conscious about how I'm walking as I feel Liam's stormy eyes on me.

I lead us towards my apartment door, and my hands are shaking like a leaf in a rainstorm and having the hardest time controlling my faculties around this man right now. I dig around my purse, scrambling to find my keys.

I take a steadying breath. It's got to be the alcohol because it can't be this man making me lose my senses.

"Are you going to open the door?" His deep, strong voice pummels into me, almost knocking the breath right out of me. *Jesus, I forgot he was here for a second.* I don't know how because he commands every space he's in. Yep, it's got to be the alcohol…

His warm hands grab the keys from my hands and shove them into the door, unlocking it for the both of us.

"After you," he growls. We both enter my apartment, and I suddenly feel naked. The need to run into my closet and find the most covering pieces of clothing is screaming out to me. I don't like feeling exposed and vulnerable. But with Liam, at this moment, I'm completely bare and unsheltered. I look behind me as he's toeing off his shoes, and I kick mine off into the corner underneath the hallway table.

I can barely take my eyes off this behemoth of a man with the linebacker stature. His bulging arms strain against the weaves of thread in his smooth powder-blue dress shirt. It's then I remember I still have his jacket on.

"Oh, here you go," I say nervously, shrugging off the jacket. His one eyebrow raises as I hand over the jacket.

He takes it, and I expect him to put it back on, but he tosses it on the bench in the hallway, making a statement that he's staying.

Why?

Unsure of where my voice comes from, I hear myself ask him, "Do you want a tour?"

Darkness flashes in his eyes, and he grunts a yes.

"Um, okay. So this is the hallway…" And with the unimpressed look on his face, I look away, pulling my lip between my teeth and step lightly, to prevent the squeaks in the floor, into the open concept kitchen and living area. "Like I said, it's not much, but it has charm." He walks further into the room, and heat crawls up my body, setting every nerve inside me on fire. My heart quickens and I feel faint.

"Can I get you anything to drink? I think there's some kind of juice, water, or a beer." He turns slowly in the living room, scrutiny folds his facial features as he glances around the room, assessing. I hold my breath; waiting for his approval gnaws at me. It shouldn't matter what he thinks, but something inside me wants to please him. To think I'm good enough.

"I'm fine, thanks," he says flatly. He turns on his heel, and his eyes finally settle on mine. A zing of electricity crackles through my body. My chest heaves heavy breaths as I feel like I'm caught in a trap. Frozen to the spot under his gaze. His footsteps are slow and deliberate as he closes the distance between us. Like a predator stalking his prey.

A dark storm swirls behind his eyes as he nears, and desire courses through my body for this hard, muscled man to take me. To throw me up against the wall and ravish me.

Tear my clothes to pieces, leaving heaps of ripped fabric on the floor. My hands clench at my side as he stops directly in front of me, a hair's breadth away. He dips down, and a giant hand pushes back some of my blonde locks and tucks it behind my ears. My head snaps to his warm hand like a magnet. And the feeling of his rough skin against my smooth face sends molten lava to my core.

"Have a good night, Lexi." His voice lingers on my name as his lips brush the corner of my lips, sending fevered chills down my spine. Leaving me an utter panting, sopping mess.

He moves away, stepping around me, and I'm doused in a cold bucket of water as he leaves my orbit. I spin around, and his hand is clasping around my doorknob, and my throat dries up. Panic sets in, and everything inside me is yelling out to stop Liam from leaving. My voice chokes out of me in a rush.

"H-have a g-good night!" Heat spreads from my core to my face, lighting it up bright red.

Liam's face cocks to the side, and I catch the corner of his eye looking at me and a small twitch of his mouth before he disappears out of my apartment. I'm left standing in silence, feeling like an idiot.

CHAPTER ELEVEN

My dick strains against the zipper of my slacks as I stalk down the hallway to the elevator.

I had to get out of Lexi's apartment quickly, as I was slowly losing my restraint. There's something about her that screams to my desire. She's like a gorgeous siren in the night, luring me in with her songs of promise.

Just as I reach the elevator, my shoulders feel noticeably lighter, and I realize I left my blazer in her apartment.

"Shit," I exhale, running my hands down my face. My teeth clench and grind together as I turn around, making my way back to her door. When I'm in front, I raise my hand to knock. Suddenly, the door flies open before my knuckles can connect with the heavy wooden door.

Lexi's hair is slightly wild, as if she's been tugging at it for a few minutes. Her face is flushed, and her chapped lips are parted in surprise as she stares at me, pupils blown, in front of her.

My cock stirs, pulsing inside my pants, and I feel my eye twitch as I look at this completely fuckable woman. She's all breathy, chest pressed out, and heaving.

"You forgot your—"

I snap.

My arms wrap around her lithe body, tugging her in tight against me until I can feel her nipples pucker against my chest. My mouth devours hers as a hand buries deep into her soft platinum hair. I coil the strands around my wrist, pulling taut, tipping her head so her mouth parts, and my tongue dives into her.

She moans, and a small shiver quakes through her body as she melts into me, arms wrapping around my neck, and fuck if I don't come right then. Her body is so responsive to me already, as my hand pushes her lower back closer to my pelvis and she arches into me. I guide us into the entryway, my tongue tangling with hers and licking every corner of her hot little mouth. She tastes like sin and glory.

I kick the door behind me shut, spin us around and pin her between my solid form and the door. I grind my hips into her, my painfully hard cock rubbing against her stomach. Her breath catches, and she loses her senses for a second and forgets to move her lips with mine.

While my one hand is still wrapped in her silky hair, I yank on it enough to pull her lips from mine. I run my tongue down her sweet skin, feeling it pebble as I drag it lower to the curve of her collarbone. My free hand runs up her fucking perfect body. Curves in all the right places.

My hand skims her midriff, and she jolts. Travelling further up, I take my time and appreciate the feeling of her against my hand, drawing out the anticipation of my touching her more intimately. My hand cups her breast, and it spills out of my grasp. It's heavy and full, and it's perfect. I've always been more of a boob man.

The pads of my thumb runs gently over her puckered nipple, which is lightly covered by the sheer tank top fabric and a thin, unpadded bra. Lexi's breath stalls once more as my finger brushes across her nipple, and then I take it between my forefinger and thumb and pinch it gently.

Her hands weave into my hair and grip as she bucks her hips into me, trying to find friction where she most wants it. Needs it. I oblige. Kneeing open her legs, I place my thigh under her heat, and she immediately starts grinding on me. She has a needy little pussy.

I growl against her lips as my hand gropes her tit a little harder, making her moan hot breaths into my mouth.

Her fingers fall out of my hair and onto my shirt, curling her fingers into the blue material. Stretching the fabric until the buttons strain, threatening to burst. My hand travels south, cupping the apex of her core. A hungry, desperate moan ripples through the room.

I can feel her heat through her jeans, knowing that she's probably soaking wet and ready for me to slide into her. She rides into my hand, frantic for stimulation.

"*Please,* Liam," she whines. Her shaky, begging voice rocks me to my core, and any bit of self-restraint I had has now snapped like a rubber band. I should pull away, but I want to sink so deep inside her that I can see my cock moving in her stomach.

My hands push up her shirt, over her breasts, and it slings around her neck. I tug one of the cups of her strapless nude bra to the side and a pert, pink nipple greets me with a standing ovation, just like Lexi will be doing when I'm done with her. My lips travel down her neck, in between the valley of her breasts, my tongue lacing the skin with every kiss. Lexi tastes sweet, like a juicy strawberry on a hot summer day.

I circle my tongue around her hardened peak, sucking on the sensitive flesh.

"Ooooh, Liam!"

My smirk wraps around her nipple as I take my teeth and lightly graze it. If she's moaning like that now, I can't fucking wait to get her on her back and show her what I can really do with my mouth. My dick hardens like steel just thinking about how fucking good her pussy will taste.

Anchoring my hands around her thighs, I lift her off the floor and wrap her legs around my waist, peeling her from the door. I carry her into the living room and drop her on her feet at the edge of the couch. My hands grapple her waist and spin her around. My fingers skim across her skin, dropping to the waist of her pants and skillfully undo the button on her jeans. I loop my fingers through the belt loops and tug them down, and they peel rapidly off her legs and wrap around her ankles. I sink to my knees with the fall of her pants.

I nudge her legs to widen her stance and push her over the arm of the couch. Her ass is wrapped like a pretty, perfect package in floral black lace panties that slope the curve of her cheeks just right. *A round, delicious peach. Supple and…* My teeth sink into one of her cheeks, and she lets out a sharp shriek. Lexi jerks and tries to stand up, but my hand is forceful as I push her back over the arm of the couch.

"Don't move."

Her skin pebbles in little bumps as a slight tremble takes over her body. My hands round her cheeks, caressing as I admire the view. Her legs twitch, and her toes curl and ankles wriggle as she waits for something to happen. So. Fucking. Patiently. My cock aches.

"Good girl." My voice is a low, sultry rumble as I inch closer to her, pressing soft, gentle kisses to her skin. Her panting grows frantic as I take my time making my way across her ass. I push her panties to the side agonizingly slow, and she grumbles something unintelligible.

I raise my hand and land a sharp, quick blow to her cheeks. She jumps and yelps as I smooth my hand over the rising pink mark and place a kiss on it.

"I won't repeat myself. Don't move until I say you can."

If Lexi's panties weren't wet before, they're fucking drenched now. The musk of her arousal lingers in my nostrils, and I press my nose to her pussy and inhale deep. A sharp breath draws from Lexi.

I press my lips against hers in a slow, purposeful kiss. My tongue sneaks out, taking a long swipe at her folds, and I come undone. *Almost.*

She's perfect. Her pussy is divine. It's like drinking a cup of ambrosia from the Gods. The nectar she leaks is like liquid cocaine, setting my senses, my blood, on fire. Just this little taste isn't enough.

My tongue plunges into her without warning, and she sucks in a surprised breath. "*Yes,*" Lexi moans. My balls tense up, and I feel the few beads of pre-cum dampen my boxers as my dick throbs with burgeoning release. I slip my tongue through her folds, flicking the tip of my tongue on her clit. "Ooooh…" she moans louder, arching her hips as close to my face as possible.

I press down on her back, my fingers spread wide to firmly keep her in place while my other hand parts her lips so I have more access.

I roll my tongue with long, languid licks to her sensitive clit, and between every few passes, I dip my tongue deep into her entrance. As her body relaxes, I slip two fingers into her, pumping in and out in slow torture, *just* missing that spot on purpose. "Please," Lexi pants.

I pull my face away from her, a string of saliva drips between us. "A needy little slut, aren't you?"

CHAPTER TWELVE

LEXI

"A needy little slut, aren't you?"

Liam's voice is dark, coarse, and rumbles against my skin. I should be disgusted by the filthy words he's using, but I just get wetter.

"Mmm… You are. And you like it, don't you? Look how fucking wet your pussy is for me." I breathe in sharp when his tongue settles on me again but is faster and rougher.

"L-L-Liam!" I barely recognize the voice coming from my mouth, let alone the lust coursing through my body because of this man. I feel the juices slipping down my leg as he ravishes me with his mouth, and my legs tremble as I try to hold myself together. I'm close. *So close.*

Squeaks, moans, and other nondescript noises tumble from my lips. "Fuck yes. I'm close, Liam." My blood boils as his fingers inside me hook, stroking my G-spot with the perfect amount of pressure. My knees are weak, and my legs turn to jelly. "*Please,*" I beg for release.

In one fluid motion, everything stops. His fingers withdraw, and his tongue is no longer touching me, and I'm hit with a crash of adrenaline. Panting and confused, I turn my head to look over my shoulder when he slams his thick length into me in one thrust.

"Ahhhh!" Surprised, I wonder when the hell he unzipped and put a condom on, but at this point I'm not complaining.

"Fuck, you're tight," he growls, lowering his torso over me, his chest hair tickling against my back. He sinks his teeth into my shoulder. "You feel so good. Look at you taking my cock so well."

His lips brush against the shell of my ear, and a hand wraps around my neck, lifting me closer to him.

"My good little slut," he whispers as he withdraws and slams into me slowly. His hips rock against my backside, and the slapping of our skin echoes throughout my living room. "Right?" His fingers tighten around my neck, waiting for an answer.

"Yes." My voice is barely a whisper. His hand snakes around my waist, dives between my legs and pinches my clit. Liam's hand works my sensitive mound while pistoning into me, his large, throbbing cock sliding in deep until he's crashing off my cervix. A twinge of pain makes my legs shake, but it's a pleasurable pain.

He continues to thrust hard, powerful strokes, shaking my entire body. His cock hardens inside me like a steel rod, and with each brush against my G-spot, my toes curl little by little as I race to the finish line. My channel squeezes around him, gripping him, not wanting him to exit me.

His strokes grow deeper, harder, and in rigid movements. "Fuck, baby. I'm gonna come."

A whimper escapes me as starbursts form behind my eyes. I jut forward with every powerful thrust, and I feel a tiny bead of sweat drip onto my back and roll down my side. He's panting and growling like a rabid animal, trying to hold on longer, to not lose control.

"Liam," I whisper, low and sultry, to encourage him to finish. "I'm almost there." And with the right touch…*there it is.* His fingers expertly circle my clit for another blissful swirl, and I shatter.

His throbbing cock pulses into me as he rocks in motion with his hot seed expelling into me. "Fuck," Liam says, his fingers curling into my hips tight before letting go and withdrawing himself from me. My heart sinks with the sudden emptiness. Loneliness.

At a turtle's pace, I stand up and turn to face him, anxiety like a live wire sparking in my body. I try not to stare at him, but it's hard when he's built the way he is. He's like a masterpiece, carved from marble, chiselled to perfection. The ridges between each ab—eight, I counted shamelessly—are deep little valleys, expertly separating each definition. His shoulders are broad, like a linebacker, and his arms…Ooooh, his arms. Bulging muscles with ropy veins wrap around the muscles under his flesh.

He's mesmerizing, beautiful, and all the other words that escape my mind as I blatantly stare at Liam. A deep chuckle rumbles into the room as he slips the condom off his dick and ties it off.

"Like what you see, dove?" It's the name that does it for me. My heart flutters in my chest in time with the butterflies in my stomach. "Come on, now. Don't play coy. I just had my dick deep inside you. You can admit that you're staring; It's not like I mind." Liam's voice is teasing as his lips curl into a smug grin.

I bite the inside of my cheek, my teeth pressing too hard, a metallic taste fills my mouth. *What the fuck is he doing to me?* I'm fucking leaking down my leg again just *thinking* about how he just had his cock deep inside me. I stifle a moan, moving my teeth to my lips to bite it back. Liam's grin grows like the Cheshire Cat's, all bright, perfect white teeth.

With the condom dangling from his fingers, he swaggers over to me, pulls me in from around my waist with his empty hand, smashing his lips to mine. His wet tongue slips between my lips, aggressively tangling with mine before he lets go. "Where's your washroom?" he purrs, moving his lips to the shell of my ear, gently grazing it.

"Down the hall," I breathlessly whisper. He pulls away, leaving me shivering in the absence of his heat. His giant hand covers an ass cheek and grips it hard. Then he stalks away, used condom in hand, and disappears behind the bathroom door.

Uh, what now?

I feel stupid for standing here, half-naked.

I gather my clothes and head down the hallway to my bedroom, tossing them into the basket in the corner. Rolling my bottom lip in between my teeth, I dig through my dresser to find something cozy to wear. My ears stay perked up, waiting to hear him emerge from the washroom.

Once I'm dressed, I pick at my cuticles as I walk down the hallway, heading towards the kitchen to grab a drink because my throat suddenly feels like the Sahara Desert. My nerves are like live wires inside my body right now and lighting up every synapsis in my brain. I round the island that has the sink in it, that faces the open concept living room and consequently the direction of the bathroom.

I can't look away from the door, waiting on pins and needles until he emerges from the washroom, and I have to face him. My skin prickles as I wait, my anxiety increasing, like the rise of a roller coaster to the peak, waiting for the drop, the crash.

This man does something to me, and I'm not sure why. Maybe it's because I've lived almost like a hermit to men this last year, or maybe it's because this man is insanely hot and he gets under my skin. Or maybe it's the taboo of it all—my ex-boyfriend's friend.

My heart sinks as guilt comes crashing in.

Oh, fuck. What did I do? I shouldn't have gone there. But he was standing there, at my door, looking all manly and like he was holding back all sorts of restraint. I wanted to snap the thin thread that held it all together. I *wanted* him to take me. I wanted to see just how far I could push him. And I'm coming to realize that little liaison wasn't enough.

I suck my bottom lip in between my teeth, lightly scraping against it as I fill my glass with water, still staring in the direction of the washroom. *How long does it take to dispose of a condom and clean up?*

CHAPTER THIRTEEN

LIAM

Fuck. Fuck. Fuck.

CHAPTER FOURTEEN

LEXI

My adrenaline surges as thoughts flurry through my head. What if I pushed him too far?

I shouldn't have done this. I shouldn't have let it get this far. This is killing me. Why isn't he coming out?

Just as the thought crosses my mind, the bathroom door snicks open, and the water glass overflows. I jump, my eyes snapping down to my hand holding the glass, and it almost slips from my grasp. My lungs expand as I take a deep breath, steadying myself, trying to shake off these nerves.

I feel him standing in front of me before I see or hear him. I'm so hyperaware of him, it scares me. I've never been so—I don't know. I can't explain it. Liam just makes me *feel*.

I finally allow my eyes to raise, following up his impeccably dressed torso, to the firm line of his jaw, to the piercing storm behind his eyes. He looks cool, calm, collected, but his eyes look conflicted, confused, concerned. My heart flutters like a nervous butterfly trapped in a cage. His grey eyes are beautiful chaos, and I find myself getting lost in them.

He clears his throat, and his lips part slightly, like he's lost what he's about to say.

"I should go." His hands dive deep into his pockets of his slacks as he looks around my apartment, playing it cool. Or is he playing it cool? Is he just as unaffected with what just happened between us as I'm affected by it? Did I misread the emotions playing in his eyes?

As he turns back to face me, he definitely looks collected now. Not an ounce of anything in his eyes, except maybe boredom. *I should have known this was going to happen. He's a playboy after all, just like the rest of the men in this city.*

"Yeah, probably," I say, my tone frosty. I tried playing it cool, but that was more frozen. *Shit.* He stares at me for a beat longer before he dips his head, gathers his jacket, and heads out of my apartment for the second time tonight. This time, I know he's not coming back.

• • •

I watch my door for an unhealthy amount of time—I won't admit it was almost twenty minutes I stood there, at the sink, waiting for him to come back. But it definitely was one of my weaker moments. When I finally collect myself, my body deflates as I let out a long, defeated sigh. I walk back to the front hallway of my apartment and grab my iPhone out of my purse, the group chat lit up.

Lillian: *Um, so what the hell happened?*
Abby: *I'd like to second that! Get it, girl!*
Lillian: *No. Do not "get it." I called dibs.*

I roll my eyes reading the messages, skimming through the rest of them, thankful Henry has nothing to say about the issue at hand. However, a small green gremlin inside me snarls and bares his teeth at Lillian's *dibs* comment. Like fuck if she called dibs. The snarling inside me simmers when I remember I just hooked up with him, but my stomach somersaults when I remember how things were left. Fucking confusing.

My bare feet smack against the wooden floor as I drag myself to the couch, letting my body sink into the cushions like they're swallowing me whole. My legs dangle over the arm of the couch, and I remember how a little over an hour ago he was ramming his thick cock inside me. I squeeze my legs together, suppressing the desire building inside me.

I'm pathetic. Unlocking my phone, I pull up Instagram and search his name. My face burns, which I can imagine just how much I resemble a tomato because I'm acting like a little teenage stalker and finding this man on social media. Just to get more of him. Like I said, I'm pathetic.

There are a few silly videos from his university days, drunken words, laughter, dancing with his friends, and drunk Liam back in university is the cutest side I've seen of him so far. He's this cheeky, happy moron, and I mean it in the sweetest way possible. My finger glides across the screen like a tiny figure skater, scrolling through years of posts, and before I know it, it's almost 1 AM. I've gone down a spiralling hole of Liam West, and I still can't get enough.

I have to force myself to close the app and push myself off the couch. As I stand, I realize just how sore my cheeks are from smiling at all his posts. I trudge into my room, my eyes sucked dry from staring at my phone for hours, and I strip down to my panties and bra and climb into bed. Wriggling under the covers, I get cozy and roll onto my side and plug my phone in and turn on all my seven alarms for the morning.

I tuck an arm under the pillow while the other one wraps around my down pillow and let out a long yawn. My eyes drift closed, and I'm ready to sleep...*almost*. My hand creeps over to where my phone rests on the bedside table, and I bring it under the covers with my head and continue scrolling, watching videos, and looking at pictures of Liam until my eyes have no other choice but to shut.

I've got it bad.

CHAPTER FIFTEEN

Liam

It's been three fucking days, and I can't get Lexi out of my head.

I feel like a complete asshole, running out of her apartment like a little bitch. I should have said something. Fuck, even something like *Thank you for the amazing fuck* would have been better than *I should go*. Why am I such a goddamn asshole? Why does she make me so nervous?

After I pulled out of her, my insides instantly turned to ice. It felt like losing a piece of me. My only saving grace were the moments I could hide in the washroom. My hands were gripping the counter, knuckles turning white, as I refused to look at myself, wondering what the hell I did. Lexi's a friend's ex. She should be off-limits. I broke the stupid bro code. A swirling hurricane of guilt wrecked my gut as I tried to pull myself together.

No luck.

When I left the washroom, I could feel her presence in the air. I know I was in her apartment, but there's a difference between being there and feeling her there. Her spirit just lingered in the air, like a fine misting of perfume. Her apartment seemed more cheery than her disposition. Everything is in pastel and bright colours. Pale-yellow walls with turquoise frames hanging on them. A dusty-rose couch with a lavender accent chair, each decorated with funky patterned throw pillows.

Her taste is everything opposite to mine. The dull greys or deep blues. The colours that surround her apartment scream lively and bubbly, but so far all I've seen from her is nerves. Maybe *I* make her nervous.

A knock on my office door pulls me from my thoughts of Lexi moaning, and I have to adjust my position in my chair from the uncomfortable boner I'm sporting.

"Jade and Moores are on the hunt." Charlie pops her head into my office. Her chocolatey brown eyes roll as she scrunches her nose, making this horrible face. My lips press together, trying to suppress a grin.

"Any idea why?"

"Nope." She shakes her head. Her glossy raven strands swish around her. "Good luck, though. Apparently, you're being whispered about why they're furious."

My head cocks to the side, and I pull my eyebrows together, utterly confused as to why it would have something to do with me.

"Eeek!" Charlie jumps, disappearing from the crack in my door. "Y-yes, he's here. One second." She pops her head back in. "Jade and Moores are here to see you." Disappearing once again, but only for a moment, until she opens the door wide and steps aside for the two polished old men with scowls on their faces stalking through the doorway.

Jade seems less wound up than Moores. These men look impeccable for sixty-eight and seventy. Moores is a little thicker, a small beer gut, but hardly noticeable. His greys are practically white, but he keeps everything short and clean. Moustache, hair, and no beard. Jade is the more youthful one. Still has that salt-and-pepper hair, styled with a swoop to the side. Honestly, I'm still surprised they're working and not retired, but that's what greedy bastards do. Work until they die.

They both, however, are squinting so hard, I can't tell what their eye colours are. Moores's face is stained blood red and looks like he's about to blow a gasket. The heat that's rising off the top of his head is like looking at the pavement on a hot summer day and there's that shimmer in the air. Jade, more collected, but still very pissed for some unknown reason, just looks like a stern father. Hard, rigid jaw, angry, furrowed eyebrows, and tight, thin lips.

"Jade. Moores. What can I do for you?" I say, getting to my feet and adjusting my sport coat and buttoning it up.

"You're fucking fired, you little fucking prick!" Moores snaps. Jade rests a hand on Moores' shoulder.

"*Daniel*," he warns. "Let me handle this." My stomach sinks, and it takes everything inside me not to react. My head tingles a little as I try to get my breathing under control. To keep my cool. My eyes slide back and forth between Moores and Jade.

"What's this about?" My tone is flat, trying to be unaffected by Moores's outburst. My hands curl into tight fists as I shove them deep into my pockets. Jade's eyes twitch as he studies me before answering.

"There are rumours floating around the office that you dropped Gilbert and Sons, your largest—"

"Ahem???" Moores interjects.

"*Our*"—Jade's eyes dart to Moores and scrunches his lips together, then turns his attention back to me. The room is suffocating with tension—"largest client." I shake my head in confusion, closing my eyes to take a moment and process what he just said.

"What?" I ask, in total confusion. "Why the fuck would I drop the Gilbert account? That just makes no sense." I look down at my computer and start typing furiously, pulling up their account.

CLOSED.

"What. The. Fuck," I whisper. My hands weave through my golden hair, squeezing tight. My stomach drops again, this time falling to the floor. I hazard a glance towards Moores and Jade. "I don't know what the fuck happened. But I'll fix this."

"See that you do," Jade confirms. "This is your one and only warning."

Moores scoffs at Jade, mortified. He turns his burning glare at me, and if looks could kill, I'd be a pile of ash on the floor. "Are you fucking—"

"Let's go, Daniel." He pats his hand on Moores's shoulder and leads the way out. Moores gives me a final glare and exits my office.

After a moment, I allow the anger to rise inside me like a tidal wave. How in the fuck did the account close? Also, why the fuck was Moores so quick to turn on me? It doesn't make fucking sense. At least Jade has his head on straight still. I understand completely why they'd be fucking pissed. *I'm* fucking pissed. I plop down into my chair and start sending an email to Gilbert right away, trying to fix this situation.

A light knock on my door sounds before it opens gently. "Um, sir? Is everything alright?" Charlie asks, sweetly. *No, everything is not al-fucking-right.*

"Yeah. Just be prepared to leave at any moment. We may have a meeting to go to urgently. Take lunch now."

"But it's only 10 AM, sir."

"Take it now, or you might not get it. You have a half hour. Go." Charlie nods, closing the door behind her in a hurry.

My email dings, and I turn my attention back to the screen.

From: Gilbert and Sons
Subject: FWD: Account Closure
See below. Received this early this morning. Thanks, Sandy Gilbert Gilbert and Sons

From: Liam West
Subject: Account Closure

Dear Sandy,
It is with my deepest apologies that we have decided to cease working with you, and have thus successfully closed your account. The remaining balance of fees for last month will be billed and sent to your office, along with any other documents needed.

Thank you for your patronage,

Liam West
Accounts Division Manager

What in the actual fuck is going on? I didn't send this.
I look at my outbox. And there it is. The last message was sent at 1:40 AM. *Fuck me.*
Someone's setting me up.

CHAPTER SIXTEEN

Someone is fucking with me.

That's the only thing I've been able to think about the last few days. But I can't think of who the fuck it could be. I swear if I grind my teeth any more from all the stress, I'm going to need dentures before I'm thirty-five.

I've spent the last four days sleeping at the office, working around the clock trying to make sure none of my other clients were tampered with and trying to figure out who did this. Fucking sabotage.

But I still don't know who would do it, and why now? Everyone knows I have my eyes set on partner. Hell, it's common knowledge—I've been after it for years. The guys from work I'm close with don't seem likely culprits, but who the fuck knows? Not me, that's for sure. But I'll figure it out. What bothers me most is that Moores jumped right to firing me without waiting for an explanation. That seems a little strange to me. What I don't understand is why he would be the one sabotaging me, if I even believe it.

Luckily, nothing else has happened. Maybe it's just some vicious prank. But something nags at me in the back of my mind. Like I forgot something…

Oh, shit. Lexi.

I'm such an asshole. I know I don't technically owe her anything, but fuck. I've skipped out on all the classes I've signed up for as well. She probably thinks I'm avoiding her. I kind of am, but not intentionally. Now that she's on my mind, I can't escape her. Her slightly disappointed face when I left, the loneliness glistening in her eyes. Fuck. I regret leaving as much as I do going back to her place.

I quickly check her website for the class schedule to see when her last class is finished for the night so I can meet her there and talk. I need to explain why I've been gone. I make a few clicks as I navigate her site and finally find the calendar. Her last class ends at 5 PM tonight. That'll give me some time to finish up here and head over there.

I text my driving service that's on standby that I'll need a ride in an hour and a half. It'll take roughly thirty minutes to get there, so I bust through my work and make sure everything is secure and change my passwords again. I've taken to changing them every two days to make sure no one has access to anything. It's a fucking pain in the ass, but until I know things will not get fucked up again...

• • •

As 4:30 PM rolls around, I grab my things in a hurry, stuffing my phone, keys, and wallet into my slacks. Grabbing my navy Armani blazer off the back of my office door, I hustle to the elevator in record time to avoid all the people trickling out of the office. When I reach the lobby, the sleek black SUV with dark tinted windows rolls up and parks proudly at the entrance of the building.

The driver, Sam, gets out of the vehicle, rounding the front end and opening up the door for me as I exit the building. Tipping my head to him in greeting, I duck inside the back of the car and rattle off where we're headed. Once the driver is back in the car and pulling away from the curb, I dig my phone out of my pocket and send a quick message to Rhys and Brandt.

Me: *Might be late to watch the game. Meet you at the bar.*

They both respond with a thumbs-up emoji, and I tuck my phone into the inside breast pocket of my jacket as my foot bounces uncontrollably from nerves. Not sure if it's from seeing Lexi again, meeting up with Brandt afterwards, or maybe both. Shit. I'll have to tell Brandt I fucked Lexi. I groan to myself, and I notice Sam's wondering eyes perk up through the rearview mirror. I close my eyes, dropping my head into my hands as I scrub my face and feel the slight prickle of a beard growing. This just isn't my week.

• • •

Sam pulls the car up around the corner of Dundas and Bay Street near the side of the building before jumping out of the vehicle and opening the door for me. I thank him by handing him a hundred-dollar bill from my wallet as a tip. Sticking my wallet back into my pants, I check my TAG Heuer Carrera watch that gleams in the late afternoon fall sun, making sure I haven't missed her. I'm just a few minutes past the ending of her class; she usually sticks around afterwards to clean. My heart makes an erratic thump when I realize I'm going to catch her.

I push open the glass door to her gym, Yoga and Cycle, and a little bell dings overhead. I quickly pass through the doorway only for my feet to stop abruptly and plant firmly on the ground. My hands clench into fists as my teeth grind together. I think I might have even growled like a wolf.

There, standing a few feet away, is Lexi looking all gorgeous, sweaty, and glowing while she talks to that gangly nerd-fucker from the bar. Something sinister deep inside me worms its way into every inch of me. Seeping like poison and possessing me to do something I never normally would. She hasn't realized I'm here yet, and that makes this beast inside me fucking livid.

CHAPTER

SEVENTEEN

A week…It's been *seven fucking days*. And nothing. Sure, he doesn't have my number, but really, he knows where I work! He's supposed to be attending the classes, for shit's sake.

A sliver of doubt plants itself inside me, and my buckets full of anxiety sprinkle onto it. I try not to let the seed grow, but it's taking root. *What the fuck did I do? Was I too easy?* No. Stop it, Lexi. This isn't like you. You're better than a man that doesn't give you the time of day. You've done hook-ups before. This is no different.

I wrestle with my subconscious all day while going through the motions during my workout classes. I half-heartedly put the minimal effort in during my classes, but thankfully no one seemed to notice. All week I couldn't stop thinking about Liam. Every waking and sleeping thought was about him. What was he doing? Why hasn't he reached out yet? Why is he skipping classes? Is he ignoring me? Was I that lame of a lay? These thoughts cycle round and round inside my head, making me dizzier than spin class.

My phone beeps, and my watch vibrates on my wrist. I glance at it quickly and groan when Lillian's name pops up on the screen. Sighing, I unlock my phone and check the message.

Lillian: *Girl, I need deets on that man. Can you get me his number?*

Lillian needs to screw off. I know Liam isn't mine to claim, but Lillian? Really? The little green monster inside me is turning all of my thoughts towards Lill poisonous at this point. I clench my teeth as my feet swirl faster on the pedals of the bike, gradually getting so fast one of my students calls out to me. Snapping out of my daze, *again*, I mumble an apology and end the class early. My being distracted will only give them injuries.

As class is wrapping up, I cheer everyone on. "Good work today! See you tomorrow!" The crowd thins, and I make my way out of the classroom and into the entryway where the receptionist, Jan, sits. Bending over the counter, Jan pushes a water bottle towards me. His eyebrows shoot up into his hairline and nods to someone behind me. I give a slight groan, slapping on my fake business smile, straighten, and turn around.

Andy, one of my regulars, and the guy from the bar the other night, stands before me. His floppy chestnut hair is damp, falling into his eyes. Today he's sans glasses. My smile wavers slightly as I haven't been in the chatty mood lately. Jan packs up his things and slips out, leaving me alone with Andy.

"Hey, Andy. How was class today?" Inside I'm counting down the minutes until this conversation can end and I can go home and wallow for no real good reason.

"It was good. You're great at this, Lexi. If you hadn't already opened your own gym, I would suggest you should," he chuckles, and I humour him with a chuckle of my own, but it falls flat. His eyes twinkle as my fake laugh leaves my lips. His eyes flicker between mine, like he's building up the courage to ask me something. *Anything but that... please.* As his lips part to say something, I cut him off with my own questions.

"You know, I've never asked what you do for a living. You seem to live and breathe working out lately. What is it that you do that allows your schedule to be so flexible?" His eyes shine, and a large smile grows across his face, like he just won a prize.

"Well, actually I own my own small tech and software company. It's just a small startup right now..." He continues talking in detail about what he does, and I try to keep my eyes from glazing over, the conversation just not something I can hold my attention to. It beats him asking me out, which I feel like he was going to do. Even if he was someone I'd consider dating—he's not—I don't know if I'd be able to go on any dates right now. My head is so fucking confused, and my ego is bruised from this shit with Liam.

I know it was just a random hookup, but it was amazing. And it can't just be me who feels this explosive chemistry between us. If I'm being honest with myself, there was a flicker of it when I first met him, too, back when I was still with Brandt. I just don't know what to do or how to move on from this right now. There really isn't anything to move past which makes it harder in a way.

Andy's smile grows and chuckles, and I follow suit, trying to keep up in this conversation I haven't been paying attention to.

"So what do you think?"

I blink, completely confused.

"I'm sorry." A flush creeps across my skin. "What was the question again?" My nerves vibrate and jolt, hoping that I didn't just miss him asking me out. Praying it was a different question altogether.

"I was wondering if you'd—"

"Lexi," a deep, growling voice cuts off Andy and makes me jump in the process. Whirling around, I come face-to-face with the man that has blown me off for the last week. His narrowed grey eyes are dark and stormy as his jaw clenches. After the shock wears off, I fold my arms across my chest, trying to match his level of intensity. *He's the one who's pissed? It should be me.* Fucker.

"I'm in the middle of a conversation, Liam. You'll have to wait." Each word leaves my lips in an icy coating. As I turn to face Andy, pretending to feign interest in what he was going to say, a warm, giant hand wraps around my bi-cep, stopping me from turning completely. "Excuse you," I snap at Liam, yanking my arm away from him.

"We need to talk. *Alone.*" Liam's eyes dart to Andy, glowering at him. Andy looks like he shrank three feet, but is still trying to act as though he's unaffected. I admire Andy's attempt. I inhale a deep breath, blowing out a long sigh as I turn to apologize to Andy.

"I'm sorry, Andy. Can we continue this another time? I have something I need to take care of." His face looks like a boiled tomato. Red, puffy, and I swear there's steam rolling off his cheeks. His eye twitches as well. His eyes roll close as he draws a deep breath, the colour draining from his face.

"Sure, Lexi. I'll see you tomorrow." Liam snorts behind me, and I whip my head to level him with a deadly glare. He just shrugs his shoulders and looks away, his eye catching on a video playing on the TV in the corner of the lob-by. Redirecting my attention to Andy, I give him a weak, sympathetic smile and wish him a good night as he gathers his stuff and leaves. The moment the door closes, I throw a punch to Liam's arm, cracking a few of my knuckles, and a smug grin pulls at his lips. *Fucker.* It probably hurt me more than it hurt him.

"What the fuck was that all about? You don't get to come in here and act all alpha-hole when I'm talking to someone just because you want your turn. You can wait like a fucking adult. Also, you don't have any right to demand my time or attention after leaving me high and dry after the other night. And before you give me any lame-ass excuse—"

"You're right."

"Huh?" I must not have heard him correctly.

"I said, you're right." Nope. I did hear him correctly.

"Of course I'm right." I try to keep my tone even and confident, but I think it falls a little flat. My mind is drawing a blank on what I was just saying to him. I just stare at him, completely speechless. Liam's face relaxes, his rigid, clenched jaw releases, and his eyes soften. He takes a half step forward, and I match him with a step back. His eyebrows pull together in what looks like frustration. His arm shoots out, snaking around my waist and pulling me in close. His other hand weaves itself into the hair behind my ear, brushing the few loose strands back. He pulls me in tight against his hard, marbled chest, and my breathing deepens in rapid succession. He dips his head slowly, almost like giving me time to pull away, but I don't stop him. My heart is thundering in my chest, my body is screaming for him to kiss me. My lips part as he inches closer.

His lips are warm and plush as they brush against mine, but he stops there. Lingering, leaving us in limbo. "I'm sorry," he whispers against my lips. My breath catches at his apology, and just like that, everything I thought I was mad about is wiped away. I barely nod my head before his lips crash against mine, his arm squeezing my waist even more. His fingers grip my hair as he tilts my head back to deepen the kiss.

His tongue is soft with languid strokes as it explores my mouth, tangling with my tongue. His hand falls from my hair and trails down my body, palming my breast before travelling lower and gripping my ass.

"Fuck, Lexi," he whispers against my cheek as his lips move across my jaw line, pressing kisses behind my ear and trailing them down my neck. "You taste so fucking good."

CHAPTER EIGHTEEN

LIAM

She's everything I've been craving the last week. Light and sweet. A ray of sunshine in my otherwise lonely existence. Her perfect heart-shaped lips are full and soft as mine ravish hers. Her skin is sweet, with a hint of salt from the sweat on her skin from her classes for the day, but it only revs my engine more, making me wish it was because of me she was sweating. *Fuck. I need to be inside her.*

My lips break away from hers, and a soft whimper escapes her lips. Her eyes are still closed, drawing measured breaths before she opens them and looks at me.

"Give me your number."

"Okay," she answers breathlessly, a small shiver runs down her spine. Thankfully it wasn't an argument, because I wasn't asking. I slide my phone out of my pocket and hand it to her, and she enters her contact information.

"I've got to go now, but I'll message you." Her face drops, and I feel her heart and hopes dropping as well. "I've got plans, but I just needed to see you." She nods her head with her lips pressed thinly together.

"Okay, I'll talk to you later," she says, half-heartedly. It pains me because I know she doesn't believe me, and can I blame her? I blew her off for the last week. I tuck my hand under her chin and tilt it ever so slightly, then I press my lips to her forehead, a promise that I will message her later. She allows her body to melt into me just a little. "I've got to go. See you later, dove." A small sigh tangles with her breath. Regrettably, I have to let go of her. This neediness I have for her is new to me. I've never felt so strongly the need to protect someone. When I finally release, her face drops into a sad expression. I turn away, walking out the door without looking back because if I do, I know I won't leave.

· · ·

The sports bar is bursting with patrons, and the noise pours out of the entrance. It takes me a few moments to navigate through the crowd, that's close to violating fire code, to find Rhys and Brandt. They're nestled down at the far end of the room near the bar in a small four-person booth. I push my way between people to get over there and slide in opposite Rhys and Brandt.

"Sorry I'm a little late," I say as I flag down a waitress; they both give me a noncommittal shrug. The server pops over in her tight black dress that ends a little higher than her mid-thigh. A dark-grey quarter apron wraps around her waist twice. She smiles sweetly as she takes my order, waiting a few seconds and staring at me a beat longer than necessary before walking away. Rhys's head cocks and glances between me and the server with confusion, but then shakes it off.

"You've been MIA for the last few weeks," Rhys says. "What's been going on?" A small sliver of guilt coils inside me as I glance at Brandt, unsure if I should, or *want* to tell him about Lexi.

"Um, some shit at work is going down. Someone tried to drop one of my biggest clients, and someone's framing me for it, or it's just a really fucked up prank. Nothing else has happened since. So I'm just hoping its a fucked up prank."

Both Rhys and Brandt look at me, grimaces on their faces. "That's not good, man. What did Jade and Moores say?" Brandt asks, bringing his beer bottle to his mouth, taking a swig from it. I sigh, scrubbing my face.

"Nothing good. Moores fucking lost it on me, yelling and shit, threatening to fire me. But Jade talked him down. Gave me one warning not to let anything else happen. As if it was my fucking fault. I guess the only reason why I didn't get my ass handed to me is because I have a great relationship with the owner and his son, and was able to salvage it and keep them on.

"The part that really fucking gets to me is that I am *so* fucking close to the—" The waitress places my tumbler of rye and bottle of beers in front of me "—thank you—" I say without a glance at the server, but continue on with my conversation "—so close to the promotion of partner that I can't afford any more fucking screw-ups. And this one might even have cost me it if I hadn't been able to bring the Gilberts back on."

"Did you figure out how it happened?" Brandt asks.

"Someone used my email and basically said we're dropping them. And didn't delete any trace of it either." Brandt goes quiet, and I can see the gears turning in his head. He glances down at his beer and swishes the contents in it around.

"That sucks, man. I don't even know what to say. Think it's any of the guys you're close with at work fucking with you?" Rhys asks. I'm quiet as I contemplate this, thinking if Richie, Gavin, or Kane would have any ulterior motives to fuck with me, other than being funny jerks. But as I think about it, neither of them would use such a bold, risky move to fuck with me as a joke. It's a move that ruins one's career, and I don't think they'd do that. *I hope not*, at least.

I shake my head, trying to not think about it too much. I don't want any paranoia seeping into my thoughts about those guys. I'm as close to them as I am to Brandt and Rhys, if not closer. "Naw, I don't think so. They're good guys. I honestly don't think they'd do anything to fuck me over like that. They're all on the top of their game, and no one wants partner like I do. They're happy just rolling in the cash they make and fucking pretty women."

Rhys chuckles, "Aren't we all?" Both Brandt and I give him a sideways look, and he shrugs. "What? Riley is fucking hot, even more so as a mother. Those two girls got me wrapped around their fingers, and I'm not ashamed to admit it." Rhys was a stubborn ass for what went down between him and Riley. And as far as I'm concerned, he better worship the ground she walks on for putting up with his shit and taking him back. If you ask me, she should have made him work harder for it. I love Rhys, but man did he fuck up big time with her, and he's lucky she even gave him the time of day, child or not.

"Speaking of pretty women," Rhys trails off, looking towards the waitress that's over at another table, glancing over here, staring me down. When all three of us look over at her, pink kisses her skin as it spreads across her cheeks, and she looks away from us fast. "You gonna make a move on her tonight? She's basically drooling for your dick."

Unsure of what to say, I glance down at the tumbler in my hand. Instead of saying anything, I pick it up and swallow the entire contents in the glass. Brandt and Rhys give each other a weird glance. "So…Is that a no?" Rhys asks. I clear my throat, avoiding looking at the guys. "Oh man, you met someone didn't you? Well, who the fuck is she?"

"It's, uh, no one," I lie.

"Sure doesn't sound like no one. You would be bragging about it right now if it was no one." Rhys presses. "C'mon, boy, speak." As if I'm a dog and will listen to his command. Asshole. Brandt smirks but gives me a curious stare. I look away, feeling a pit forming in the bottom of my gut.

"We know her," Brandt says, his eyes piercing me, brows pinched together. Rhys's eyes widen with a wicked grin.

"Honestly, it's nothing. We just hooked up once."

Rhys sputters a laugh. "Oh God, he's practically in love, then." My hand curls around the beer bottle, my strength threatening to shatter the glass. "He looks guilty when he looks at you, Brandt. I bet it's someone you've been with, like Selena or something."

This piques Brandt's interest, staring at me with expectant eyes. *Fuck.* I just need to tell them.

"It's Lexi."

CHAPTER NINETEEN

"Lexi?"

Rhys is full on loving this. He's laughing and shaking his head. But it's Brandt that worries me. He's staring at me, his eyes narrowed.

He's pissed.

"Don't fuck with her," Brandt growls.

"A little late now, Brandt. He's already railed her," Rhys howls. His shoulders shake with the ferocity of his laughter bursting from his chest.

"Not what I mean," Brandt says. "Don't fuck with her just because you can. She's been hurt enough."

"Yeah, by you," I murmur under my breath. Brandt's face hardens, and I'm positive that he heard me.

"What I mean is, if you're just fucking her, using her, or whatever, just don't. She deserves more than that. You have no idea how much I wish I didn't hurt her."

Rhys finally zips his trap shut and looks away, pretending to watch the game on the television. Shouting nonsense at the screen that matches what others are yelling, as if he's been paying attention this whole time. *Coward.*

"Are you dating her now?"

I don't know what the fuck we're doing at this point. But all I know is there's something inside me that craves her. Something that's innately feral when I see her with another man, like this evening. My teeth clench together as I recall the images of that scrawny meat bag of a man touching her as they talked. The muscles in my jaw feather.

"If you're not going to date her, just stay away," Brandt says, a warning to me that I should probably heed. But instead I provoke him further.

"You gave up the right to speak on her behalf when you let her go. What her and I do, or don't do, is none of your business." Brandt sighs, looking away from me. His shoulders sag, and he relaxes into his seat.

"You're right. Just, please, be careful with her. She deserves more than a passing fuck buddy."

I'm stunned, and Rhys seems to be as well. We're both staring at Brandt with questioning looks. He backed down too quickly for me to be sure that he means it.

"So you're fine with whatever Lexi and I do?"

Brandt tenses, his hand twitching before he grasps his bottle and shrugs.

"Like you said, its really none of my business." He doesn't say anything again, except relating to the game.

• • •

A few hours later, back at home, my phone burns a hole in my pocket. The knowledge of having Lexi's number is driving me insane. It's taking every ounce of my self-control to not text her. Not to call her and hear her voice say my name. Just imagining my name on her lips makes my cock throb with an incredible desire I've never felt before. Thinking of her luscious pink lips parting in a moan, her round, supple breasts bouncing as I rock into her. Her nails digging into my back, biting into the skin, as I mark her skin with my mouth.

Before I know it, my phone is in my hand, and I'm messaging her something I hope I won't regret.

Liam: *Hey sexy.*

The dots appear on the screen, disappear, then reappear. It takes her a few seconds to respond.

Lexi: *Um. Who's this?*
Liam: *Don't play coy, dove. You know who this is.*

The dots appear and disappear again as I wait for her response, but it never comes. Growing impatient, my fingers fly across the screen, typing out another message.

Liam: *You can't honestly expect me to think you forgot whose cock was inside you, making your pussy clench so deliciously tight. Maybe you'll remember how I made you moan my name. Or how well I teased that pretty little clit of yours...*

I wait for her answer, anxious and insanely turned on. I fucked myself with this one. Sitting in my bed, I prop the pillow up behind me and lean into the headboard. My hand grips the bulge in my pants, trying to hold off the need to fucking rub one out. I do nothing but stare at the dots that bounce and then vanish. Over and over again. *Is this her way of torturing me?* Fuck, she's going to be the death of me. Finally my phone dings with her response.

Lexi: *BOB?*

White-hot anger sears through my veins.

Liam: *Who. The. Fuck. Is. Bob?*
Lexi: *Not Bob.*
Lexi: *B.O.B... My Battery Operated Boyfriend.*

I chuckle, although it comes out more like a growl.

Liam: *As long as it's only my real cock inside you, I don't care about any of these BOBs.*

Lexi: *Maybe you should care...These BOBs know how to get the job done. Oh, and he's doing a fantastic job. Right. Now.*

My cock rages against my boxers, roaring to be released and buried deep into her pussy. In a few swift movements, I'm dressed and texting my driver to be ready in five minutes. A quick pass with my toothbrush and I'm out the door.

CHAPTER

TWENTY

LEXI

My bottom lip is pinched between my teeth as I grin at my phone.

Desire pools in my core, making me long to be filled with Liam's cock. I can't stop reading his fucking sexy message, over and over.

Liam: *You can't honestly expect me to think you forgot whose cock was inside you, making your pussy clench so deliciously tight. Maybe you'll remember how I made you moan my name. Or how well I teased that pretty little clit of yours…*

I've never found sexting to be hot, but damn did he set my skin on fire. And of course I remember everything about that night. Even as angry as I am for him essentially ghosting me, it still plays on repeat in my mind. I don't know if I'll ever be able to get it off my mind. I partially worry that Liam has ruined me forever. Like no other man is ever going to measure up to how he can fuck.

There's just something, some natural chemistry or something, that just makes everything more intense. Maybe it has something to do with the taboo of it all. Ex's best friend, the trope that's beloved in romance novels. The fact that he should be off-limits speaks to my burning desire to have this man. But there's also the way he looks at me, like I'm finally being seen for the first time. It's only me.

There's a knock at my door, and I wonder who the hell it could be at this time of night. Not to mention who was able to get past the entryway without buzzing up. I don't know how I would have pissed off any neighbours as I'm currently sitting in the dark in my bedroom. I slink off my bed and grab my turquoise silky housecoat that hangs off the back of my door and wrap it around my body. The knocking at the door grows louder and impatient. *Who the fuck could it be?* Anxiety prickles inside of me, terrified of who might be on the other side. But as I near the door, something inside me tells me I already know who it is. My heart is pounding harder than ever before, even though I know, without a doubt, I'm safe. The man that's on the other side of the door will never do anything to hurt me, willingly. I don't know why or how I know this, but I do.

I wrap my hand around the handle while the other one unlocks the three different mechanisms on the door, and before I let him in, I draw a long breath. It does nothing to settle the jumbles and vibrations jolting inside me. Turning the door handle, I open the door slowly, Liam's imposing body gradually comes into view, and my heart stutters in my chest. He's standing there, staring down at me with fire burning in his eyes. His lip twitches briefly wiping the scowl off his face, but he doesn't make a move. We stand there, staring at each other, and I have to clench my thighs together because of the way he's looking at me.

My chest heaves rapidly as I try to regain the control of my breathing, but it's useless around him. Anytime he's near me, I lose all sense and control of my faculties. His eyes never waver from mine, and I can see the storm brewing behind his greys. I can see the confliction, the restraint passing through him in his eyes, letting me know he's just as affected as I am about him. The silence is deafening that surrounds us; all that I hear is the thrumming of my heartbeat and the faint ticking of the clock that's on the wall behind me. Something about this feels familiar. Like a repeat of the other night.

I swallow, thinking of something to say. *Anything* to say, but nothing comes. When suddenly Liam's body comes crashing into mine, his hands threading through my hair as he tips my head back and crushes his lips against mine, diving tongue first into my mouth.

"*Fuck, Lexi,*" he murmurs against my lips. "I need to teach you a lesson about teasing me." His voice is demanding, exacting. He steps inside my apartment, kicking the door closed behind him. His strong body leans against mine until he's pressing me up against the wall. His hands fall to mine, tangling my wrists in his hands and holding them over my head. Liam dips his head down, his lips finding my collarbone, and sinks his teeth into my flesh.

"Aaahh," I whimper, choking on a breath. I feel his lips curl into a smile against my skin, and his tongue flickers out, lapping at the area he just bit, soothing the sting. He traces kisses back up my neck, into my jaw, and behind my ear. Featherlight movements that make goosebumps pepper my skin.

"Your skin tastes so good, dove." His fingers move to the sash on my housecoat, deftly tugging, undoing it slowly. I attempt to keep my knees from buckling from this slow torture he's making me endure. When the wrap is finally undone, he pushes it to the side and kisses down along my neckline, pressing kisses along my cleavage, his lips brushing against the lacy trim of my nightie. "You're so goddamn sexy. Did you know I was going to show up? Is that why you're dressed like a fucking courtesan? My little, perfect slut."

Before he lets go of my wrists, he growls, "Don't move your hands." Another demand, and I nod, hypnotized by his voice. His hands skim my body, groping my breasts, flicking my nipples with his fingers, as his eyes never leave mine. It's so intimate, so…unnerving. His hands continue to travel—roam—my body. His hands pause at the dips in my hips, fitting perfectly. He trails them to the back, eclipsing the globes on my ass, palming them and squeezing. His fingers slowly gather the silky fabric of my nightie until my ass is exposed. "Mmm." A gravelly appreciation rumbles in his throat. "A G-string?" he asks, as he grabs the string between my cheeks and snaps it, jolting me in surprise. "Turquoise looks good on you…But you know what I think? I think red looks even better," he grumbles into my neck before latching onto me, and sucking hard. Marking me.

"*Liam*," I whisper, almost begging.

"Yes, baby?"

It takes all my nerves to speak up. "Please don't mark me. It's not professional." He growls.

"Then how else will everyone know you're *mine*?"

"I-I'm not *anyone's*," I stammer.

"No?" His hand moves to the front, his fingers pressing against the thin fabric on my pussy, which betrays me. "Then why are you fucking soaked through for me? It is for *me*, correct?" My breath catches, and I don't say anything. His nose brushes against my collarbone as his fingers tease me through the fabric. I resist chasing his touch, keeping my hips planted firmly against the wall. When I don't say anything, he chuckles. "Told you…You're mine."

His finger sneaks behind the fabric of my panties and dips into my wet entrance for a moment, before he pulls it out and brings his fingers to his lips and sucks. "You're so goddamn delectable. I need more."

CHAPTER TWENTY-ONE

LIAM

The moment her arousal touches my tongue, it's like taking a hit of heroin. She's a drug, and only she can satisfy my craving. My hands palm her thighs right beneath the crest of her cheeks, and I hoist her up, wrapping her legs around my waist. Her arms automatically wrap around my neck. I walk us down the hallway to her bedroom. A dim light filters out of one door into the hallway, and I follow the light.

Her bedroom is feminine, light, and airy. The same kind of pastels and light colours from her living room continues in here. Her walls are a pale yellow, her plush bedspread is rosy pinks, pale purples, and soft-green florals.

There's an accent chair in the corner of her room but it's draped in clothing and purses, a catch-all for things she's probably planning on wearing again, or something of a discard pile instead of putting them back into her closet. I suppress a smile. All women are similar. My mother and sister do the same thing.

I walk us over to her bed, dropping her down, and she lands on her back, her pale blonde hair cascading and haloing around her. I reach between her legs, hooking my fingers around the strings at her hips, pulling down her panties until I can flick them across the room. I take a good long look at her, admiring her beauty. Her knees are bent, but her pretty pussy peeks out between her legs just giving me enough of a show. Her nightgown is bunched up to her waist, her stomach is hollow with little nodules flexing every time she breathes. Her neck is red from the assault of my lips, my mark turning from red to a darker, murky shade.

"I was right and wrong," I murmur, my lips tugging into a smirk. Her eyes glaze over with silent questions, brows puckering. "You do look good in red. But you also look good in purple." Her lips part, and she draws in a sharp breath as her hand snaps to her neck, covering the mark I left behind. Her face dousing in crimson. "Don't be embarrassed, dove. You look fucking beautiful. Now, on your knees." Lexi hesitates, looking confused in the change of praise to demand. "Don't make me ask again, Lexi," I growl. She presses up on her forearms, slowly flipping over until her ass is in the air and pointed directly at me. Her nightgown is still hoisted over her waist, she makes a move to adjust it. "Don't. It's perfect. You're perfect," I say, admiring the view of her full ass and pussy on display for me.

I take a step closer and trail my fingers from her clit to her slick folds. She gasps, a slight moan of need on her lips. I withdraw my hand, and she whimpers so quietly, it could almost be missed. *Almost.* "Ahh, still a greedy little pussy, isn't she?" My hand opens and lands a sharp, but gentle blow to her pussy. She mewls like a cat, jumping out of her skin.

"What was that for?" she asks, breathlessly.

"For teasing me earlier." Another sharp blow to her pussy has juices leaking down her leg, and she's moaning. My fingers soothe the sting, swirling around her clit, building up her orgasm. Lexi's panting, moaning, and an utter mess. She's so fucking wet. As her arousal dribbles down her thigh, the small lamp that shines in the corner catches the wetness, making it glisten. I play with her clit, and take my time, circling around the spot she wants it most. Every so often I dip my fingers in her entrance and lubricate them with her juices just to tease her some more. She whimpers, trying to rock her body to catch more friction, and each time she does this, I back off. "Don't like being teased, do you my little dove? Well, neither do I." This time, I cup my hand and land another smack to her pussy, her legs wobbling from the pleasurable pain.

"*Please, Liam,*" she begs. Her lilted voice sounds so sweet as it's barely a whisper, floating in the air.

"Please, what?"

She pants, dropping her head between her shoulders,

her fingers curling into the covers. Like she's mad she's having to beg and ask for what she wants.

"Please, *what?*" I demand. She draws in a deep breath.

"Please…please let me come," she groans, displeased she had to ask. I smirk, burying the laughter in my chest with clearing of my throat. I'm glad she can't see how much I'm enjoying this. My cock aches and I squeeze it, fighting back the insane desire I feel. *Not today.* I take a few moments of silence to pretend to contemplate her request. "*Please??*" She asks impatiently, wiggling her ass a little.

"Hmm… No, I don't think so. Not tonight." A wicked smile blooms on my face. Lexi jolts upright, turns towards me, flushed and outraged. Her eyes are narrow and sharp as they throw daggers at me.

"What?!" she asks incredulously. "What the fuck do you mean 'no?'" She slowly shuffles off the bed and stands tall, not quite reaching my shoulders. Her eyes are blazing, and her jaw is clenched. Lexi's face only grows more furious as my smirk grows.

"It means exactly as it sounds. No. Not tonight. That's what you get for teasing me, to be teased in return." I grab her wrist, pull her into my chest, and plant a long, rough kiss on her lips. She automatically gets lost in the contact, opening her mouth to mine, allowing my tongue to slip in and lick every corner. I pull away rapidly, and head towards the door, leaving her stunned in my wake.

"Fuck you!" she hollers after me. I cock my head to the side and chuckle as I call back at her.

"Not yet, but you will be."

CHAPTER TWENTY-TWO

The next week is as tedious and tantalizing as the other night when Liam stopped by.

Liam seems to be hot one minute, then cold the next. He goes from one day texting me at all hours, then nothing for two days. It's infuriating and confusing, but aside from all that, I can't get this man off my mind. I find myself drawn to my phone, looking at it, unlocking the screen every fifteen minutes to make sure I didn't miss one of his messages.

I don't know what's happening right now between us, but part of me is thrilled at the attention. And maybe that's all this is, but it feels like more. I want it to be *more*. Liam gives me something I haven't felt in a really long time, if not ever. Most of our interactions have been revolving around sex, and that's fine. I just hope there's more to this than just mind-blowing sex. But if that's all there is, then I'll take it and ride the high until it fizzles out. But I really hope there's something here. Just as I'm thinking about messaging Liam, a message dings on my phone. I unlock it and read the message.

Lillian: *Hey, want to come out with me tonight? Abby and Henry are being very vague about their plans.*
Lexi: *It's probably because they're doing it. Haven't you noticed them acting weird when we all get together?*
Lillian: *WHAT? How have I never noticed this? Do you really think they're fucking?*

I sigh at my screen. Lillian is so oblivious to anything around her unless it involves her. I love her dearly, but fucking hell, she needs to pull her head out of her ass sometimes.

Lexi: *Idk how you've never noticed before. But it's fairly recent.*
Lillian: *So, are you going to come out with me tonight?*

I debate this question for a few minutes, and I come up with no good answer. It's a Friday night, and as much as I was hoping to hear from Liam, or even see him, I've received no messages all day. I can't be this chick that sits at home waiting for a guy. I don't want to be that girl anymore. I don't want to be the one who waits for some guy to finally realize she's worth something. Feeling as though I've decided, I message Lillian back that I'll meet her in an hour.

• • •

We've settled on a bar that's close to my place as I'm centred in the downtown Entertainment District. Surrounded by all the bars and fun places to hang out at night. We pick a little Korean barbecue place a few blocks down from the bar we're planning on dancing at. This tiny Korean place, Seoul Smoke BBQ, is crammed to the edges with tables, all of them full. My heart sinks as I was really looking forward to eating here tonight. Something about Korean food speaks to my stomach before I drown myself in liquor.

A sharp nudge into my ribs, and I glare at Lillian. She nods her head, pressing me to look in the far left corner's direction. There in the back with a bench/table combo that can accommodate up to eight people sits Liam and three guys that look vaguely familiar. I tear my eyes away, my heart racing in my chest, blood pounding in my ears. Lillian leans in, and I smell her powerful floral fragrance, but her voice is lost, drowning in the crowd.

"What?" I shout. I'm distracted momentarily as I feel as though someone is watching me. The hairs on the back of my neck prickle, and I look around to see if anyone is staring at me. I don't see anything, but a creepy chill washes over me. But Lillian's voice crashes through, bringing me back.

"Follow me," she shouts back, a wicked and cunning glint in her eyes. As she leads us towards Liam's table, I suddenly feel insecure. Am I dressed okay? Is my make-up smeared? *Oh my god… What if he thinks I'm following him??* Dread washes over me as my heart is now frantically beating in my chest. My vision tunnels, and it feels like everything around us is moving in slow motion, but we're running at *Flash* speed. I feel my heart beating in my throat, and I take a few deep breaths before we reach the table to settle down. Thankfully, they haven't noticed us.

"Hey boys," Lillian coos. She places her hand on her hip, while the other ruffles her short curly hair on top. Her bleached blonde hair is short on the sides, while it's a few inches long on the top, enough to make tiny ringlets. Her curls are styled in a tight fauxhawk-looking nest of hair. Grey eyes find mine, and I feel the stare down to my core. Heat simmers in my blood, and a jolt of desire shoots straight to my pussy. I can feel the desire seeping out of me, dampening my panties. The other three men ignore me as their stares roam all over Lillian in her tight burgundy wrap dress, paired with her black and red Louboutins. One of the guys sitting closest to Liam smirks in distaste at Lillian, grabs his drink, and gulps it down. Lillian's face soon matches her dress when she realizes she's been dissed. Her confidence only wavers for a second before she's shaking it off.

"Mind if we join you?" Her eyes look to Liam and feast on him. He looks at the trio and shrugs.

"Guess it's okay. Take a seat."

Lillian doesn't hesitate to take Liam up on his offer, joining the table, making the guy who's sitting in front of Liam shuffle down so she can sit in his direct eye line. The one beside Lillian actually stands up, motioning me to take his spot. I hesitantly move to sit down, and he takes the spot beside the guy that's sitting by Liam. I'm not directly in front of Liam, but his eyes are on me nonetheless. I feel them roaming my body, a hungry, possessive stare.

Liam's attention is torn away from me when Lillian's finger trails along his forearm, and his eyes narrow at the touch, his brows pinching together. "Well, aren't you going to introduce us, Liam?" Lillian batts her eyelashes at Liam before roaming her eyes over the other men at the table. The irritated one sitting beside Liam scoffs and looks away, making Lill's face redden again.

"The grumpy one to my left is Gavin, Kane is on the end, and beside Lexi is Richie. Stay away from him, he's a pervert and a sex addict."

"Ha ha," Richie laughs humourlessly. "Fuck you, bud." He turns to the busy restaurant and tries to flag down the server with his tanned arm that's roped with muscles. I glance away from him quickly but feel Liam's eyes burning into me, so I turn to face him and level him with one of my own deathly stares. Then the fucker smirks, like it's cute that I'm trying to challenge him. My phone vibrates in my clutch, and I pull it out, and there's a message waiting from Liam. Shocked, I glance at him, wondering how the hell he was able to send me a message and I didn't even see him pull out his phone.

I'm a little nervous as I open the message.

Liam: *Don't even fucking think of flirting with one of these assholes.*

I grin at the screen, wondering how long it would take to drive him to caveman status. I wasn't even thinking of flirting with any of his friends, but now that he's planted that idea in my head…Maybe it's time to have some fun watching him lose his composure. I purse my lips, trying to stifle the grin and maniacal laugh that's bound to burst from me if I'm not careful.

Lillian starts up a conversation, asking how they all know each other and what they do for a living. I'm not really paying attention as I plot my move on who to hit on. I take in each of his friends, wondering which one would fuck with him more. Each man is handsome in their own way, which is ridiculous to be seated with so many sexy men at one table. Thank goodness this isn't a bar, or Lillian and I would be the envy of all the single ladies in the room.

Gavin, the grumpy one has a rigid scowl on his face, his blue eyes cold and unforgiving. His body is tense, as if our presence is unwarranted or unwanted, which for him, probably is true. His large hand stays wrapped around his beer, while the other pushes away his dinner, his face paling like he's going to be sick. His thick waves of chestnut hair fall onto his forehead, creeping into his eyes, making him look dark and dangerous. Probably not the right person to fuck with, nor flirt with. I'm sure he can turn it on and off like a professional, but something about him screams *leave me alone.*

Richie, who's beside me, is a total no. He reeks of alcohol, and every woman that walks past, his eyes trail right along behind them, his head swivelling on his neck like an owl. His deep olive skin speaks to his European culture, Italian I'm betting or maybe Portuguese. He feels like a slimeball though. And the fact that Liam made that comment, I don't want Richie to get the wrong idea.

Then my gaze lands on Kane. Arguably the most attractive of all four of them, after Liam, of course. His back hair is thick and slicked back as though he just came from work, and possibly did considering he's still wearing his suit. His calm green eyes are kind and welcoming, but there's a hint of darkness behind them. Something…sinister? It's definitely a quality that draws you in, making a perfect trap for the predator to catch his prey. His shoulders are wide and sturdy, and his arms strain against the fabric of his blazer. He looks like he could throw you around like a rag doll and make you scream, begging him to stop. Yes, I think he'll do.

My eyes flash over to Liam's. His eyes are narrowed, angry, and unwavering as he stares me down, making small motions with his head as he listens, or pretends, to Lillian.

One small flick of my lips, and I'm giving him a sickly-sweet grin.

Game on.

CHAPTER TWENTY-THREE

She's playing with fire. And I don't give a fuck if she gets burned.

Because I will be the one holding the match.

I slide my phone out of my pocket, hiding it under the table as I type out a message to Lexi.

Liam: *You're going to lose this game, dove. Don't play in the big leagues if you're not ready to take the loss.*

I smirk when I see her typing a response, a flurry of fingers skittering across the screen.

Lexi: *Go big or go home. That's what they say, right?*
Lexi: *I wonder just how big Kane is and if he's willing to go home...*

Holy fucking hell. This chick has some fire in her.

Liam: *Challenge accepted.*

I take my eyes off my screen for a moment and catch the rosy tint to her skin that's illuminated by her screen. Fuck, she looks gorgeous. Her perfect lips are stained red, plump, and kissable. Her cleavage is shown in a tasteful, yet generous helping thanks to a push up bra, no doubt. Her skin is creamy and almost translucent—shimmery— against the black mini dress she's wearing. She gives me a tight smile, full of mirth, as she turns to Kane and engages him in conversation. My jaw ticks for a second, but then I turn my attention to Lillian, who's been vying for my attention all night.

"So, *Lillian*," I say in a low, gravelly rumble. Earning me a sideways glance from Lexi. "You look fucking gorgeous tonight. What were you ladies planning on doing tonight?"

Lillian shakes out her shoulders, pressing her breasts forward a bit, hoping to get me to glance down. I play into her game, and raise the stakes with Lexi. I glance down at Lillian's cleavage, but it doesn't compare. Lexi's breath catches and I smirk. My eyes flick back up to Lillian's face, and she looks like she just won the lottery. There are stars in her eyes, and her smile is confident and proud.

"We were just going to go out dancing after dinner," she purrs. Her fingers trail along my arm and makes my hair stand on end, and not in a good way. It doesn't feel right, her touch feels wrong. There's only one woman's touch I want on me, and she's trying to flirt with my buddy. Instead of letting Lillian take control, I flip my hand over and trap hers in mine, holding it in place. More or less to stop the incessant tickling, but it works twofold, as I see Lexi's eyes grow wide, her face reddening and flustered.

"Yes, we were going to go dancing," Lexi turns her attention to Kane. He's eating up the attention she's giving him. They all know who's fucking her, so I'm not sure why he's playing into her games. "Unless...*someone* has a better offer. Then I'm game." She flashes him her most flirtatious smile, batting her eyelashes and biting her lower lip. Kane's eyebrows raise into his hairline, surprised by her forward comment, I'm guessing. He gets a wicked smirk on his face.

"And what if *I'm* offering?"

Lexi flushes, her lips parting, unsure of what to say. She makes a few incoherent noises before actually saying anything.

"I, uh. Um, yeah." She quickly shakes it off, rolling her shoulders and flicking her soft blonde hair over her shoulders. "Well, I'm *willing*." Her eyes flick to me, and a feral beast is roaring to get out. I know this is all an act—a game—but on the off chance Kane or Lexi takes it too far, I'll be fucking damned. I don't know about Lexi, but Kane doesn't like to lose a challenge. It's why he's one of our better lawyers and onboarding specialists for the clients at the firm. He's a panther in Armani clothing, waiting to pounce on his prey. Not willing to let it slip through his claws. And Lexi will be no exception.

I clear my throat, ripping my hand away from Lillian's, and her body sags, leaving her feeling rejected. My eyes land on Lexi.

"Don't you have an early class tomorrow morning? Why are you even going out dancing and drinking?" My voice comes out harsher than intended. But Lexi levels me with a glare and a smirk.

"Hm…One, why do you know my schedule?" Her voice fills with joyous challenge. "Are you stalking me? And, two, why does it matter what I do? You're not my father, my boyfriend, or even my *fuck* buddy." She shrugs her shoulders nonchalantly. "Kane, do you share this same notion? That I shouldn't be out on a 'work' night?"

Kane's lips curl into a twisted little smile, knowing exactly what's going on, and he plays right into it. I don't know if it's to fuck with me, or if he's just getting a kick out of this exchange. Probably both.

"Oh, I definitely don't share that notion. I find that exhausting your body the night before a workday can sometimes be therapeutic and rejuvenating if done with a certain activity." He's looking her dead in the eyes, and I can see the flush creeping across her alabaster skin. Her chest is rising rapidly, accentuating the curve of her cleavage, and I catch Kane glancing down at it. *Fucker's going to get decked.*

I watch as Kane laces his fingers with Lexi's. Something inside me snaps, and I can't take this game any longer. I stand up abruptly, and everyone turns to face me with curious looks but Kane and Lexi. Her eyes are on their intertwined hands, while his eyes stay locked onto her face. I clear my throat annoyingly loud and obnoxious until Lexi's foggy eyes lift from their hands to my face.

"A word, Lexi?" I grumble, and she snaps out of her daze, her breathing still rapid. She dips her head in a curt nod, stands, and follows my lead as I take us towards the washrooms.

• • •

"What the fuck was that, little dove?" I growl low as my lips brush her ear, my body pressing her into the wall, and her hands pushing against my shoulders. She shivers against me, and I feel the pebbling of her nipples through the top of her dress. "Do you want to test my patience?" My hands skim the curves of her body until my hand reaches the hem of the skirt. I snake my hand up, and move my body so that I'm shielding her from anyone who walks down this dim corridor. My hands seek her heat, revelling in the warmth that I find. Her panties are soaked through, clinging to her skin as I move them to the side.

"Tsk, tsk. What a naughty little slut," I murmur in her ear. Her breath stutters as my finger slides into her with ease. I pump once, twice, before adding another finger. The heel of my palm rubbing against her clit. "Do you want to keep playing games, my dove? Shall we play one right now?"

Lexi moans, biting her lip to keep the sound from getting louder. My chuckle comes out dark and playful. "Is that a yes?" Another moan slips from her lips as she rolls her hips. "Let's play how long it'll take me to make you come?" She's panting, and her fingers curl into my charcoal T-shirt, grabbing fiercely until her knuckles blanch. "By the looks of it, it's a game I'm going to win. And quickly too."

My lips crush against hers, my teeth pulling at her bottom lip. Biting and nipping it as she gasps for air, and my tongue soothes the bite. I plunge my tongue into her mouth, moving deeper as my fingers explore deeper into her channel. Hooking them, I find that perfect spot. As I stroke it, keeping a regular rhythm, gradually gathering speed, I use my thumb to rub gentle circles on her clit. It's not long before she's panting wildly, and I use my mouth to keep her quiet. My lips ravage hers, swallowing her moans. She's incoherent, chasing her orgasm, but I hear footsteps heading this way.

I rub frantically, pumping my fingers harder and faster until she lifts her leg and hooks it around my waist, giving me more access. I plunder deeper inside her still, feeling her wetness dripping down my hands.

"Li-Li-mmmm," she moans into my mouth; almost ready to tumble over the edge. I keep pumping into her, slowly downshifting my speed, not quite ready to let her orgasm. The steps are getting closer, and I feel Lexi's body tensing, coming to the realization of where we are and what just happened. Her hand leaves my shoulder, and she grabs my wrist and rips it out of her. Her face burns with embarrassment as she frantically fixes her dress and hair. Her fingers wiping at the edges of her lips, trying to reduce the smearing of lipstick.

"*Fuck*," she whispers. "*Fuck, fuck.*" The clicking of shoes stops just behind me.

"Lexi?" A husky, feminine voice calls out. Lillian. Lexi goes completely rigid, her eyes are as wide as the moon.

"Uh, yep! Coming!" I glower at Lexi, and she must read my thoughts. "Uh, actually, I'm not feeling so well. I think Liam's going to take me home."

CHAPTER TWENTY-FOUR

Lexi

"Liam's going to take me home."

But as we leave the restaurant, he takes off in the opposite direction. He pulls his phone out of his pocket and messages someone.

"Uh, where are we going?" I ask, my legs working double time to keep up with his long, purposeful strides. A black SUV swerves up to the sidewalk where we are and parks. A little wave of apprehension washes over me. "Liam?" He turns and looks at me.

"My place." He opens the door and helps me in, nodding to the driver in the front seat. "Home, please." The driver pulls away from the side of the road and merges back into the traffic. Liam then pushes a button on the side of the door and a partition rises, blocking out the front cab of the car, leaving me and Liam utterly alone.

His large hands grab hold of my thighs and tear me from my seat, placing me on his lap. I straddle him, my skirt bunching around my hips as he digs his hands into my hair and pulls my head in close. His lips encase mine in a rough, heated kiss. His kiss is impetuous, rushed, and charged. A clashing of teeth and lips. His hands untangle from my hair and rest on my hips before gripping them. He guides my hips, rotating and rolling them against his crotch, pushing me down closer to him, showing me just how much he wants me. His cock throbs between my legs, growing harder and longer with each pass of my hips.

"Fucking hell, Lexi," he mumbles against my lips. "You're going to be the death of me."

• • •

A short ten minute ride of kissing and dry humping has me all but leaking from my pussy. Thankfully Liam's jeans are a dark wash denim, and it's dark enough outside where the wet spot on his pants is virtually invisible. Liam barely waits for the car to come to a complete stop before he's opening the door and carrying me out of the car. My feet finally reach the pavement, and he takes a moment to adjust himself, tucking his cock into his waistband. He laces his fingers with mine and tugs me along, trailing behind him as he takes us into his building.

He punches the forty-ninth floor, so close to the penthouse. He pushes me to the opposite side of the elevator, and just stares at me. Like a hunter studying its prey. My stomach crawls up my throat as his gaze penetrates me. Shifting my balance nervously, I try to look away, find something to focus on, but all I can see is him. After what seems like an eternity, the elevator finally dings, and Liam presses his thumb to a tiny glass square on the elevator panel, and the doors slide open. He holds out his hand, and I place mine in his, and he guides me out of the elevator into a large, grand entryway.

"What—This is where you live?" A cocky smirk grows on his face. "You live in a penthouse?"

"*The* penthouse." My head whips around to face him.

"The penthouse? How? What?" I'm at a loss for words. This is an elaborate penthouse. A two-storey penthouse, to be exact. There's marble flooring, opulent sconces, glittering, dangling chandeliers. Gold, brass, or silver in different nooks and crannies of the main entrance. A large, luxurious two-door walk-in front closet. My eyes are filled with curiosity and wonderment as I look around the foyer—and it's a true foyer at that. A small table adorned with brass legs and a marble top sits proudly between two cream-coloured armchairs, one with a white fuzzy blanket draped over the back.

Liam leads me further into his home, and a large, open staircase wraps away from the wall, giving a grand entrance feeling to the room. As if a princess or a lady should descend these stairs in a gorgeous gown. On the wall above the stairs is a large hand-painted mural. A mix of colours blending together to make a beautiful field of lavender. Rows upon rows of lavender on a hot day in the countryside. Looking at this painting I can feel the warmth it exudes, the way the sunlight kisses my skin in the summer. How on a hot day, you can feel overcome with chills from the warmth that the sun beats down on you.

None of this seems like Liam's taste. And I know he has money, but just how much? To afford something like this in the Toronto area? It's like something out of a fairytale or romance novel. I look over at Liam, wonderstruck. He just shrugs and gives me a cocky smirk.

"I had a client who had no sons, daughters, or any family members to pass this place onto. So when he died, he gave this place to me. He always used to call me 'the son he never had.' I've only recently moved in here, so it's not quite my taste in decor."

"A client just *gave* you this place? A whole fucking penthouse? This place has got to be worth—"

"Five million dollars, give or take."

"Five…*Five million dollars?* And that just rolls off your tongue like it means nothing?" Liam shrugs.

"It's only money. There are far more valuable things in life."

I look at him, shocked. Stunned. Flabbergasted. Whatever else, you name it. And the nonchalant attitude he sports along with this irritates me. Suddenly, I feel out of my depths being here. He sighs, scrubbing his eyes when he sees my face.

"I only mean that I grew up with nothing, so I learned to never take things for granted. I worked my ass off to get everything I own, everything I have. I'm a ruthless business-man when I have to be, I'm a caring friend when I need to be, and I'm someone's greatest comfort when they have no one. I've learned to adapt to be who I need to in order to get where I am today. I don't see this place as anything other than a place where I sleep, eat, and fuck. Just like any other condo or house I could have. Before this, I was just renting. But when this opportunity came for a place that was fully paid for, I said fuck it and moved in because why not?"

I glance around the sitting room and take it all in. The two couches facing opposite of each other with the two arm chairs in the middle facing the large, floor-to-ceiling windows that overlook Toronto.

"I'm planning on getting this place renovated and decorated closer to my style. I can't stand the timely look, a little gaudy for me. But like I said, it's just a place to eat, sleep, and fuck. The rest will come eventually." There's a pregnant pause between us as I continue my assessment of this space. "Would you like a tour?" I turn to look at him, and his eyes simmer playfully.

"Sure," I whisper. Darkness flickers across his gaze, and his lips upturn into a sexy, mischievous grin.

"I know where the first stop on our tour will be." He grabs my hand and drags me behind him until we reach the bottom of the stairs. He then lifts me into his arms, bridal style, and takes the steps two at a time. It's like we're flying up the stairs with how fast he's going. Liam keeps a steady pace until he's reached two double doors that are closed. The arm that's supporting my torso slides, and the hand that's gripping me lets go, forcing me to hold my own weight by tightening my arms that are laced around his neck. The latch to the door clicks, and he nudges it open with his foot. He walks us into the middle of the room and tosses me onto the bed from the foot. I land somewhere in the middle of the soft mattress. Liam stalks around the corner and turns on a lamp on one of the nightstands.

When the light illuminates the room, I'm surrounded by a modern four-post bed, with intricate swirls and loops cut out of the headboard. The room is painted a dark navy, so dark it's almost black in the dim lighting. The marble floors peek out of a charcoal throw rug the size of the room, leaving only a two foot gap from the walls. As I look forward, I notice a large white-painted slab in the middle of the wall with a fireplace crackling underneath it.

"What's with the boring white square?"

Liam chuckles, reaches into the top drawer of his nightstand and pulls out a remote. A whirring noise fills the room, and an image flickers onto the wall. I glance up, and a stream of light pours outward to the wall, bits of dust coiling and twirling in the fractured light. "*Ooohhh*, it's for a projector. That makes sense now."

Liam grins, pulling down the top layers of the bedspread, and strips down naked while he pauses between articles of clothing to pull up Netflix and put on some true crime documentary. I must give him a horribly screwed up face because he barks out a laugh as he slides into the bed, pulling the covers up around his waist.

"I thought we were coming here to fuck?"

"So impatient, my dove. Strip down and get into bed with me. There'll be time for fucking later. Right now, I just want to watch this show and forget about how Kane's hands were touching you tonight."

CHAPTER TWENTY-FIVE

I spent the rest of the weekend at Liam's. It was a strange sensation to barely know someone for as short a time as we have and spend literally all weekend together fucking, talking, and goofing around. It was actually a nice change for once, to feel overwhelmingly welcomed and wanted. To have someone's undivided attention on me. Even when I was with Brandt, I always felt like something was missing. Like he was partially out the door, just waiting for...well, Elissa.

I was just a means of passing time for him, and I'm starting to realize that was the hardest part. It wasn't the fact that I loved him and he broke my heart, it was that I felt insignificant, or he treated me like I was insignificant once the right person came back around. This weekend with Liam has shown me that I can be someone's sole universe, even if it's just for a moment in time.

Every conversation, laugh, and witty banter between us this weekend has me only falling harder for this man. I still feel like we're only starting to get to know each other, but deep down it's like my soul recognizes him—knows him. But before I let myself get in too deep with him, like I did Brandt, I really need to take this slow. Make sure he won't hurt me. He hasn't outright said anything yet, but I don't want to wait for someone to finally decide I'm worth it.

I bend over, lacing my shoes in my office for the first class back from the weekend. These 6 AM classes are for the intermediate students who want to push themselves as an extra warm-up before our next session at 6 AM. They get a blast of cardio for forty-five minutes, then a short break before we start up again into a regular, full sixty minute class. The regular class is more about endurance building, playing with the bike's tension, whereas the other class is really just to warm up the joints and muscles by pedalling as fast as you can and working up a sweat.

As the class filters in, my mind wanders off back to this weekend and the sexy man I spent it with. I'm staring down, looking at my bike goofily, as a shadow casts over me, almost scaring the shit out of me. I place my phone on the pedestal beside me and look up.

"Jesus, Andy. You almost scared me half to death," I say, placing my hand over my chest. A smile that probably is meant to be sweet but comes off creepy sprawls across his face.

"Mind if I chat with you after class today? Considering our time was cut short last time…"

An uneasiness falls over me, plummeting my stomach to my feet. "Um, sure. I guess if we have time. Is everything okay?"

Andy smiles again, and gives me a wink. "Everything's fine. We'll talk after." He shoots me finger guns and another wink before he walks away. I try to suppress a creeped-out shiver that rolls through my body, but am unsuccessful. I shudder and shake it off as I prepare for class, hooking up my phone to the Bluetooth speaker surround sound. I'm scrolling through my Spotify playlists I've crafted, trying to find one that will set the tone for the class when a message pops up on my screen.

Liam: *Morning dove. I'll see your sexy ass shortly. Enjoy your first class.*

My heart leaps from my chest, and butterflies take flight in my stomach. It takes everything inside me not to squeal at this moment. Something this weekend between us just clicked. But I'm still terrified it's only on my side. I exit the conversation, feeling hopeful and energetic to start my day. I find an uplifting soundtrack and press play as I wait for the students to find a bike and get settled in for class.

• • •

After class is over, I almost forgot that Andy wanted to talk to me. I know I shouldn't be mean and dismiss him, but knowing what he was almost going to ask me after last class, I'd rather just avoid him and the awkward conversation and not risk hurting him. Sometimes Andy can be intense, and almost clingy. I know he has a crush on me, anyone with eyes can see that, but sometimes he acts like it's more than a crush. Sometimes, and almost too often, I think it's not coincidental we show up at the same places. I gather my stuff from the stand beside my bike quickly, unclipping my feet from the pedals. Making my way to the door in a hasty fashion, I dodge everyone in the classroom that's wanting to talk to me. "Sorry! Nature calls!" I holler. Rushing to my office, I close the door behind me and lock it.

I waste about ten minutes in my office, but make good use of my time sorting files. I check the monitor in the corner of the room that has multiple angles of my security feed. Andy no longer seems to be waiting around anymore. I sigh in relief, pile the leftover papers neatly on my desk, and make my way to the door. I need at least ten minutes to wipe all the bikes down before the next class, so I need to hustle. When I open the door, my heart drops in my chest and I almost pee myself. Andy is standing right in the doorway, blocking me in.

"Uh, Andy. What are you doing?" An uncomfortable shiver breaks over my body, the fine hairs on my arms pricking to attention. A sinking feeling in my gut takes hold, and I'm suddenly aware that he's blocking the only exit from my office.

"We never got to chat." His words are chilling and leave me with an eerie feeling. His face doesn't help the situation either. His eyes are lit up, wide, almost crazy looking. Andy's brows are wild and raised. His smile is baring his teeth and tight.

"Oh, uh…Sorry about that, Andy. I got caught up. Can we do this later? There's only a few minutes before the next class, and I have to prepare—" He steps towards me, forcing me to take a step back into my office. His grin only grows, looking more like a deranged Cheshire. My throat and mouth dry up, and I find it difficult to swallow. Andy leers at me as he takes another step into my office, and I have to shuffle back. "A-Andy? I really have to go now. People will be arriving any min—"

"What the fuck is going on here?" My heart leaps in my chest as Liam's growling voice cuts me off. Andy stiffens, his nose twitching in annoyance. His eyes roll closed as he takes a breath before turning around to face Liam. Something in Andy shifts, and he becomes this nervous, nerdy persona that I know so well. The seemingly innocent man that I thought he was.

"Uh…Oh, we were just chatting. N-n-nothing else. I sh-sh-should go now. See you next time, Lexi." And he scurries past Liam, gathering his things and rushing out of the gym but not before one final glance backwards, and something dark flickers in his eyes. Once he's gone I can finally breathe. I release a giant breath I didn't realize I was holding. Liam grabs my wrist, pulls me into him, and wraps me in his arms. The warmth radiating off of him calms me, and I melt into him, relaxing and snuggling my head into his chest.

"What was that all about?"

"I honestly don't know. He just kind of cornered me as I was coming out of my office." My voice comes out shaky, and I take another breath to relax my nerves. I step out of Liam's arms as people start coming in for the 6 AM class. "I've got to get ready. Are you joining this class?" His smirk sets off a kaleidoscope of butterflies, swooping and looping in my chest.

"Why else would I be here at the ass crack of dawn?" I take a moment to appreciate the man standing before me. He's got a tight black Under Armour T-shirt on that clings to every hard ridge of his body, and it leaves very little to the imagination. But lucky for me I know exactly what his rippling chest of muscles looks like. My eyes glance down at the black basketball shorts he's wearing, down to the black Nikes he's got on his feet. His calves are perfect half-moons with corded muscles. As I glance back up, I notice his bulge has grown in the last few seconds. "If you don't stop checking me out," he growls. "You're going to have to cancel your class, and I'm going to fuck you on your desk."

Heat rushes to my face, and I sigh. I would rather be getting railed on my desk right now, now that I know that it's an option.

"Is that a promise or a threat?" I ask in a sickly-sweet voice, batting my lashes, and biting my lip for good measure. Liam's face shadows over, a wicked playful look in his eyes.

"Don't test me, dove. We all know what happens when you test my patience."

"Hmm…But isn't that half the fun?"

CHAPTER TWENTY-SIX

Fuck. Fuck. Fuck.

I furiously type away into the client management system trying to find another one of my bigger accounts.

Gone.

Like they never existed.

Not like last time, when it said the Gilberts were cancelled. I've got to fix this before Jade and Moores find out. This is not fucking good. White, searing-hot anger flashes through me, and I squeeze my mouse until it shatters in my hand, and I whip the pieces across the room. What the fuck is going on? Why is someone trying to fuck with me?

I grab my phone out of my pocket and dial Brandt. "Hello?"

"Hey man. I need your help. Remember when I told you about someone fucking with me at work? Well, it's happened again. But this time they deleted an account entirely."

"Fuck man, that sucks. What can I do?"

"I hate to ask, but it's my ass on the line. Think one of your IT guys can figure out what the fuck happened and restore the info?" There's a small pause on Brandt's part, and I just hope it's not hesitation. But I hear the clacking of the keyboard and clicks of his mouse.

"I can send Jessie over in fifteen minutes to do some work on your servers. I'll even have her upgrade some of your firewalls on your computer and on the servers."

"Thanks, man," I sigh in relief. "Also…One more thing. Can you have her bring me a new mouse?"

• • •

Two hours later and I'm fucking sweating, pacing my office as Jessie is working her IT magic. Her chestnut hair is swept up into a messy knot that sits at the top of her head, stray pieces sticking out along her hairline. A smattering of freckles cross the bridge of her nose, and her lapis lazuli eyes are sharp as they laser focus on the screens in front of her. Her XPS 17 Dell laptop is plugged into my MacBook Pro running diagnostics, and she shuffles between the two setups, trying to find the root cause of the issues, and hopefully the perpetrator.

"Uh, Liam?"

I stop dead in my tracks, spinning on my heel to face Jessie.

"Yeah, can you please stop pacing? It's starting to give me anxiety now, and making me fucking dizzy." Her eyes glance up to me and back down at the screens. "Actually, I'm hungry, and since, you know, you're doing nothing but pacing, why don't you make yourself useful and go get us some greasy food. I work better when there's grease on my fingers and fries in my belly."

I smirk. "Sure, what do you want?"

"Honestly, Big Joe's is my favourite."

"But that's all the way in Scarborough."

"Yes, but if someone were doing *me* a favour, I'd be super generous to them and go out of my way to get them exactly what they wanted. Especially since they're so close to restoring lost information. So I *get* to choose what I want, that'd be Big Joe's please. Double bacon cheeseburger, all the toppings, and extra large fries with Cajun spice. Ooooh, and a frozen lemonade. Please and thank you. Okay, byeeeeee."

She stands up from the desk, ushering me out of the office. This petite but voluptuous, five-foot, five-inch woman is pushing me out the door and asking for something a man my size would eat. I laugh, shaking my head as I text my driver to meet me downstairs. I guess it's to Scarborough I go.

• • •

When I get back, literally everything seems to be in chaos. People are scrambling around the different floors of the office, papers are flying everywhere, and even some people are throwing everything. I race to my office to see what happened. Jessie is sitting there typing like a mad woman.

"C'mon, c'mon, you fucker. Show me who you are," she mumbles to herself.

"What the fuck is going on?" I demand. She pops a sucker into her mouth and holds up a finger to me, indicating I need to wait patiently for an answer. Like fuck. I walk around the desk, dropping her sachet of food on the corner of the desk, and lean over her shoulders. I look at the screen, and all I see is code. Do I know what it means? Not a fucking clue, but her fingers are still flying across the keyboard, and she's muttering to herself.

"Let's see you get out of this… Hahahaha." Her maniacal laughter worries me a little bit about her sanity. "No, no, no. FUCK!" She shoves the keyboard away from her, pushing it in defeat, throwing her hands up in the air. I look at her with a worried look as she spins around to face me. "Well, you have a hacker. In the whole system. I was able to restore the lost information, but the person doing this is good. They know what they're doing and hid their traceability. The only thing I can see is that they're not within the vicinity of the building when doing this, so I don't think it's someone here."

"Wait, so you're saying you were fighting with the hacker just now?"

Jessie grins, a sparkle dances in her eyes.

"Oh yeah. The highlight of my day, even though I lost the fucker. Managed to escape my trap before I could get his IP and location."

"So why was everyone freaking out?"

"Oh, that. The hacker is diabolical. You must have really pissed someone off. They made a huge diversion to access your personal information on the server by making it look like the stock market was crashing. They rerouted all of your company feeds to their own made-up stats, and everyone started losing it. It was pandemonium."

"They accessed my personal information?" My eye twitches, and I immediately get a migraine.

"Yeah, they did. But don't worry too much. It's all of your old information. I verified. I got your new address to cross check what information was correct."

I cock my head at her. "How did you manage that?"

Jessie's face lets a grin slip, and she blushes. "Er, I may or may not have hacked Service Ontario."

"What?"

Jessie shrugs. "I mean, the firewalls are like baby gates. They suck incredibly."

"So, what's going to stop this hacker from getting my information from Service Ontario as well?"

"Oh, that hacker probably won't be able to get it."

"But you just said the firewalls are like baby gates."

Jessie looks bored trying to explain this to me. She reaches over to the bag from Big Joe's I bought for her. She uncrinkles the bag and pulls out a few fries and stuffs them into her mouth.

"Yeah, they are," she says in between chewing. "For me. Not some amateur hacker. Don't worry, once I'm done updating your server, firewalls, and computer security, they won't be able to get back in again."

"And how do you know this?"

Jessie gives me a pathetic looking smirk, as if she's genuinely offended she has to explain her prowess.

"Because I built both Harrington Tech and CGC Infrastructure on their servers. Even the black hats I've contacted to help me make sure everything is secure? They couldn't hack it."

I'm shocked by this information. I knew Jessie was good, but I didn't know how good.

"Then why are you only working for Collins Global Collective?" She shrugs, stuffing the double bacon cheeseburger into her mouth and ripping off a piece.

"I dunno," she says around a bite. "Brandt pays really well, and I get to do as I please. Too much responsibility having my own company. And don't even get me started on all the red tape and bullshit surrounding the government." She's quiet and thoughtful for a moment. "It's nice to be part of something, part of someone's company that actually cares. A company that actually appreciates you." She shakes off whatever is lingering in her mind. "Anyway, once I'm done securing everything, you won't have to worry again. But until then, please do me a favour and just leave. Your pacing is incredibly annoying."

I chuckle as I pack up my things to leave, looking over to her, seeing her sucking a finger clean of salt and grease.

CHAPTER TWENTY-SEVEN

LIAM

When I get home from work, early no less, I decide to go for a run to work off some of this pent-up energy and anger I have. I can't believe there's a person trying to fuck with me. What the hell have I done to piss someone off? I can't think of anyone who would want to get revenge on me for something. Yes, I play hard and fast with business deals, but I haven't ever been ruthless. Not to the point where someone would want to fuck me over.

I'm just about to head out the door when my phone goes off, ringing incessantly. I groan as I dig it out of my shorts, and it's Russell Jade calling me. There's a sinking feeling dragging me down as I answer the phone.

"Hello—"

"So why the hell are you not at work when the entire building is melting down because of the stock market crash?"

I sigh. "Look, it's not a crash. I figured out what's been going on lately. Someone's been hacking into our server to mess with us. I have someone from a friend's company, who's totally trustworthy, looking into our firmware, firewalls, and tightening everything up. She's in my office—"

"Wait? You have someone from outside the company without our permission doing shit to our servers, *and* she's a female. What the fuck are you thinking, West? We need someone exceptional, not some *girl* who plays around with computers for fun."

"Woah, woah. You're more upset that there's a *woman* working on the security issues rather than the security issues themselves?"

"Look, son. I know you're still young and this whole liberal act for equality is a good movement in the right direction, but they're just certain things that men understand more." So much for the run to offset my anger. He continues on about how women are still inferior to men in the workplace, and that they're still years away from being of any real use, especially in the tech world. "Sure, there's a few that can handle their own in that cutthroat environment but…"

I can't listen to him drone on, attempting to give me a lecture about women in the workplace. The fact that he's more worried about a woman doing the job than the fact that someone hacked our systems speaks volume to his character that I never really noticed before. I always thought Jade was the level-headed one. I knew he was still old-school in some of his ways, but he never showed his prejudice quite the way he is now.

"I'm going to stop you there, Jade. I assure you Jessie Sinclair is the best coder in all of Canada, and—"

"Wait, Jessie Sinclair? The one who basically revamped all of Harrington Tech and CGC's tech divisions by his own two hands? Well, why the fuck did you not say that, boy? I've heard he was the best. You had me worried there when you said a woman was working on it. I don't care if he has his assistant with him doing some work here and there," he prattles on, his misogyny showing.

"No, you misunderstand me, Mr. Jade. Jessie Sinclair *is* a woman. She's the best coder. I've got her on a temporary loan from my friend who owns CGC." Jade clears his throat, and doesn't say anything. I swear there are crickets in the phone from the silence that's coming from his end of the call. "Everything okay, sir?" I grit my teeth, rolling my eyes.

"Um, yes. Carry on. I'll see you tomorrow at the office."

Irritation sets in, and I no longer feel like going for that run. Luckily my phone goes off and distracts me. Lexi's name pops up on my screen, and a smile tugs at my lips.

Lexi: *What are you doing right now?*
Liam: *What's it to you?*

Lexi: *Oh, I'm just feeling a little lonely and don't quite feel like playing by myself tonight.*

My cock stirs at her words, an eager fella wanting to get out and play.

Liam: *Should I come over then?*
Lexi: *Only if you want to. I won't turn away the company.*

I spin on my heels, and go back upstairs to my bedroom to change and freshen up, then I'm out the door in ten minutes. It doesn't take long to get to Lexi's apartment. She buzzes me up, and before I can even knock on the door, she's pulling me in by the collar, pressing her lips and body against mine. Her hand grips my hair, pulling me into her deeper as her other one drapes around my neck, bringing her to her tiptoes.

"I need you right now," she whispers breathlessly against my mouth. She grabs my hand and tugs me down the hallway to her bedroom. Her fingers are thin, fragile little twigs compared to my large, thick logs. I marvel at the feeling of how her hand fits perfectly with mine. The contrast between them and how strong mine are that I could protect her no matter what. I like that feeling. *I think I really like her.*

Lexi lets go of my hand, and steps away, facing me. Once she's a few paces away, she starts to strip. Leisurely and seductively removing one piece of clothing at a time until she's down to her bra and panties. Her arms wrap around her back, pushing her chest out slightly as she unclasps her bra, letting it fall to the floor. Her large round breasts are perfect with their hardened pink nipples. I'm already hard as a rock from this tantalizing strip show. Her fingers hook into the band of her panties, and she pulls them down agonizingly slow. She steps out of the one side, and flicks the cheeky panties towards me with the other foot. I catch them midair, bunching them up into a ball, and bring them to my nose and inhale deeply. Her arousal clings to the lacy fabric.

"Fuck, you smell so good," I groan. A pink hue washes over her skin as she rolls her bottom lip between her teeth. Her cheeks burn brighter as I stuff the wad of panties in my pocket to keep. It's my turn to strip, and I take my time dragging my T-shirt over my head, only allowing a few inches of my rigid stomach and chest to show at a time. I toss the shirt to the side and start undoing my jeans next, but this time letting them drop to the ground with a thump—my cell phone and wallet in the pockets. Her mouth parts with a gasp of excitement when my cock springs free without the confines of boxers. I step outside my pants, a cocky smirk on my face, stripping my socks off with my feet as I go, until I'm completely naked too.

I wrap my hand around my throbbing, engorged cock, pumping it once, twice, three times. I stalk towards her, water pooling in my mouth. Salivating like a fucking dog waiting for a bite of steak. "Lay down on the bed, and spread those pretty legs, dove." Lexi backs up until the backs of her knees hit the bed, and she flops down, raising herself on her arms as she shuffles back. I trap her ankles in my hands, pulling her back to the edge of the bed, sinking to my knees.

"I *need* to taste you," I groan. Suddenly feeling like a man parched walking through the desert, I press my mouth to her core and drink up her nectar. "You're already so wet, my dove," I mumble against her pussy. She moans, and squirms underneath me, and I press my hand to her stomach, holding her down.

My tongue swirls around her clit, and she draws a deep breath, letting her body melt into the mattress. My lips latch around her clit, sucking it hard.

"Liam," she moans. I smirk against her as I slide two fingers into her; her thighs clench my head as I rub her G-spot. "Fuck, that feels so good," she pants. I thrust my fingers faster inside her, my tongue licking and circling her clit, alternating between matching my finger's pace and going slower.

"I don't think I can… *Liam*," she moans. She's close, I can feel her pussy tightening. I add a third finger, filling her, while I alternate between sucking and licking her clit. She starts to shake. "I'm so close, Liam. Oh god, yessss."

She shatters, her pussy fluttering around my fingers, clenching hard and almost painful. She's moaning and panting, "*Ohh, mmmmm.*" Her chest is rising and falling hard, she's struggling to breathe as I slow my pace, lapping up all of her. Crawling over top of her, I pull her with me into the centre of the bed.

"We're not done just yet."

CHAPTER TWENTY-EIGHT

LEXI

Having Liam over and fucking weren't my intentions when I finished work today.

Getting home freaked me out. As I approach my door, it's slightly ajar, making all my warning bells blare. I stand outside my hallway, not stupid enough to enter alone, and call my landlord. It takes him ten minutes to get upstairs and enter the apartment with me. His hand is heavy with a baseball bat. I should've called the cops, but a small voice told me there was no one here. Whoever it was is long gone. Roddy, the landlord, is an ex-marine from the US. It was one of the reasons I rented this place. Something about him felt safe.

I follow Roddy around the apartment, clearing each room before I enter after him, making sure nothing was stolen—nothing was.

"I've never heard of people breaking in and stealin' nothin'," Roddy says. "Just to be safe, I'm gonna change your lock t'marra. I'll get one of them fancy ones. Hopefully, that'll keep anyone out." My anxious heart relaxes, and I sigh in relief.

"Thanks, Roddy. I really appreciate it." He nods curtly.

"Got anyone that can stay with ya tonight, kid? I just don't want you bein' alone t'night."

My mind only drifts to one person I could possibly want beside me tonight.

"Yeah, of course. I have someone I can think of. Thanks, Roddy."

"Well, then. Have a good night, kiddo. I'll see you tomorrow."

• • •

A few hours later, Liam's here, and we're tangled up in my bed sheets, huffing away after the last hour's exertions. Liam lets go of me and starts to slide out of the bed. My heart plummets to my feet and anxiety drowns me.

"No, stay," I say, rushing to sit up without the sheets falling off me. He looks at me, eyes concerned. "Please?" He smiles, and my heart skips a beat.

"I was just going to the washroom. But I'll stay the night if you insist." He gives me a wink and walks out of the bedroom and into the washroom. I settle back into bed, and my skin feels like it's pricking with pins and needles, not because they fell asleep, but the anxiety I feel with Liam leaving me all alone in my room. An uneasy feeling falls over me as I tug the sheets closer to my body and look around the room, trying to see anything out of the ordinary in my room, but I see nothing. Just darkened shapes and outlines of the stuff around my room is all I can see, even with my eyes adjusted to the lighting.

I reach over to my nightstand and grab my phone and quickly shuffle through the messages in Lillian, Henry, and Abby's group chat. They're talking about the night that I went out with Liam, and Lillian's making it seem like it's a huge deal.

Lillian: *You should have seen the way he was staring her down as she was flirting with his friend. He looked like he was going to rip someone's head off. I tried distracting him and keeping his attention on me. Clearly, he has eyes for only Lexi.*
Abby: *Awww, that's so cute! *heart eye emoji**
Abby: *Their babies would be soooo adorable. Omg, I'm obsessed.*
Lillian: *Ugh, don't go there. My poor little heart can't take it.*
Henry: *What heart? The one made of ice? *crying laugh emoji**
Lillian: *Wow. Rude much?*

The flush of the toilet rings through the room, and I scramble to close my messages so that Liam doesn't see, dropping my phone onto the ground with a clatter. I jump up from the bed, toss the covers off of me, and grab my phone. I'm on my hands and knees with my ass up in the air, when a deep voice rumbles behind me.

"What're you doing down there? I can't complain though. I like this view." His words are playful and seductive, and heat swirls in my belly. Temporarily making me forget about the conversation that's lit up on the screen when I feel his body hovering an inch over me. "Cute babies they say?" His voice is soft and deep as it rumbles in my ear. My heart stops in my chest, and I swallow the bile rising in my throat as my skin burns, igniting across my body like a wick dipped in gasoline.

Panic sets in, and I'm completely mortified by my friends and vow to disembowel them the next time I see them.

"I mean, we're pretty fucking solid at the practice of making them…I would imagine our efforts would be rewarded with cute babies."

My panic only escalates, and I feel like I'm suffocating or having a heart attack. My body can't decide what's going on. I look at Liam over my shoulder with wide eyes, my heart trying to restart itself.

"What the fuck?"

Liam cracks a gigantic, playful smile full of pearly white teeth. "I'm kidding. But we do have amazing sex." There's a few small thumps of my heart as our eyes really connect, and there's a moment of silence between us. "Here," Liam whispers, wrapping an arm around my waist. "Let's get back into bed." He stops pulling on me when he sees the confusion in my eyes. "What?"

"You're not…scared off?"

"Because of your ridiculous friends? It's not like you're trying to get pregnant," he says, standing full height, his face contorting into concern. "Are you?" his voice warily asking the question. I shoot to my feet, my hand gripping my phone, feeling so strong I might break it.

"I am *not* trying to get fucking pregnant. Believe me, that's the last thing I want right now, especially with you."

Liam's face falls, and his body hardens momentarily before washing away turning into a neutral slate. I draw in a breath, sighing. "That's...that's not what I meant. I just meant—"

"I get it. I know what you meant." Liam's words are clipped and icy.

"No, you don't. I just mean, if *anyone* it couldn't be you. Fuck, we shouldn't even be doing this." I flap my hands motioning between us. "You're my ex's friend. I don't want to hurt him, even though he hurt me. If he were to find out—"

"He knows." My heart stops again for what feels like the hundredth time tonight.

"What?"

Liam repeats himself. "He knows. I told him already."

My world stops, my breathing stutters. I'm at a loss for words. It takes me a few minutes to process his words. My inner turmoil is messy and chaotic as I have conflicting feelings about Brandt knowing, and what it ultimately means for me and Liam. I know we're just hooking up right now, but Liam's growing to be something more to me. I don't know how to explain it, but I feel like it's right somehow. However, the anxiety that grips me now that I know Brandt knows, faint lingering feelings come forward, and it's like they're punching me in the gut.

"If you're worried, he doesn't care. He might even actually support this. Us." He's calm, almost flippant about it.

My world seems to crumble at his words. *Did I really mean so little to Brandt? Does he really not care that I'm sleeping with his friend?* Liam's words chip away at my self-confidence, until it finally shatters. Although I've moved on, or at least I think I have, the fact that Brandt doesn't care still affects me. I really and truly was a rebound just like I feared. I never really stood a chance, did I?

An awkward silence falls between us, and I can't shake this unsettling feeling that's growing inside me. I thought I was over it, but it still hurts. Maybe even more because of how callous Liam is about it. I've never been someone who was so insecure before. I've never felt so fragile after Brandt dumped me. I was slowly getting my confidence back thanks to Liam. I thought I finally healed my heart, until those words came pouring out of Liam's mouth.

If you're worried, he doesn't care.

Trapped in my own thoughts, I barely realize that Liam is across the room getting dressed. It takes me a full minute to switch off my depressing thoughts and finally look at him. Feeling exposed, I cross my legs and wrap my hands around my chest.

"Are you leaving?" My voice is weak, pathetic, and sad. I sound like a shell of myself. Liam doesn't say anything as he pulls his T-shirt over his head, just giving me a curt nod. "Oh…"

"I think it's just best I leave. After all, you're right. We shouldn't even be doing this." He's so cold. The icy air rolls off him like opening a freezer on a hot summer day, leaving me with the chills. I open my mouth to respond, and he shakes his head, running a hand through his hair. "Goodbye, Lexi. I'll let myself out."

CHAPTER TWENTY-NINE

LIAM

What did I get myself into? I should have known better than this. But Lexi, she's so…intoxicating.

Here I am, letting myself get closer to her, falling deeper into her spell. And all along she still cares about Brandt. I knew she had feelings for him, but I thought she was over it. However, as soon as I mentioned Brandt and how he didn't care if we were fucking, something inside her seemed to break.

I curse myself for being so careless with how I told her, but she pisses me off. We're standing there, naked, and she decides to say that we shouldn't even be fucking. Basically calling whatever this is between us a mistake.

My hands clench into tight fists, and I grit my teeth as I walk down the hallway to the elevator. It's hard to stay mad when her scent lingers on my skin, when I can still feel her between my fingers, when her face is so clear in my mind of how she looks when she comes on my cock. *Fuck.*

Before I know it, I'm spinning around on my heels, marching back to her apartment. My mind is flurrying with words, anger, and lust. I don't even knock on the door, I open it, letting it swing open, and it slams against the wall. Small legs come tiptoeing around the corner as Lexi wraps her housecoat around herself, pulling it tight against her. Her eyes are wide. My perfect dove, scared at the sight of me.

"You don't just get to dismiss me like that, Lexi." Her head tilts, her brows pinch together as she pulls her housecoat tighter. "You don't get to just decide if we should be doing this or not. You don't get to be upset about another man when I'm the one fucking you. When I'm the one who's here. When I'm the one who's making you come so fucking hard. You don't get to think or utter another man's name." I step closer to her, gripping my hand around her wrist, tugging her into me. Her body clashes with mine, her chest heaving breaths. I dip my head closer to hers, our lips brushing. My voice is low, gravelly, as I speak against her mouth. "It's only my name that will be leaving your lips." My hand grabs her chin, and my thumb pulls down her bottom lip. "And only me you'll be thinking about."

The room is silent, not even the clock ticking registers in my mind. It's only me and her, and her breathing. It's so quiet, I hear the pounding of her heart against her ribcage. I inch closer until her hot breath laces with mine. My blood boils for her, my heart calls to her. I descend slowly, taking her lips with mine in a careful, purposeful kiss. When she kisses me back, the beast inside me breaks free. Iron bars are pulled wide, and I'm raging. My hands wrap around her slim, cut waist, pulling her into me tighter. Our mouths clash, tongues tangle together, as my hands round her full ass and drop to her thick, hard thighs. I grab them, hoisting her up and locking her around my waist as I spin us around and crush her into the wall behind me. With one hand, I undo my zipper and free my hardened-steel cock before sliding it against her wet lips.

"You're so fucking wet for me, dove. Just try to tell me that you get this wet for anyone else. Tell me that your pussy weeps for them like it does me."

"*Liam*," she moans.

"That's right, baby. It's my name on your lips. I'm taking you bare. That way you know who owns your pussy, your body, your mind. Hold on, dove."

I barely give her a second before I'm plunging into her deep, making her scream out in ecstasy. I slide in so easily, so effortlessly. "You're taking my cock so well." I drop my head to hers, closing my eyes for a moment. Her soft, warm walls clench around me, sucking me in deeper. Feeling her without any barrier feels like fucking heaven. I revel in the wet warmth, trying to contain myself and not come right on the spot. "Your pussy feels so damn good."

I slowly withdraw to the tip, and Lexi grips onto the collar of my shirt by the nape of my neck, holding on for dear life. I rotate my hips, finding the right angle and thrust, deep and hard. My stroke rocks her to the core, stealing her breath. I rock again, this time harder and deeper. "Oh, God," she moans. The corner of my lip upturns, and I'm grinning like a fool as I claim her lips. She kisses me back fervently. Her breasts press into me with heavy breaths. My hands support her weight around her ass, pulling her cheeks apart, allowing my cock to sink in deeper.

"Who does this fucking pussy belong to?" I growl.

"*You*," she moans breathlessly. My mouth devours hers, my tongue licking every corner. Her nails dig into the back of my neck, and they pierce my skin, but fuck if I don't love the feeling.

"Fuck, Lexi. This pussy..." My hips flex as I piston into her, and she's riding my cock, matching me thrust for thrust. I'm slowly losing restraint as my cock glides in and out of her so smoothly. Lexi's panting, and I can feel her on the precipice of coming. Her mouth breaks from mine, her head lulling against the wall with her mouth gaping. "Eyes on me, dove." Her squeezed eyes open, locking onto mine, her pupils are dilated, and her hazel eyes are glazed over in lust. "I want to watch when you come on my dick." She gasps, and I feel a faint flutter of her walls, her climax close.

I reach between us, and my finger finds her clit and rubs small circles.

"Oh God, Liam, I can't... *Liam...*" She shatters, her pussy milking my climax from me.

"Fuck, Lexi," I moan, spilling my hot seed inside her. I come hard and fast, but it doesn't seem to stop. Something about marking her with my cum buried deep inside her pussy makes it that much hotter. Knowing that she'll be dripping with my cum only feeds the territorial beast inside me. I connect my forehead with hers, both of us panting and catching our breaths. She's sated. Her eyes shine with pleasure and contentment. A small shiver runs down her spine causing her to shift, and I feel me leaking out of her. The pearly, viscous liquid runs down her thigh, and I take my hand, wiping it up and pressing it back to her entrance.

"I suppose we should go get cleaned up," I say. Lexi softly nods her head. "But not you. I want you to have me inside you all night as I sleep next to you. I want you to remember who the fuck is dripping out of you." I withdraw from her, setting her down on her feet gently while placing a kiss on her forehead. "Go get to bed—naked. I'll be there in a minute." She squeezes past me, and I feel her pebbled nipples slide against my chest. I take a moment to compose myself, adjusting my pants. I worry for a second if we were too loud, but I shrug, padding over to the door, shutting and locking it up. Luckily she doesn't seem to have nosy neighbours.

CHAPTER THIRTY

The next day, as I'm leaving Lexi's apartment, I check my phone and notice I missed fifteen calls.

I stop dead in my tracks and scroll through the calls from my driver, Adam, and my building's security line. There's a bunch of text messages as well from Ivan, but also Brandt and Rhys wondering where the hell I am. I'm so fucking confused.

My first call is to Adam.

"Fuckin' eh. At least your ass is alive," he says, his Irish accent thick.

"What the fuck is going on?"

"Someone broke into your flat. When security couldn't get a hold of you, they called me. Apparently, a bunch of shite is broken."

A dark ribbon of rage weaves itself around every organ in my body and squeezes. It feels like a shadow darkening my life. "Do they know who it was?" My voice is gritty and low.

"Naw. I guess whoever it was jammed the signals for the security cameras."

"Fuck," I yell. Flagging down a cab, I end the call. Who the fuck would be able to break into my place? I'm supposed to have the top-of-the-line security. One of the reasons why I moved into the place I inherited. This can't be a coincidence. First work, now this? Someone has to be targeting me. But why?

• • •

Three days later, I have Jessie Sinclair back in my office along with a private security guard I've hired.

"Alright, I need you two to work together. I don't know what the fuck is going on, but someone is trying to fuck with me. You've seen it first hand already, Jessie. I need you and Ivan to figure out what the hell needs to be done to up my security at my place and figure out who it is."

Jessie nods and Ivan stands still, his large muscular body rigid in place. The man is a beast. He's much larger than me, with dark hair and a firm jaw. He's an ex-soldier, and he stands like one. Feet slightly apart, chest out, hands folding behind his back. The only real notion he gives me that he comprehended it is a quick, curt nod. It happened so fast, or the movement was so minimal, I almost missed it. Jessie's eyes keep shifting to the side to glance at him. Either she finds him attractive or is intimidated by him, but I almost think nothing intimidates Jessie. She's outspoken and doesn't care what people think.

Just then, a knock sounds on my door, and Kane stands there, nose in his phone, completely distracted. I notice Jessie shift to see who it is, and her breath catches as red splashes up to her ears. She flicks her head forward again, biting her lip, and tries to remain calm. Kane is oblivious to the guests I have in my office.

"You going to the bar tonight with us, or are you hooking up with Lexi again?"

Jessie hazards a peek, but whips around just as fast as the first time. *Curious.*

"I'll probably come out for a few drinks."

Kane nods, and slowly raises his head. "What the fuck is with G.I Joe over here?" His thumb points in the direction of Ivan. Jessie sits a little taller, pushing her chest out, tossing her hair over her shoulder. She opens her laptop and pretends to work. My eyes shift from Jessie to Ivan.

"Ivan Berchard, Jessie Sinclair, meet Kane Denton. Kane, meet Ivan, the private security I've hired. And Jessie Sinclair is the IT specialist and self-proclaimed hacker from Brandt's company." Jessie's hands tremble as she turns around, clasping them in her lap. Her brown hair swishes along her shoulders as she turns around to greet him. When Jessie is fully facing him, Kane's eyes open slightly and narrow, as if caught by an angry surprise. Kane's face remains hardened as he nods to both of them, but barely takes his eyes off Jessie.

"We'll talk later, then," Kane says. But I'm not so sure he's talking to me or Jessie. "Ivan. *Jessie.*"

Jessie's face drains of all its colour as she gives a weak smile and a polite nod. Kane doesn't move for a minute, his eyes fixed on Jessie. He finally leaves, and I hear Jessie let out a breath she was holding. *What the fuck happened there?* I brush it off as I have more important things to worry about. I clear my throat, redirecting Jessie's attention back to me.

"Anyway, what I need to happen is a revamp of all the security of my condo. I want high-tech everything. Fingerprint scans, facial recognition, the works. I want to be notified if there's a fucking ant in my place. So I need you," I say, redirecting my attention to Ivan, "to work with Jessie, giving her the names of all the high-tech, top-of-the-line equipment. Jessie"—I turn back to face her—"will install it with your help and hack the coding to make it more secure." Jessie is typing down notes while Ivan stares at me blankly. "Got it? And don't worry about expense. It's the last thing on my fucking mind right now. I need to figure out who's fucking with me."

I wrap up the meeting and send them both on their way to get to work. I hoped that after having this meeting, my nerves would settle a little, but they're still shot to hell. I push away from my desk and pack my shit up while I press the call button on my phone for my assistant.

"Yes, sir?"

"Clear the rest of my schedule for the day, please." My assistant confirms, and I grab my things and go. I stop off at home, throw a quick cardio session in, and get ready to meet the boys. Choosing a pair of dark denim jeans, paired with a black T-shirt, I pick out one of my platinum Rolexes that has a black interface and a tiny diamond underneath the twelve. I stop in the bathroom to style my hair; the caramel strands swooping into perfection. As I give myself a once over, I notice that my shirt moulds to my body like a second skin. It hugs every muscle and ridge, defining everything. I walk out of the washroom to my closet and grab a grey zip hoodie and throw it on, as the mid-September air is growing chilly at night.

I head towards the door of my apartment and stop by the entry hallway table, sifting through the mail that was left here by the housekeeper. There's a fancy pearl envelope with my name on it in calligraphy and no return address. I know what it is. I've known it was on its way for a while now. Brandt and Elissa's wedding invitation. A knot forms in my stomach thinking about them. Once upon a time, Elissa and I had a thing. It was really a one-night stand, but she intrigued me, and I was interested in more. Or at least a few nights more of great sex. But Brandt and her were destined to be together, if you believe in that sort of thing. I didn't. Until Lexi.

Sighing, I open the envelope and see they set the date for mid-October. It's a month away, give or take a few days. The inside of the invitation addresses *Liam and Guest.* My mind immediately thinks of Lexi as my guest, but I think better of it. She probably wouldn't want to attend Brandt's wedding, but I desperately want her to go with me. I want Lexi draped on my arm, showing everyone that she's mine. Showing Brandt whom he's missed out on because Lexi is fucking amazing.

God fucking dammit.

I've got it bad.

CHAPTER THIRTY-ONE

LEXI

Over the last few weeks, Liam and I have spent a lot of time together. Almost every day we're texting each other constantly, and every night one of us ends up at the other's place. I feel like I'm really starting to fall for him. I never thought my heart would be willing to let someone in so easily again, but there he is. Liam, consuming my every thought, filling every space in my heart. Repairing it crack by crack. He's slowly glueing me back together, making me feel like I'm worthy of someone, of love. He's the best thing that's happened to me in a while. Whenever I think of him, my heart does this flip in my chest, setting off a swirl of butterflies. I'm giddy every time a text message beeps and it's him.

My hand wraps around the gold wedding band that hangs from a platinum chain around my neck. My heart darkens and weeps for my grandfather. I miss him terribly. He taught me what love was. He was the only role model I had growing up. Both of my parents died in a car accident when I was a baby, and my grandparents took me in. When I was about five, my grandmother died of breast cancer, and my grandfather never really recovered. All I had was him, and he me. He'd let me stay up late, telling me wonderful stories of my parents and their love, their wedding. He also told me about Gramma. How he loved her from the first moment he met her.

They were in their first year of college, and she was carrying a stack of textbooks over to the shelf in the campus bookstore. Gramma had just started working there to help pay for her campus living during the second semester. Grandpa saw her coming down the aisle he was in looking for a biology textbook, and he noticed too late that she couldn't see where she was going, and she ran right into him. All the books dropped from her arms, clattering to the ground, and a few of them broke at the spine. Grandpa took a knee to help her collect her things and noticed her sniffing, holding back tears. He said that when she finally realized he was there, she had the most vibrant aquamarine eyes he'd ever seen. He said it was like their souls connected in that moment, and everything else disappeared.

From that moment on, they were never apart. They spent every waking moment together. They had their ups and downs like any couple. Their love burned bright, and their fights were volatile, but he said passion always fuelled everything. One minute they were shouting at each other, and the next they were ripping each other's clothes off. Grandpa used to say, "People say to find someone who loves you more than you love them. That way, you never get hurt. But I think you need to find someone who ignites passion inside you. Someone who sets your skin on fire, someone who touches every nerve, someone who makes you feel like you're vibrating. That's what Gramma was to me. Someone who sparked all the passion inside of me. The good and the bad. That's what I want for you, Lexi."

And I don't think I've ever let that go. My biggest fear is never finding what he and my Gramma had. Squeezing the gold ring tighter, my heart aches remembering my grandfather.

I think I might have found that with Liam. I feel the charge, the pull. I feel like he lights things inside me I've never known. But I hope like hell he feels it too. I don't think I could go through another heartbreak because this time I don't think I'd recover. I'm in too deep with him.

The buzzer to my apartment goes off, distracting me from my thoughts. My heart leaps, knowing instantly who it is. I rush to the door, almost tripping over my own feet. Once I reach the buzzer, I take a moment to collect myself, brushing my blonde locks out of my face and letting them waterfall over my shoulders. I quickly ruffle the flowing tank top, making sure it's not snagged anywhere. I wipe my hands down the rough denim texture of my jeans, exhaling loudly before answering the buzzing.

"Hello?" I ask, trying to keep my cool. I'm so excited my heart's beating in my throat.

"Hey, dove. Let me up." His voice is so sexy even over the crappy intercom system. Without responding, I press the buzzer, letting him up. I pace the entire four and a half minutes and twenty-three seconds he takes to get to my door. It baffles me how I'm so nervous to see him. We're going on day sixteen of seeing each other, and tonight I plan on asking what this is between us. I need to know before I fall any deeper. Because if I'm just passing time for him, if I don't mean the same to him as he means to me, I can't do this anymore. It'll only hurt worse down the line. I can't keep investing time in these guys that only see me as a stepping stone. I deserve to be someone's everything.

The knock I've been waiting for finally sounds on my door. I draw a deep breath, and it settles my nerves. I twist the knob on the door and open it slowly, and there he is. *Liam.* Standing there looking so perfect in dark jeans, a grey T-shirt, and a leather jacket. My mouth goes bone dry as my eyes rove over him. His wide shoulders and arms fill out the leather jacket, the definition of his muscles are still seen through the tight, unforgiving material. My eyes finally zone in on the bouquet of daisies—my favourite— and my heart melts. I feel the heat rushing to my face, and a small sting in my eyes as I blink back tears of happiness. No one has bought me flowers in years.

"Come in," I choke out, clearing my throat. I sweep the door open, sidestepping to let him in. He brushes past me, placing a soft kiss into my hairline, passing me the bouquet.

"Hey baby," he says. His voice flows over my skin like warmed honey and milk, moisturizing me. His touch says warm, but the rest of him screams tense. He barely looks at me, walking past and toeing off his shoes. Something's up. I know he has a lot on his plate right now, but he's acting nervous.

"Liam? What's wrong?" He looks at me confused.

"Huh? Oh, nothing." His words say one thing, but his tone and actions say another. I want to press, but I don't want him to close down. But he opens up instead. "So I don't know how you feel about this, but I have a wedding to go to in two weeks. I was wondering if you wanted to go with me?" My eyes search his, wondering if this has been why he seems so nervous. Does this invite mean we're on the same page? Ready to move forward and be something more? I part my lips to speak, but he stops me. "I know we haven't really discussed us, and things are going well, but I have a plus one and thought it'd be fun to have you there."

My heart sinks a little. So I'm just filling the extra invitation he got. He's not thinking this as taking a step forward, at least that's what it sounds like. It'd just be *fun* to have me there with him so he's not bored or lonely. Not sure why he'd need me though, I'm sure there'd be plenty of women there that would want to spend the night with him. The negative, insecure part of my brain destroys any hope I had of a discussion of us tonight. But there's a sliver of me that holds onto hope. He wouldn't ask me to go two weeks in advance if he really thought so little of me, would he? He's clearly thinking we'll still be doing *whatever* this is between us.

I decide with this chaos running through my mind, I might as well just come out and ask.

"Isn't a wedding a little…relationship-y?"

"What the fuck does that mean?" His eyes narrow, and I suddenly feel nervous.

"I mean, we're just sleeping together, right? Isn't that a little serious of a step?" I ask weakly, second-guessing why the frick I opened my mouth. His eyes grow dark, and goosebumps pepper my skin. He's all dark and predatory.

"We're not *just* sleeping together," he growls.

"Well, I don't know what we're doing then! We've never really talked about it."

"You're mine."

I sigh, exasperated.

"Okay, sure. But what does that mean? Are we dating? Because all we do is stay in and fuck. We've never once gone out." He looks at me with confusion etched all over his face.

"I just brought you flowers?"

"Hah…Okay. So that's the determining factor of establishing what we are?" I groan, confusing myself. Where am I even going with this conversation? Where do I even want it to go? *Do I want him to call me his girlfriend?*

"You want us to label whatever this is between us?"

"Yes…No…I don't know?"

He steps closer to me, forcing me to back up, thudding lightly into the wall. He grabs my hand and lifts it to his mouth, pressing kisses and nibbling into the palm. He spreads my fingers wide, places kisses on the pads of my fingertips.

"Want me to call you my...*girlfriend*?" He lowers our hands and steps closer, tracing his nose along the column of my neck, trailing his tongue along the same path. My breath hitches, the air clogging up my throat. My head spins, as he's dangerously close, teasing my skin, breathing hot air onto my neck. My core clenches as he dangles that word, *girlfriend*, and his hand trails up my thigh and cups my heat.

CHAPTER THIRTY-TWO

LIAM

Girlfriend.

The way that rolls off my tongue feels nice.

Is it necessary? No. As long as I know she's mine, then I don't care what the fuck she labels us. If it makes her feel more secure, then why the hell not?

I've never had a real "girlfriend" before. Sure, there was that Brittany chick in elementary school, but we were over before the end of the week because Bradley was better at hockey than me. And things in grade six don't count anyway. I think we held hands once. I've had a few women I've kept around for a few weeks here and there as a convenient lay, but I'd never consider them my *girlfriend*. There were no expectations or rules. But with Lexi, I feel the need for rules, boundaries. I don't want to worry about who's touching her or kissing her. Just thinking about a faceless man near her sends me into a white-hot rage. So if that word girlfriend prevents that from happening, then she's my girlfriend.

I'm standing a hair's breadth away from her, so close our lips are almost brushing, and I can feel the heat from her mouth escaping in silent pants. My cock jerks in my pants as I picture her sexy little mouth wrapped around my shaft, sucking me off. How her hot, wet mouth feels against my skin. How her tongue flicks along the prominent vein, tracing it up to the tip before swirling around like she's sucking a lollipop.

"It really doesn't matter what you call us," I say. My hand trails up her curves until it reaches her breast. I palm it, my thumb rubbing the taut nipple poking through the thin materials of her shirt and bra. "As long as you know you're mine." My lips eclipse hers, taking her hard and demanding. My tongue lashes against her lips, and she parts hers for me, allowing my tongue full access to her mouth. My hand cups her jaw, tilting it up further, allowing me deeper access, and she moans as I explore her mouth. Lexi's skin under my fingers peppers with goosebumps, her skin fevered. Her arms wrap tight around my neck, winding around like a boa constrictor. Her nails biting into my neck like fangs. I feel her heart thrashing in her chest, the pulse in her neck throbbing.

I pull away, tapping her ass playfully. "So are you coming?" A live wire of nerves wracks my body as I wait for her answer. I don't know why I'm nervous. It's not like I told her whose wedding it is… Lexi looks at me with a blank face and glassy, lust-filled eyes. She takes a second to come back down to earth, blinking away the fog.

"Coming where?"

"The wedding. Will you be my date?" She tries to suppress the massive grin spreading over her face, but fails miserably. Her cheeks tinge pink.

"Yes, of course…" she says. "*Boyfriend,*" she murmurs under her breath, thinking that I can't hear it. I chuckle to myself, heading into her kitchen to cook us some dinner.

• • •

The next two weeks fly by, and my nerves grow increasingly chaotic until I feel like I'm physically vibrating. And I have a small inkling why.

"Dude, chill the fuck out. Your leg shaking is going to knock the entire table over," Rhys complains. "It's like you're the nervous one getting married." I give Rhys a death glare, and Brandt looks unaffected. Maybe a small twinkle of amusement in his eye. We're all at the bar for Brandt's bachelor party before the big day tomorrow. We just spent the day out on the links hitting balls, and now we're at the hotel bar drinking.

Brandt and Elissa's wedding is at a vineyard just outside of Barrie. Tonight the men are staying at a hotel nearby while the women are staying at the bed and breakfast that's at the vineyard. The girls themselves are having their own bachelorette party tonight as well, although I wonder what they could be doing since it's just Elissa, Riley, and Riley and Rhys's daughter.

"Fuck, sorry," I say, forcing myself to sit still.

"What's got you all fucked up?" Rhys asks. Brandt's his quiet, usual self, just listening to the conversation.

"Uh, my date."

Brandt's eyes are now lit up with curiosity, and Rhys looks confused.

"Why would you be nervous about your date?" My eyes shift from Rhys to Brandt, and both of them look concerned.

"Uh, I'm bringing Lexi." Rhys' eyes widen in excitement, and Brandt just looks…pissed? Annoyed? "And…I didn't tell her whose wedding it was."

Rhys bursts out laughing, some of his rum spilling out of the tumbler in his hand, and Brandt rolls his eyes and shakes his head.

"I'm sorry," Rhys says between gulps of laughter. "But how the fuck did you explain where you were going tonight? You just left her up in her hotel room?"

I tighten my lips into a thin line and look away. "She's not here yet. She's driving up tomorrow morning before the ceremony."

This makes Rhys laugh even harder, and Brandt just looks unimpressed.

"So you invited her to my wedding—her ex's wedding—and didn't feel like you needed to inform her of whose it is?" Brandt grumbles. Yes, I feel slightly bad for not telling Lexi about whose wedding it is, but can anyone blame me? If she knew it was Brandt's wedding, there's no way she would have agreed, and I didn't want to show up stag to this wedding specifically. I shrug, keeping my eyes focused on the weird loopy, twisted stone statue in the corner of the hotel's bar. Staring at it, it settles me a little. Like it's representing how I feel about this situation I'm in. Yes, it's weird, twisted, but it's also beautiful all at the same time.

"It's not like that, okay? The subject of whose wedding just never came up." I mean, it's not a lie. A lie by omission, yes. But not an *actual* lie.

"Dude, you're fucked," Rhys quips. "She's going to be so pissed." My gut sinks; although I already know this, I chose to ignore the glaring obvious.

The server comes by, collecting the empty glasses, and Rhys orders another round for us. "So is this thing serious between you and Lexi?" Rhys asks. His eyes shift to Brandt to check his reaction, but he's a slab of marble. Unmoving. "I mean, it's got to be, right? If you're considering bringing her to Brandt's wedding."

I shrug, trying to play it cool. I suppose we are serious now, considering she's my girlfriend and I'm bringing her to a wedding. She's more than just a good lay to me. She's...Lexi.

"I guess so. I mean, it's been a few months now, and she asked what we were. She's more than a fuck buddy. I really like her. Now, is that enough fucking girl talk for you lovesick puppies?"

Brandt and Rhys both snort into their drinks that the server just dropped off. "Just wait, dude. If you're not already, you'll be whipped, and hard." Just hearing Rhys say this, it dawns on me that it may already be too late. She's already becoming everything to me. I look forward to the nights we spend together, whether it's at my place or hers. I like how she lounges in her dirty, ragged sweat pants and holey crop top, with a blonde knot on the top of her head. Even like that, she's beautiful. But the way her lips move when they say my name is the most gorgeous thing of all.

My phone vibrates in my pocket, and I pull it out, and waiting for me is a text message from Lexi.

Lexi: *My bed is so cold and lonely without you here. :(*

Oh yeah, I'm in fucking trouble.

CHAPTER THIRTY-THREE

The drive to the wedding venue didn't take very long, but it was scenic. Long stretches of highway with open rolling fields. A nice change from the hustle and bustle and traffic of Toronto. I glance to the passenger seat at the small gift I bought. The small box is wrapped in a dusty-rose floral paper and matching ribbon tied around the package. It's just some silly iced tea spoons. But what do you get the marrying couple you don't even know? Fuck. I don't even know whose wedding it is. Obviously someone close to Liam because he had to be there the night before the wedding. The fact that I didn't even question whose wedding it is scares me a little bit. I'm so deep into my feelings for Liam and the fact that we defined whatever we were into an actual couple that I didn't even think about asking him anything about the wedding. I suppose I didn't even have to get a gift, knowing Liam probably took care of it himself, but it felt too weird showing up alone for the wedding without something for the happy couple.

I pull into the driveway, dust kicking up behind me from the dirt and gravel clouding my rearview mirror, at the small inn where Liam rented us a room for the night. It's right down the road from the wedding venue, which worked out perfectly. I was surprised Liam was able to secure a different place to stay, and this inn had rooms left being so close to the venue, I'd have thought we'd be booking in Barrie for the night and driving. So either all the guests are staying in a hotel in the city, or they're all from around here. Originally, I thought we'd be staying at the venue's bed and breakfast, but considering the bride and groom probably want their night in seclusion, it makes sense that we'd be at a different location. I shake it off, trying not to think about it too hard. I'm here now, and that's all that matters.

I collect my things from the trunk of my car, and my suitcase bumps along behind me through the chalky dirt and gravel parking lot. Thankfully, my dress is safe from nature in the garment bag, and I made the conscious decision not to get ready until I got here. Birds dance and sing in the light and crisp air of mid-October as I walk towards the inn. The light, cool breeze is enough to elicit shivers and the use of a light sweater, even under a warm sun. But the breeze is pleasant, earthy, unlike the chaotic streets of Toronto.

My bag clunks behind me as I step up the creaking wooden floorboards of the hazelnut-stained porch, which wraps around the perimeter of the house. The two-storeyed farmhouse feels like old southern -charm with its faded and peeling robin's-egg blue and the aged, intricate floral murals of dull pinks and greens that have been hand-painted in random spots over multiple siding slats. The heavy oak door stands proud and solid in the middle, with two large bay windows on either side—the perfect nook for lazing around on a Sunday afternoon with a good book. This place feels like it's straight out of a novel from the scenes of a small-town romance.

I get lost in the fantasies of Liam and me in a place like this; no inhibitions, just freedom. Snuggling by the fireplace, the fire crackling in the background. Wrapped in each other's arms, sweaty limbs tangled together, hearts beating as one, like secret words whispered between lovers.

"Excuse me, miss. Can I help you?" The lady at the front desk asks, tearing me away from a beautiful dream. I shake it off and walk over to the desk to check in.

"Yes, sorry. Just admiring the beautiful place," I say, twirling around, taking in the charming atmosphere. The main floor has two rooms off the entryway, but feels open concept by the double-wide archways. Directly across from me are stairs that lead up to the rooms. The two main rooms are decorated with delicate floral wallpaper, and the gleaming hardwood floors have antique-looking rugs placed strategically throughout to make the rooms look larger and welcoming. Scrumptious scents of buttery garlic and bread waft in the air from a closed-off room near the back, but a burst of scent comes through every time a server pushes the swinging door open.

I walk over to the desk, dragging my luggage behind me. "I was told Liam West left a key for me to his room. I'm Lexi Gardener." The lady offers me a warm smile as her hazel eyes flick from me to the screen as she types and clicks away at the computer.

"Ah, there you are. Room 12," she says. "My name is Aliana, and I'll be the attendant on shift tonight if you need anything. Just pick up the phone and press zero to get the front desk. Our in-house restaurant is open until 9 PM, and our chef is fantastic."

"It seems like it. Something smells so good," I reply. Aliana gives me a wide smile.

"She's preparing lasagna, garlic bread, with an antipasto spread. One of her signature dishes here. The ultimate comfort food, so she says," Aliana chuckles. She turns around and fetches a brass key hanging on a fancy antique hook board. Aliana gathers a few other papers and turns back around, handing me the bundle of papers and the key adorned with a butterfly keychain. "Room 12 is the best room, in my opinion. It's the butterfly suite and probably the coziest room in the whole place. Here are some brochures for some touristy stuff to do if you don't already have plans," she explains.

"Actually, I do have plans. We're here for a wedding this weekend. It's actually just down the road at the vineyard."

Aliana's eyes light up. "Oh, that's a lovely place! Barrie's Berry Vineyard is the perfect place for a small, intimate wedding. I heard it's the most exclusive wedding they've ever had. Something about some rich, important people from Toronto. It's very popular this time of year with all the colours of fall, but I'm surprised these important people wanted such a small wedding." A sly smile appears on her face. "Can you tell me who the wedding is for? I'm just dying to know."

My mouth pops open, and no words come out as I try to figure out what to tell her. An awkward chuckle escapes my lips.

"Actually, I don't know who the wedding is for. I'm just a plus one."

Aliana's face falls, her brows pinch together.

"You didn't ask your date who the wedding was for?" Her voice drips with confusion.

"Uh…Nope," I nervously chuckle. "It didn't cross my mind at the time."

"Oh…Well, I'm sure you'll have a fantastic time. Also, their wine, which we also carry in our restaurant, is delicious."

"I'll definitely be trying it tonight! Thanks so much, Aliana."

"No problem. Just up the stairs, to the right, at the end of the hall will be your room. Please let me know if there's anything else I can do." I offer her a small smile, grab my things, and head upstairs to my room.

· · ·

When I push open the door to the room, I'm greeted by a warm, rustic bedroom. There's a four-poster king bed with plush white linens and a pale olive-green throw blanket draped over the foot of the bed. The walls are creamy with hand-painted roses and leaves around the room, some with butterflies resting on the petals. The hardwood creaks under my feet as I move into the room, but it's a welcoming sound. It gives to the ambiance of the room with the cream rug that juts out from under the bed at an angle. Across from the bed is a brick fireplace, but has since been replaced by an electric insert that crackles and licks at the glass pane.

A large bay window is off to the side that has a built-in bench with overstuffed pillows with different floral patterns and colours. Underneath is a little bookshelf, packed with some of the classics, and some contemporary reads as well. The urge to beg the owners of the inn to let me live in this room forever is overwhelming.

The bathroom is another room I'd like to live in forever. Cool teals, pastel corals, and mint greens set the calming and relaxing tone of the room. A deep, claw-foot tub stands in the middle of the room with its brass feet and golden rim of the tub. Across the top is a bamboo board with a candle, a bag of dried rose petals, a bath bomb, and some bath salts. In the corner is a walk-in waterfall shower, surrounded by glass walls. The tiles are white and grey except for the accent piece that wraps around the length of the wall and looks like sea glass, and an inkling that they were handpicked at the beach.

This is a room I could easily lose time in. Thankfully, I had the good sense to use the shower at my place before leaving or else I'd never leave this washroom. I exit back into the main bedroom, plopping my suitcase onto the bed. The zipper saws as I open it, and I grab my toiletries, hair products, and makeup bag. My arms burst with all my stuff, and I walk into the washroom and spread my products and equipment out on the double-sink, white marble countertop. I slip my phone out of my leggings pocket and open the music app and start up my favourite playlist. *Paint the Town Red* by Doja Cat pumps into the air as I pull the scrunchy from my hair, letting the long blonde hair tumble down my shoulders. I grab the spray bottle of water, prepping my hair, and plug in my Dyson Airwrap to start getting ready for the wedding.

An hour later, as I'm putting the finishing touches of my makeup on, a giant, warm hand wraps around my waist and I jump, smearing a run of lipstick off my upper lip onto my cheek.

"Jesus Christ, Liam! You scared the hell out of me."

A deep chuckle rumbles in his chest, and it settles the rapid beating of my scared heart. He steps up behind me, pushing my long waves to the other shoulder, and his nose trails up the column of my neck. His lips press gentle kisses onto my skin, sending jolts of desire down my spine. My hand reaches up, tangling in his caramel hair, tugging into my fist as his kiss grows heated.

"*Liam...*" My breathless plea for more, but we don't have time. "I need to finish getting ready. And fix my lipstick. We don't have time. The ceremony starts in forty minutes."

"That's plenty of time, dove," he says in between kisses.

CHAPTER THIRTY-FOUR

LEXI

His lips trail down the length of my neck as he pulls aside the neckline of my T-shirt, down my shoulder, following with kisses. Goosebumps raise across my skin, triggering me to shiver. His arm wraps around my ribs, and his hand covers a breast as his fingers paw into me.

"Liam, please. I need to—"

"Shhh, dove. I need to taste you. It's been too long."

His hands drop to my hips and spin me around as his hands move in a flash, ripping my pants and panties down to my ankles. Then, with his hands back on my hips, he lifts me onto the edge of the counter. As he places kisses down my torso, stopping to bite my nipples through my shirt and bra, I'm lost in the moment. My hand slips, knocking over tubes and palettes of my expensive makeup collection, By Mario. They clatter into the sink and onto the floor.

Liam kisses down the length of my body as he sinks to his knees. Heat pools at my core as I pant. His hands wrap around my thighs, giving them a light tug, teetering me on the edge of the counter. His fingers expertly part my folds, my arousal dribbling out of my entrance.

"Hold on tight, dove. I'm a starved man, and this pussy looks delicious."

He hooks my legs over his shoulders as my hands grip the edge of the counter, and I barely grab hold before he dives into me. His head nuzzles in between my legs, his tongue assaulting my clit with harsh, rapid lashes. The moment his mouth seals around my clit and sucks, my back arches, and my hands scramble to grab fists full of hair.

I feel his lips smile against me as I writhe against him. His tongue dives deep into my core as his thumb takes a turn to circle my clit.

"There's my good little slut," he says, between languid licks.

"Oh, God…Liam," I pant, tugging on his hair. Chasing my orgasm, I roll my body against his face, climbing higher and higher, as his mouth moves back to my clit, sucking hard. Slurping me down, he plunges three fingers into me, curving them just so, until he presses *that* button and I detonate. I explode around his fingers, stars bursting behind my eyes, pulse after pulse of pleasure. I ride the waves out as he laps up my arousal lazily.

I collapse back against the mirror in a boneless heap, coming down from the high, but it's not enough. I need to be filled with him. There's an empty hollowness inside me that only he can fill.

Liam gets to his feet, licking his glistening lips from my come, his eyes still full of hunger. He glances down at the TAG Heuer watch on his wrist. A thrill shoots through my body as his stormy gaze lifts and locks onto my eyes, and I see the flecks of steely grey mixed with acid-washed denim. A wolfish, dangerous grin sprawls across Liam's face.

He rips me off the counter, spinning me around so I'm facing ourselves in the mirror. Liam's hands grasp the hem of my shirt, tearing it off, unclasps my bra and tosses them aside. He lifts my hips until I am reaching tall on my tip-toes, legs spread wide. His belt jingles as he quickly undoes his pants. He notches the silky crown of his cock at my soaking entrance, coating it in my arousal.

"There's still time. Guess you'll be going to the wedding with my come leaking out of you. Get ready little dove, you'll be screaming my name in a minute."

• • •

Thirty minutes later, I slide out of my car, clenching my legs together while I gather the skirt of my emerald dress in my hands. The task is difficult enough as it is without Liam smirking and chuckling to himself over my dilemma. I bend into the car to grab the present I bought. He wasn't fucking around when he said he was going to fill me with his come. He almost didn't give me my panties to wear, but there's no way in fucking hell I'm attending a wedding without panties on, *especially* when I have semen dripping out of me.

My hips sway a little more than usual as I try to keep my entrance blocked by my legs as I walk, but Liam has different thoughts. His arm wraps around my waist, pulling me in tight to his body, effectively stopping my hips from being able to sway. He drops his mouth down beside my ear and grumbles into it.

"Be a good girl and stop squirming. I want you to remember that you're mine." I shoot him a sideways glare. His lips are gentle as they press a kiss into my hairline. "Did I mention? You look stunning today, dove." How can this man be so filthy one second, but then be completely heart-melting the next? Every day with Liam, I tumble into the abyss of feelings that I thought I'd never have again. If I ever even truly felt this way before.

I know what I felt for Brandt was real. It almost destroyed every piece of me that was confident and so sure of myself. I think I fell in love with the idea of being in love. Brandt is a great man, truly kind and wonderful. I don't for one second believe he meant to hurt me on purpose, but it was still a sharp blow to my self-worth. It was definitely a low moment for me, and until Liam, I didn't know if I'd ever feel like myself again.

There's something about Liam I'm just drawn to, and if I'm honest with myself, I think I felt it from the first moment I met him. And maybe things really do happen for a reason. Maybe I met Brandt in order to get to Liam. I rarely buy into the whole "fate" thing, but I don't know?

There's something that just clicks with us. I feel it, and I know he feels it, too. I can feel it in the way his lips touch mine, the way his fingers graze my skin and set it on fire. The way one look from him can level the walls I've erected so completely.

As we walk into the vineyard's main building, his arm snugly around my waist, I realize I'm truly and utterly fucked if this ends, because I think I've known from the start that this thing that's between us is something that can destroy me. Even worse than before. It feels like this man owns part of my soul, and I don't know if I can live without it.

I've fallen for this man, hard.

Oh shit.

I'm in love with Liam West.

CHAPTER THIRTY-FIVE

LIAM

I hold Lexi closer to me as we walk through the entrance to the main building at the vineyard. The building's walls wrap around with floor-to-ceiling windows. The decor is clean, rustic. It's like they've copied and pasted it right out of a bridal magazine. Lexi's heels click along the hallway to the back entrance.

"So, whose wedding is this?" she asks. I feel her hazel eyes glancing at the side of my cheek. My gut twists inside, and a small wave of nausea comes over me. I pull my lips tight as I think of an answer that won't make her run.

"Just a friend's wedding."

Lexi stops abruptly. "What aren't you telling me?" Her head cocks, her long blonde hair falls from one shoulder to behind the other one, and her brows pinch together. I pause, clenching my eyes shut, taking a deep breath before I turn to face her. My hands curl into fists, and my nails dig into my palms.

Fuck.

"Liam, what's going on?"

I turn, scrubbing my face with a large exhale. "Lexi, look. I—"

"Westie!" a familiar voice shouts down the hallway behind me. I tense, and Lexi leans to the side to look around me, and her face drains of its colour. Rhys comes up behind me and claps me on the shoulder. "Glad you could finally make it, fucker. Thought you were gonna be late. Brandt would have had your ass. Oh, hi, Lexi." At least he gives Lexi a genuine smile.

Lexi's eyes glisten, wavering between me and Rhys. Her eyes are wild and wide, her lips folded into her mouth, biting back her emotions.

"Brandt?" she asks weakly. She stares into my eyes, and I can feel her heart breaking. Rapidly, her chest heaves with each breath. "Is it *his* wedding you brought me to?"

I feel Rhys stiffen beside me, and I see him shaking his head out of the corner of my eye, his black hair tastefully dishevelled.

"Oh shit. You didn't tell her yet?" He whispers something under his breath and excuses himself. "Hey, Lexi? You look beautiful, by the way. See you in there, West."

Rhys says before turning around and leaving us standing in silence.

"Lex—"

She holds up a polished hand, shoving the gift into my chest. "Don't. Just…don't." Lexi stares down at her shoes, her hand rubbing her forehead.

"I have to go," I murmur. "I need to take my spot."

"Wait, you didn't just bring me as a plus one, but you're actually *in* the wedding and leaving me alone with all of Brandt's and Elissa's friends and family while you're off doing wedding stuff today?"

"It's not that kind of wedding—"

"Just stop," she whispers, her eyes finding mine for a moment. "Get going. I'll be there in a minute." She looks away, hurt etching all her features on her face.

"You're staying?" I ask hopefully. My hands fiddle with the ribbon wrapped around the present.

"Rhys has already seen me. I have no choice but to show up now. *Please go,*" she pleads. "I just need a moment."

I open my mouth to say something, anything. But nothing comes out. I give her a curt nod, turn on my heel, and walk down the long, lonely hallway without Lexi by my side.

• • •

The ceremony starts, and I'm standing under the gazebo beside Rhys and Brandt. My eyes scan the crowd for my blonde dove. My shining light. I know I screwed up not telling her about Brandt's wedding. It was careless, but I was afraid she wouldn't come with me. Which sounds completely fucking stupid, but I just wanted her here on my arm. The guys already know about us, so what's the big deal?

I finally find her. My heart relaxes in my chest, relieved she's still here, even if she's sitting in the back of the rows, looking like she's ready to flee. Her eyes connect with mine, and my lips upturn, my heart warming. Her face is void of any emotion as her eyes flutter shut and she draws a deep breath, breaking our eye contact and looking elsewhere. A strand of her blonde hair blows across her face, shielding her from my stare. Lexi's hand reaches up, tucking the strand behind her ear.

The music shifts in the air, and she rises with the rest of the attendees, watching Elissa round the corner of the building. My eyes flick from Lexi to watch Elissa enter. It's no use denying she's glowing. Her cinnamon hair twisted into a low bun, adorned with a rose-gold and pearl hair comb. The rose and gold colours of her makeup only enhance her natural beauty. Her body is wrapped in an off-the-shoulder champagne lace dress with quarter-length sleeves, and it fits her body like a glove, pouring down her silhouette, showing off all her curves and flaring at the bottom of the skirt.

But even as beautiful as Elissa is, I can't keep my eyes off the woman who consumes me long enough to admire the bride.

Lexi is all I see. All I need.

I hope I didn't just fuck this up.

• • •

The rest of the ceremony is only twenty minutes. A quick exchange of vows, the standard kiss, and the happy couple go off with a photographer to take photos. When I'm finally free, I break from the obligations of being a groomsman and rush off to look for Lexi. I find her huddling in the corner, biting the inside of her cheek and muttering to herself. I smile to myself, a spark of happiness that she's stayed this long.

She must hear me approach because she straightens, her body settling into a rigid stance, almost like she's moulding invisible armour around herself. Her hazel eyes connect with mine, and I feel my heart crack a little. Her heart-shaped lips upturn in a weak smile.

"You looked handsome up there," she breathes. She sucks in her bottom lip and bites down. I exhale the breath I didn't realize I was holding. I was terrified she was going to say something else. "But I think I'm going to head out now."

Something like that.

A boulder crushes into my stomach as she looks away from me.

"Lexi, dove. Please don't leave. I'm sorry I didn't tell you." Her gaze sharpens as her eyes find mine.

"Why didn't you tell me, Liam?"

"I don't know. I just—"

"The worst part of all this is I probably still would have come. Just because *you* asked me to."

"I thought you would have said no because it's Brandt's wedding."

She sighs, her eyes shutting like she's in pain, shaking her head.

"So you blindside me instead? You think that's better than coming to your friend's wedding alone? Blindsiding your *girlfriend* with her ex's wedding?" She lets out a caustic laugh. "Honestly, Liam."

"Dove, I'm sorry."

"Yeah, me too."

She takes a step forward, resting her hand on the lapel of my jacket, and presses a soft kiss to the corner of my mouth. She lingers there for a minute, and I close my eyes, burning this moment into my brain forever. Something inside me feels like it's breaking, and I don't fucking like it.

"Please don't leave like this," I beg.

"I just need some time to think, Liam." She turns to walk away, but not without another sad glance over her shoulder. "Tell Brandt and Elissa I said congratulations. I'll talk to you later."

Then she walks away, leaving me all alone.

CHAPTER THIRTY-SIX

LEXI

Liam walks away to take his position for the ceremony, leaving me with a jumble of chaos in my mind.

I'm not quite sure what to do about this information, that this is Brandt's wedding. I know I've moved on, and with Liam, but I don't know if I'm ready to see Brandt moving on so intimately. I never thought I'd be in a position where I have to decide if I'm going to attend my ex's wedding or be a coward and run.

Fucking Liam.

I already told Liam I'd stay for the ceremony, so I suck up all my feelings and confusion and head out back to where the wedding's taking place. I find a solo chair in the back with no one else in the row and take a seat, praying no one notices me or tries to ask who I'm here for—my ex, the bride, or my current boyfriend. I sigh, settling into my chair and crossing my ankles.

I try my best to avoid looking at the front, but my eyes are magnetized to the gorgeous man standing at the front. Caramel hair blowing in the light breeze, looking panty-dropping hot in his bespoke charcoal suit that grips the expanse of his chest. His arms threatening to burst the seams of the sleeves of his jacket. Stubble peppers his firm jaw, leading to his delicious, sensual lips. I tear my eyes away when my heart kicks in my chest, reminding me that Liam didn't tell me the truth about today.

I take in the rest of the venue, and it's a beautiful landscape. A large white gazebo is at the front, with rows upon rows of vines behind. In front of the gazebo are two sections of chairs on either side of the aisle, which only have about fifteen rows, each with pink chrysanthemums dotting each end chair. For two people who have an extensive network of people in their lives, this is a very intimate wedding, and I suddenly feel very out of place.

I look around at the people here, and everyone seems to fit in and is happy for the couple. Looking to the front, I try to avoid Liam's gaze, but it's impossible. My eyes seek him out like a moth seeks a flame. Our eyes lock, and it takes everything inside me to not look away because staring at him just hurts right now. The longer I look, the harder it gets to breathe because he steals my breath and suffocates me all at once.

My gaze flicks away and lands on Brandt, and my heart gives a light squeeze. He looks…happy. His green eyes are bright and vibrant among the dying colours of fall. His golden-brown hair is longer now, coiffed at the front, and he's grown a short beard. He looks handsome, rugged. He stands proudly in front of the crowd, laughing with Rhys while they all wait for the main event. Brandt's dark-blue suit shows his sculpted figure, and a champagne-coloured shirt peaks out of the jacket's opening.

As the last note of the melodic song hangs in the air, Elissa's friend Riley makes it to the gazebo, standing opposite Rhys, and a hush ripples throughout the guests and the wooden garden chairs creak as everyone stands. The piano starts an elegant instrumental rendition of *It's Always Been You* by Caleb Hearn. Everyone turns to the back, waiting for the bride to walk down the aisle.

Finally, Elissa rounds the corner, shining brilliantly in her wedding dress. Thin layers of champagne satin underneath the creamy white lace hug her curves and give Elissa the perfect hourglass shape. Her makeup is flawless golds and rose-coloured tones, with rose-gold jewelry adorning her neck and ears.

Elissa glides effortlessly over the grassy terrain in her white satin heels that poke through the flare of her skirt. A bouquet of pink and white chrysanthemums rests between her hands. I glance over at Brandt, and I swear I see a tear glistening in his eye as he radiates happiness, beaming as he looks at Elissa. They're so focused on each other, it's like no one else here matters. This moment is solely for them.

Elissa finally makes her way to the end where Brandt is, and he helps her up the gazebo steps. Her hand slips into his easily, and he leans in, brushing a kiss against her cheek. As they stand there, hand in hand, and make their vows, my heart squeezes a little and a single tear bubbles in my eye. As much as Brandt hurt me, I'm happy he's happy. That's all I really ever wanted, even if that happiness wasn't with me.

As they seal their commitment with a kiss, I join in with the crowd clapping, wiping away a stray tear that broke free. A small, genuine smile forms, and it finally feels like a weight has been lifted. Finally, letting go of the heartbreak I've been holding onto. Seeing Brandt and Elissa get their happy ending makes me hopeful for mine.

• • •

I find myself a corner away from all the other people rushing towards the happy couple, offering them their congratulations. I wring my hands, nervously trying to go over what I'm going to say to Liam when he inevitably approaches me. When I hear footsteps approaching, I steel myself and my resolve because I know one look from him and I can melt. I'll forget everything and fall into his arms, and right now I need space. I need to think.

In reality, I know he made a small mistake, and in my heart, I've honestly already forgiven him for that. But it's his not seeming to trust me to decide for myself—for us—to attend the wedding. He purposefully omitted information and kind of took my freedom of choice away, and I don't know how to feel about that. He put me in an awkward position.

When he's a foot away, I draw a deep breath before looking him in the eye.

"You looked handsome up there," I breathe. My words feel wobbly as I swallow the air that's clogging my throat. "But I think I'm going to head out now."

I hazard a glance at Liam, and his face is broken, reflecting just how badly I feel inside. I'm torn. I want to reach out to him, smooth my hand along his jaw and kiss him and tell him everything is going to be okay, but something stops me. He looks crushed, and a small niggle of guilt eats away at me.

"Lexi, dove. Please don't leave. I'm sorry I didn't tell you."

"Why didn't you tell me, Liam?"

"I don't know. I just—"

"The worst part of all this is I probably still would have come. Just because *you* asked me to." I bite back the emotions threatening to burst through me and stamp down the weakening of my resolve. Stepping a fraction closer to him, I lean in against his chest. I press a gentle kiss on the corner of his mouth. And with all the strength I can muster, I separate from him.

"Please don't leave like this," Liam begs. His hands reach out to grab mine, but I pull away.

"I just need some time to think, Liam." As I walk away, I leave my heart behind me. I glance over my shoulder. "Tell Brandt and Elissa I said congratulations."

CHAPTER THIRTY-SEVEN

LIAM

After Lexi walks away, it takes me approximately twenty minutes to arrange a car to come pick me up and take me to the inn where I can catch her and talk this thing through. But by the time I get there, all of her stuff is gone, and so is she.

I pack up my shit, haul it into the car, and have the driver take me back to Toronto. By the time we get off the DVP, I have a string of unanswered messages to her and a gnawing concern growing in my stomach. I call my bodyguard, Ivan, and have him check in on her and let me know she's safe. But that doesn't stop the turmoil from spreading inside of me.

• • •

It's been three days of hell without Lexi.

I fucked up. But it was a small mistake. So what if I didn't tell her it was her ex's wedding? It's not like I outright lied to her. *No, just a lie by omission. Which is still a lie. But also, it was her ex's wedding, dude. She had a right to know.* Shut up. Whose side are you on, anyway? *The side that's in love with Lexi.*

Fuck. I need to get her back. I need her to talk to me so I can fix this. I'm in my office, trying to work, but my mind is obviously elsewhere. I've got an important meeting with Jade and Moores coming up regarding my partnership promotion, and I can't go in there all fucked up.

Deciding I've had enough of her silence, I grab my phone from my pocket and message her.

Liam: *Lexi, please. Talk to me. I need to hear from you and if you're alright.*

It takes a few moments, but I finally, *finally* get a response.

Lexi: *Just give me time to think... Please.*

Not the response I was hoping for, but it'll do. At least she's responding. I tap my foot underneath my desk, debating on whether I should message her again or leave her be. *Fuck it.*

Liam: *Dove, I know you're upset. We just need to talk about this, please. Let me come over and talk this out. I need you, baby.*

Her reply is instant, giving me hope. But then I read the message, and my heart slams to my feet.

Lexi: *Liam, I need time to think. There's so much going on inside my head and heart right now, I need time to sort it out. I think we should take a break and both think about things.*
Liam: *What is there to think about? I made a mistake and I'm not letting you go over some stupid thing. Please, please just let me come over tonight and we can talk this out.*

My knee bounces under my desk as I wait for her reply.

LEXI

I'm staring at my phone in the middle of a spin class, wondering what the hell to do. Liam's messages are flashing up at me, making me question everything.

"Keep climbing guys!" I yell at the class without looking up. My fingers slide the messages up and down as I bite on my lip, contemplating what I'm going to do. Every cell in my body screams to say yes. Let him come over so I can see him again. So I can hold, touch, kiss, and taste him. I close my eyes and let my mind wander to what it was like the last time his fingers grazed my skin. How his lips felt against my flesh. How his arms felt wrapped around my body, holding me tight.

It was only a slight mistake, right?
I can't let it go.
I love him.
A small smile touches my lips as I type out my reply.

LIAM

Lexi: *Okay.*

My heart sings with hope.

I feel like if I can get her to talk to me, I can do anything. The last three days have been hell, but maybe this is a sign that things will be changing. For the better.

I check my watch, making sure I won't be late for the meeting. I close out of my browsers and organize my desk quickly before shoving my phone in my pocket. On the way to the boardroom, I pass Richie, Gavin, and a disgruntled-looking Kane in the kitchenette.

"Good luck, man," Richie says.

I give them a sly smile, letting them know I have this in the bag.

"I don't need luck. I'm Liam fucking West."

They all chuckle along with me. I roll my shoulders, straighten my tie, and enter the boardroom. Russell Jade and Daniel Moores sit on the far side of the table, side by side, leaving the chair opposite of them open for me.

"Gentlemen," I say, nodding to both of them. Their weathered faces are made of stone as they nod back.

"Let's make this quick," Moores interjects. "I've got tee time set in forty minutes." *Bastard.* It's just like him to be a prick when this big moment is about to happen. Jade sits there and says nothing to Moores's comment, which is only slightly worrisome.

"Let's get started," Jade says. "Liam, as you know, we've valued your hard work and dedication to your position and company since the moment you joined us years ago. You've grown so much and have been one of our most successful investment bankers in the history of the company."

"Thank you, sir." The pride I feel right now is incredible. It surges through me like a superhuman power emanating in my body. It's overwhelming; I'm close to bursting at the seams. Now is the moment I'll finally be recognized for all my hard work. All the late hours, missed family functions, time with friends I let slip through my fingers. All the sacrifices I've made will finally pay off. Finally, after three years of them putting it off, I'll finally be a partner. It's hard to contain my excitement, and I feel I'm doing it well. Or at least I think I am until I see Moores and Jade share a look of...concern? Guilt?

No, no, no, no, no.

Fuck.

Not again.

"Now, listen, son. All of that said, with recent events that have happened, we just can't talk about a partnership with you. The hacking and deleting of sensitive and important information, dropping clients. It's just not good for business, you see." My world shatters. Not fucking again. My heart sits in my throat as my hands curl into fists, blanching, holding back all the rage I'm ready to release.

"I've taken care of that. I've had the best fucking coder

strengthen your shit firewalls and security. There haven't been any incidents since." My voice is low as I glare at them, biting back all the expletives I'm dying to shout. *Fuck.* Moores is sitting there with his disgusting moustache twitching gleefully, and I want to punch his pompous face in. I've received reports from Jessie Sinclair that the hacker has been trying to penetrate our updated servers and has had no luck. And everything else has been quiet. No more break-ins or other incidents.

"And while we appreciate that you've taken care of it, our reputation is everything, and if this gets out and it's because of you…Well, you see? It would destroy the company if your name is ever on the business." Jade looks a little remorseful, but Moores is a smug prick, sitting there, smirking and tapping his fingers on the table.

Wait…

"What do you mean 'ever on the business?' This isn't another fucking delay, is it? You're taking me out of the running altogether. Just another game of yours to play. To see how willing and hard I will keep working without actually getting the recognition I deserve."

"Son, please understand," Jade interjects.

"Don't fucking *son* me. You can take your old man's speak and sayings and shove it up your ass. I should have fucking known that I would never be a partner here. I'm too successful, and I would dominate you two in decisions. You're both just threatened by me. That's why you've been putting it off for years, hoping I would somehow fuck up to the point of revoking my deserving of the title. Fuck!" I push myself away from the table, smashing my fists into the wood. The pain that splinters in my fists doesn't even register in my mind as I fume. Jade flinches, and Moores' face drains of colour. "I was never going to get partner." I laugh sardonically, placing my hands on my hips, dropping my head between my shoulders and shaking it.

"I quit."

"Wh-what?" Jade's voice is shaky.

"I said I quit." I lift my head, and my eyes snap to Jade. He looks worried, shocked.

"Now, that's just a little extreme, Liam. Please, just take a moment—"

"I've taken three years of 'moments' waiting to get partner. Each year you've put it off only to tell me now it's never going to happen. I. Fucking. Quit." I kick the chair out from behind me, and I stomp out of the boardroom. I storm past the kitchenette, and I see the guys share looks of confusion as I pass. Finally reaching my office, I slam the door shut and start packing all my shit. I don't worry about anything other than my personal shit.

There's a light rap on my door before it swings open, and the three guys come in, looking a little wary.

"Didn't go well?" Gavin says, flinching as I slam my satchel with my laptop in it on my desk.

"I quit." The guys are quiet, so quiet I think I can hear the crickets that are outside, fourteen floors down.

"Good for you," Richie quips. All of us turn sharp glares at Richie. "What? I'm just saying…It took you long enough to realize you were getting fucking strung along and do something about it. So…what are you going to do now?"

"Not sure about work. But I'm going to get my girl back."

As I'm leaving my office for the last time, my phone rings.

"Boss," Ivan's baritone voice registers over the phone when I answer it. "It's about Lexi."

CHAPTER

THIRTY-EIGHT

"Great work, everyone!"

My last fitness class is done for the day. I grab a towel and disinfectant, preparing to wipe down the bikes when a shadow casts over me. I jump, smashing my head off of someone's chin. Rubbing my head, I glance upwards and see Andy rubbing his chin.

"I'm so sorry, Andy. I wasn't expecting anyone to be standing right there."

A slow smile spreads on his face, a sparkle of humour in his eyes.

"No worries, Lexi. So…No boyfriend today?" Andy asks, his gaze shifting around the room as if he expects Liam to pop up at any moment.

"Uh, nope. Not today, I guess." His eyes settle on me, and his smile widens.

"Oh, good, good. So…how are you?" He asks with concern, as if he knows something I don't know. I cock my head, pinching my brows together in confusion.

"Um…Everything's good, thanks for asking, Andy." I flick my eyes away from him towards the door, praying that someone enters and stops this awkward conversation. I know that hope is futile because my last class for the day just left and no one else is here or will be coming in. I shift sideways to get out of his direct way and hopefully manoeuvre around him, but he sidesteps with me and blocks my exit. Anxiety rushes over my body like a tidal wave; goosebumps raise the hairs on my arms and neck. "Can I…help you with something?" I ask. His hand reaches out, caressing my cheek, and I freeze, not sure of what to do.

"It's just a shame…to see you so sad." His thumb strokes my cheek as he shakes away the chestnut hair that's fallen into his eyes. I suppress the chill that's crawling down my spine like a worm. "Liam doesn't deserve you." His voice is vacant, distant as his eyes lock mine into place, and I'm too nervous to look away. My body is screaming to run, but my head makes sure I draw measured breaths and stay calm even though my heart feels like it's going to fly out of my chest.

"Thanks," I say, cautiously. "Look, Andy, it's been a long day. Do you mind if we finish this conversation another time? I'd like to clean up and get home." *What does he even know about Liam and me to assume that Liam doesn't deserve me?* My words seem to break him from the trance-like state he was in.

"Yeah, sure." His hand drops from my face to my shoulder and squeezes it. "Things will work out for the best, don't worry." Confusion and worry etches on my face as he gives me a sincere smile, not nearly as creepy as the earlier ones. "I'll see you later." He winks, and it takes every ounce of willpower not to vomit in my mouth as he turns and leaves. When the main door clicks shut, I release a large breath, my body sagging, exhausted from the adrenaline and nerves that surge through my body. My hands tremble as I grab my phone off the table beside my stationary bike and check the time. I've got enough time to get home, shower, and change quickly before Liam comes over.

• • •

An hour later, there's a knock at my door. My nerves run wild as I rush to the door to greet Liam. It's been three days, but they've been long and hellish without him. I don't even really understand why I was so upset at this point. Sure, he lied, kind of. But it was his vulnerability influencing his choice. I can't blame him for that. Especially since Brandt and I have a history, and it wasn't until recently that I truly moved on. So I understand why he might have been hesitant to tell me whose wedding it was. It's no excuse, but I understand. It's awkward when you're dating your best friend's ex. Besides, I love Liam, and I'm at the point where I can't imagine my life without him. These last few days have been…some of the worst in my life. I need him. I can't breathe without him. Part of me is scared of what loving him means, and I think that's why I pushed him away at the wedding. I think it's because he can destroy me, completely and utterly destroy me. If he walks away, I don't know if I'll ever recover.

I quickly run my fingers through my blonde strands, fluffing my hair before opening the door. The smile I have on my face drops when I see Liam's. His eyes are distant—cold, even—and won't look directly at me. His mouth is in a firm line, and his brows are furrowed. My heart sinks in my chest, wondering what the hell is going on.

"Can I come in, please?" Liam's voice is a flatline of emotion. I nod my head and move aside so he can come in. He turns his head a fraction, nodding to someone behind him I didn't even notice was there. A large man the size of Hercules is behind him, with shorn jet-black hair. The lumbering man turns around, folding his hands behind his back. Liam crosses the threshold of my apartment and closes the door behind me.

He's quiet, and I know he doesn't say much in general, but everything about him is quiet. Like he's a ghost or shadow that moves silently. Alarm bells ring in my ears, warning me that something has changed. Something is changing. I follow him deeper into my apartment, and when he stops at the end of the entryway, I turn him around to face me, my hand resting gently on his cheek. He nuzzles his face into my hand with his own encapsulating mine.

"Liam, you're scaring me," I whisper. "What's going on?" Liam draws a deep breath, exhaling slowly as he drops his hand away from mine and backs away from me.

"This isn't going to work out." His voice is flat and devoid of emotion, still refusing to look me in the eye.

"What?" I close my eyes and shake my head in confusion.

"I said this isn't going to work out. It's over."

It feels like the floor just opened up and swallowed me whole. I don't understand what I'm hearing.

"Didn't you come here to make up? To talk things out over what happened at the wedding?"

Liam shrugs. "I guess I thought about it and you were right. We needed some time to think things out."

"But that's what these last few days were. Spent *thinking*. When you messaged me this morning…I thought…I thought you wanted to work things out." I feel like I'm dangling over the opening in the floor, hanging on for dear life, but the rope is snapping and shredding with each breath I take.

"I changed my mind."

"But…Why?" Liam gives nothing away, not even a drop of remorse or guilt. "Please don't do this. Other than the wedding, things have been really good. I forgive you, Liam. *Please* don't do this. Look at me." His eyes roll shut as he draws a deep breath, but still says nothing.

I feel the pressure building behind my eyes as he refuses to look at me. He finally moves towards me, but he doesn't stop. He pushes past me, heading back towards the door. Tears stream down my face as I plead with him not to leave. I grab his arm, trying to keep him from moving further, but it's no use. He's too strong for me and rips his arm from my grasp. He reaches the door, his hand wraps around the metal knob and pauses for a moment.

"*Please, Liam*. I love you," I choke out in between sobs. It's hard to see through the tears watering my vision, but he definitely stills and turns his head slightly. Not enough to look at me, but enough where I can see his whole profile. His hand grips the knob harder, his knuckles turning white.

"Goodbye, Lexi."

CHAPTER THIRTY-NINE

LEXI

I fall to my knees. The ground is unforgiving as the door slams shut. Tears pour from my eyes and down my face, soaking my T-shirt. It's getting harder to breathe as I heave, choking on air. The pressure inside builds, and my heart shatters into a million pieces. My body gives, and I crash further into the floor in a heavy heap. Motionless, weighed down limbs forget how to move, and my body's barely functioning. I silently pray that it's all just some big joke. I know I pushed him away, but this is just a cruel joke. *You know it's not a joke.*

Liam's gone.

What did I do? This is all my fault.

An invisible hand tightens around my throat, squeezing until I'm gasping for air. My hands find the cold chain around my neck, and I rip it off. My grandfather's ring goes flying across the room, but my heart is barely functioning enough to care, and I'm immediately met with relief. I pull my legs tight against my chest, wrapping my arms around my knees, and I stay curled in the fetal position, sobbing until my eyes flutter shut.

• • •

A gentle knock on the door stirs me from my nightmares. I take a moment and realize I've moved from the floor to the couch at some point. My eyes feel like all the moisture has been sucked out of them, and my cheeks are tight from the dried tears, but I have nothing left to shed. I sniffle, dragging my hand across my face to wipe the drool from my mouth, when another knock startles me. Completely forgetting that's what woke me. For a moment, I stare at the door, and images of Liam breaking my heart flash across my mind, and my heart lunges in my chest, but nothing surfaces. I feel...empty.

Another knock sounds, this time more impatiently.

"Earth to Lexi!" Lillian's voice rings out. I sigh, wondering what she's doing here.

"Open up!" Abby's voice bellows through the door. My brows pinch together, totally confused. I shuffle to my feet and make my way to the door. After I slide the lock, I take a deep breath before flicking the other one. I open the door, and there are my three best friends standing on the other side. Henry, Abby, and Lillian, arms full of junk food, take out, and alcohol.

"Woah, you look like shit," Lillian says, her words full of concern. "What the hell happened and whose ass am I going to kick?"

I blink, still utterly confused.

"What are you guys doing here?"

"Um…Weekly movie night? It's thirsty Thursday!"

"No…It's only Tuesday." Three pairs of eyes zero in on me, and I can feel the burn of their stares. *How have I missed two days? Oh my God, my studio!* "Where's my phone…I need to find my phone." I whip my head around and turn to go into the living room to find my phone.

"Hun, what's going on?" Lillian's voice dips into soft, dulcet tones. Her shoes clack as she follows behind me, the other two filing into the apartment after her. Lillian's eyes pierce me, and it feels like she can see right through me. "What happened with Liam? Is this why you haven't been answering our chat for the last few days?" Lillian's cool hand grabs my forearm and spins me around to face her.

My lip quivers, and the tears bubble behind my eyes. I bite my lip, trying to keep the tears at bay, shaking my head gently. "Oh, honey," Lillian whispers. She and Abby crowd around me, pulling me in for a hug, and I completely break. Again. Lillian and Abby just hold me for a moment while I hear Henry move past us towards the kitchen, taking the stuff they brought with him. He's a bit awkward when it comes to feelings and women crying. Honestly, I don't know why he hangs out with us since he's so uncomfortable, but I suspect it has something to do with Abby.

"Okay," Lillian says, breaking the circle of hugs. "Let's grab a bottle of wine—Henry!" she shouts over her shoulder at Henry before turning back to face me and Abby. "And let's drink and commiserate together."

Henry comes into the room carrying two bottles of wine, three glasses, and a bowl of popcorn, setting them all on the coffee table. Lillian and Abby link arms with me, pulling me into the living room and snuggling down on the couch together. I look around the room with wild eyes. "I need to find my phone…The studio. I probably have a million missed calls," I say as I try to push myself off the couch, but Lillian grabs onto me and forces me to stay put.

"Don't worry about your phone right now," she says soothingly.

Abby reaches forward, grabbing a bottle of wine and three of the glasses, filling them to the brim, and passing one to each of us while Henry goes to raid my fridge for some beer. Once he comes back, he sits on the loveseat across from us, and his beer hisses open as he pops the lid.

"So, what happened?" Abby asks carefully, wincing a little. I let out a sigh.

"Honestly. I don't know. Well, I do, but I don't." I sigh, leaning forward to place my wine back on the table before dropping my head in my hands.

"It's okay," Abby says, and a gentle hand rests on my back. "Take your time."

"It's all such a mess. I guess I'll start with the fact that he brought me to Brandt's wedding." Three mouths drop open, and I feel their eyes pinning me to the spot.

"Wait, what?" Lillian asks. Another sigh leaves my lips before I dive into the details, telling them everything. About how he never told me whose wedding it was, and it wasn't until just before the ceremony I found out. I let all the details spill from my lips. My words catching every once in a while as I breathe back sobs, trying to stay strong.

"So he says he wants to talk, to work things out, but when he gets here, he dumps you?" I nod my head as tears slip down my face. "Shh, don't cry," Lillian says as Abby grabs my hands and tangles our fingers together.

"Doesn't make sense," Henry says. The three of us girls look at him with puzzled expressions. "What? I just mean that he wouldn't have fought so hard to get you to speak to him after all of that, just to turn around and dump you." Henry sighs, pushing himself off the couch and heading into the kitchen. Abby, Lillian, and I stare after him in silence. The fridge door opens and then slams shut. He enters the living room again with a new beer, twisting the lid. Henry pauses as he sees the three of us waiting, expecting him to elaborate. His brows pull together, confusion etching his face.

"Do you know something we don't?" Abby asks. Henry shakes his head.

"It's simple. That guy only had eyes for you. Fuck, Lillian couldn't even grab his attention that one night, and she literally gets *everyone*. Something happened between the few hours you spoke."

"Like what?" Lillian snorts. Henry shrugs as he collapses onto the couch, kicking his feet up onto the table, taking a long pull of his beer.

"I dunno. But something clearly changed."

We all sit quietly in thoughtful silence.

What the hell changed then?

Lillian shakes her head, slapping her hands on her lap. "Doesn't matter. Fuck Liam! Let's binge drink, eat, and watch trashy reality TV for the night and forget all about you know who." Lillian's eyes lock onto mine, and I see and feel the sympathy radiating off of her. A lump forms in my throat, and a worm of guilt eats away at me for wanting to banish my friends from my apartment so I can wallow by myself. They mean well, but I just want to be alone.

Abby grabs the remote and flicks on the television, opening up the streaming service that has our favourite trashy TV shows. I relax into the couch, sulking, when Lillian hands me my glass of wine. Her face is encouraging me to drink it, so I press the cool glass to my lips and down half the glass. Lillian's lips tilt into a warm smile as her hand wraps around my wrist and squeezes. Lillian might drive me crazy, have a forceful personality, but she's the best friend I could ask for. Suddenly, I'm glad my friends showed up.

* * *

A few hours later, closer to midnight, my friends all clean up and get ready to leave for the night. Dishes clank as Henry and Abby wash them.

"Are you sure you want me to leave?" Lillian asks. "I don't mind staying the night, so you're not alone. It would force me to wake up early for once to go home and get ready for work. I'd probably be on time for once. Really, you'd be doing me a favour." I feel a laugh bubble out, and Lillian's face brightens.

"No, it's okay. I appreciate it, Lil. But I'll be fine, thanks to you guys for coming over tonight. You really pulled me out of my funk. I didn't know I needed this." Abby and Henry finish up with the dishes and walk over to where Lillian and I stand in the entryway. "Really. Thank you." Abby walks up and pulls me into a hug, followed by Henry next as he presses a light kiss into my hairline. As they're putting on their shoes and jackets, Lillian stares at me, almost like she's waiting for me to break or change my mind. Her eyes burrow into me, and her face relaxes, satisfied with what she sees. She nods her head, her arms reaching out to gather me in them. Her arms squeeze around me like a vice-grip, wheedling out a wheeze from me.

"I'm here for you Lex Luthor," she says, and I bark out a laugh at the nickname from college. "Only Superman had the fortress of solitude. So you don't need to be alone. Just call me, okay?" Her breath is hot as she murmurs in my ear, but my heart does this flip. At least I'll always have Lillian.

CHAPTER FORTY

It's been eight weeks, five days, six hours, and fifty-seven minutes since I've heard from Liam...Not that I've been counting.

I'm not stupid. I didn't expect him to reach out after he dumped me.

Okay, maybe I did. A little bit. Just to check in on me. But nothing. Silence.

I suppose it's better this way. A clean break.

Sure, tell yourself that. It's not like you haven't been crying yourself to sleep every night. Shut up.

It's been a productive two months. Lillian talked me into hiring someone to help me run the gym so I could take some time off and focus on me. I honestly don't know why it took me so long to do this before. My studio is thriving. I have more time for myself. My studio is now open for fourteen hours a day! My classes are full, and I've been adding more classes, in and outside of the studio. Erick is a yoga instructor, fitness trainer, and model. He proposed to start yoga classes out of the studio during his interview and this whole idea of how it would work. I asked him why he didn't just do it himself instead of getting a job, but he mentioned he enjoyed being part of something but not having to worry about the fine business details of things.

The women are *loving* Erick. He's so attentive, warm, and encouraging. His classes are mostly women whereas mine are a mix. I mean, I don't blame them; he is HOT. Erick is all lean, chiselled marble, ropy muscles, broad shoulders, and buns of steel. With piercing blue eyes and dark-brown, tousled hair, and a light shadow dusting his powerful jaw. I don't blame the women for drooling over him. When we first met, I thought he was checking me out during the interview. It was a little strange, but flattering, I suppose. Lillian ate him up though. I could practically smell her arousal in the air, like a cat in heat.

"I think he needs a more *intimate* interview. I volunteer to do it. We need to make sure he's not lying about all these yoga poses he can do."

Apparently, he's just as good in bed as you'd think, so says Lillian. I don't know what that means, if he's good or bad, but she seems satisfied. They're still seeing each other, and it's going well for a casual fling. I'm happy for her. At least one of us is getting regular sex.

Ugh. I miss sex.

I miss sex with Liam.

I miss Liam.

My heart hardens in my chest. Now and then, I get this overwhelming sadness that takes over. It usually has something to do with my mind wandering back to Liam. His voice, his touch, his kiss, and how I feel so naked—*absent*—without it. I've only really endured heartbreak once before, but it was nothing like this. This hollow emptiness that echoes inside me. The aching, pounding heartbeats that threaten to keep me feeling while fighting to feel numb. To feel nothing. Because that's all I want right now, is to feel nothing.

"Lexi?" Erick's resonant voice breaks through my depressing thoughts, pulling me back to our meeting.

"Sorry, Erick." His lips curl into a gentle, teasing smirk. "I was a little dazed." He chuckles.

"Yeah, I noticed. You do that a lot."

"Do I?" Erick just smiles and nods.

"Yeah, you do. What's going on in there? Anything you want to talk about?"

Erick sits across the desk from me, leaning back in his chair, one arm slung over the back as his other hand taps the temple on his head three times. His eyes sparkle with intrigue. He leans forward, raising one eyebrow, like he's waiting on bated breath. Like a dog waiting for a bone.

"No, not really. I'm afraid it's all business up in here," I lie. "Should we continue discussing next month's schedule for classes?"

Erick's eyes narrow a fraction before an ease ripples over his face like he's bored with this conversation.

"Sure," he says, shrugging.

"How are the yoga classes going outside the studio?" Erick's face lightens.

"Really popular, actually. We need to start thinking about what we're going to do because it's too cold to have classes outside and the snow will probably start soon."

"I'm already one step ahead of you," I say, my voice lifting an octave higher. I'm so excited about this new adventure I've been planning. "I'm going to purchase the small office next door that's for sale and expand the studio to another two rooms."

The current space is three rooms, plus a full bathroom, in total. My office, the medium-sized lobby, and the classroom. The office next door would add another two rooms, plus another bathroom. Once I knock a wall down, I can have an open gym facility with weights and treadmills and a lobby, two classrooms, two private washrooms for people to use, along with my office. It's the perfect next step. I can run two classes at one time while offering an open gym for the members to use in between classes if they wish.

"That's awesome, Lexi. And such a good idea because I know a lot of clients are upset right now that I had to stop teaching the extra yoga classes we were running outside the gym. So it'll be good to have the extra space."

Erick and I sit there, going over the schedule into the new year. We only have a few days left before Christmas break for the studio, so we need to hammer out this schedule and February's, too, because come March, I'll probably be closed for renovations. Just as we're wrapping up, there's a light knock on the door. My eyes don't leave the page I'm writing out, but I see Erick shift in his chair.

"Mind if I have a word with you?" A familiar voice asks.

"Hey, Andy. Good to see you!" Erick says in his best customer service voice. "What brings you here? Classes are done for the day."

"Actually, I need to speak to Lexi…Alone, if you don't mind." Andy's voice sounds rather tense, so I look up from the paper calendar with quizzical eyes. Andy's skin is flushed and dewy. Almost as if he's been sweating. His chestnut-brown hair is mussed, like hands have been raking through it repeatedly. Erick turns to face me, and his brows pinch in confusion. He shrugs, stands, and excuses himself from my office as Andy slinks inside.

"Uh, what can I do for you, Andy? Is everything alright?" Andy's eyes nervously flit around my office, and his hands wring together.

"Yeah. Yes. Everything is okay. I was just…just wondering if maybe you'd want to go out tonight with me?"

I should be a little shocked by this question, but in all honesty, I'm not. I've always tried to avoid him after classes and whatnot because I had an inkling he's been trying to work up the courage to ask me out. Andy's a nice guy, but I really don't feel anything towards him, or anyone right now for that matter. Well, except for one person. It's better to let him down gently.

"Aw, Andy. That's so sweet of you to ask. But I've just gotten out of a relationship, and it kind of destroyed me.

I'm still healing from it. It wouldn't be fair to you, or any-one for that matter, if I decided to date right now."

"Oh…I see." His shoulders deflate with whatever ounce of courage he had stored in his body. "What about just din-ner as friends?" he winces as he asks.

"I'm sorry…I would love to, but I actually do already have plans with my friends tonight for my birthday." Pity and shame washes over me as I rattle off my explanation. It sounds like an excuse, but it's the honest truth. I glance at my phone, and the time flashing back at me lets me know that I'm running behind if I'm going to get to the club on time. I still have to go home and get ready.

"It's your birthday? Happy birthday!" Andy says.

"Thanks," I say, pushing away from my desk as I gather the papers and shove them into one of the paper trays on my desk. "But I really need to go if I'm going to make it on time. Can we talk later, Andy?"

Andy nods his head, a gentle, sad smile on his face. He steps aside as I brush past him, stuffing my phone into the pocket in my leggings. As I'm putting on my coat, I turn to find Erick standing nearby with a smirk on his face. I can see the laughter dancing in his eyes. He definitely overheard the conversation. Narrowing my eyes at Erick, I say, "Can you please lock up for me tonight? I need to get going."

"Yeah, yeah. I'll see you in a bit." I feel a burning stare roam over me, and my nerves prickle inside me.

A sinking, tingling feeling takes over, and I find myself saying, "Yeah. Just make sure Lillian is on time tonight." As if to clear the air, although I have nothing to clarify with anyone, but just the way I feel Andy's stare burning through me, something compelled me to clarify. I allow myself a brief glance at Andy and give him a gentle smile. "Good night, both of you," I say as I make a hasty exit out of the studio.

I need a stiff drink.

CHAPTER FORTY-ONE

Liam

"Dude, come out with us tonight. You need to chill. You've been doing nothing but brooding and snapping at everyone the last two months," Richie says in a rather annoying whiny voice.

I snap my attention to Richie, and he shrinks in the chair across from me at Griddle Cakes. The server comes around and drops our food off at the table with a flirtatious smile and batting her thick lashes. As she walks away, Richie's eyes roam up and down her body as they zero in on her ass, or so I assume.

"I am not brooding and snapping," I grunt, picking up my fork and stabbing it into a piece of French toast. Stuffing the bite into my mouth, I grumble under my breath about how annoying Richie is being. I catch him smirking out of the corner of my eye. *Asshole.*

"Sure, let's both pretend that everything is fine. Come out with us tonight. You need to let off some steam, obviously. With starting up your own company and whatever the hell happened between you and Lexi"—I cringe when he says her name; my heart lurches in my chest— "you just need to hang out. Get shit-faced. Get laid. *Something* to put you back in the right spirit."

I don't want to get back into the *right spirit.* Whatever the fuck he means by that. This has been the worst two months of my life. First, I quit my job because the dicks that own that company were never going to give me partner. Second, starting up my own company has been a shit show. With all the permits, licensing, and lawyers…it's been exhausting. To the point where I fall asleep at my computer in my office at home or on the kitchen island. Third, I feel empty, drained, and broken without Lexi. I know I broke it off, but it was for her safety. I would never willingly destroy that woman unless it had something to do with her safety.

• • •

The day I was supposed to beg Lexi to work things out after Brandt's wedding, I received a call from Ivan.

"Boss. It's about Lexi." It's like ice-cold water doused my body.

"What happened?" My voice echoes in the stairwell I slipped into to take the call.

"A few weeks ago, her apartment was broken into, around the same time as yours. I don't think it's a coincidence." My insides churn, a sickening feeling gurgles in my stomach. A slight panic rises within me.

"Neither do I."

"What do you want to do?"

I close my eyes, sighing, as my hand grips the phone, wishing I could smash it into tiny pieces. As if that would make things better. I know where this is headed, but still I ask.

"What do you recommend?" My voice breaks through my gritted teeth.

"I suggest a sweep of her apartment and possibly distancing yourself from her until we find out who's responsible for all this."

"She's working now. Do your sweep, and let me know what you come up with." I hang up the phone, and I smash the bar to the metal door, flinging the door wide open. I burst back into the hallway, grab the box with my things in it, and find the elevator and leave.

Lexi's place got broken into because of *me*. I can't protect her if I don't know who's doing this to me. First of all, I don't even know why someone is out to get me. Sure, I have rivals within the industry, but nothing that would or should cause breaking and entering. My mind is reeling on the way back to my place when I get another phone call.

"Ivan…"

"Whoever it was put cameras in her apartment. They've been watching her."

I grind my teeth together so hard I feel bits of gravelly tooth dust in my mouth. My pulse rages inside me, my heart thundering in my chest. "I called Jessie while I was there. She was going to disconnect them remotely, but is leaving them live so she can trace the IP address."

"No. I want them disconnected." My knuckles curl into tight white fists, the tips of my nails bite into my skin.

"I don't think that's a good idea, sir. Leaving them live is the best way to catch the son of a bitch. If we disconnect them and they decide to check the cameras, they'll know something happened and maybe make a move."

Fuck.

"Fine," I growl. "Just have Jessie monitor the feed at all times. I want to know when the bastard is active on the stream and for how long. Have Jessie send me daily reports on the matter. Tell her I don't care what it costs."

"Got it." The phone beeps, ending the call.

What the fuck have I done to piss someone off that they threaten me at work? Threaten my girl? I just don't understand.

Tendrils of blonde hair and vibrant, hopeful hazel eyes flash through my mind. Full, lush, kissable lips whisper memories on my flesh as I think about Lexi. A shadow of darkness, of sadness, eclipses my heart as a lump forms in my throat. There's only one thing I can do right now to protect her. If I stay away, if I end things with her, there's no more leverage to use her against me.

• • •

"So are you coming or what?" Richie asks, tearing me away from the memory of the worst day of my life. I'm not in the mood to go out, drink, or get laid when I constantly see the broken pieces of Lexi's soul and heart shattering from the day I ended things. I can still hear her broken cries echoing in the darkest parts of my mind whenever it's quiet. It took everything I had to walk away from her. To keep her safe. But I'm so burnt out and worn down, maybe a night out with the guys is just what I need.

"I guess I could use a drink."

Richie's dark eyes light up like a kid's on Christmas. He slaps his hands on the table, jolting my plate of food so that it rattles. "Fuckin' eh!" Richie grabs his fork like a shovel and uses it to hoover food into his mouth, making this annoying, revolting moan with every bite he noshes between his teeth. My lip curls in disgust as I bring my coffee mug up to my mouth to take a sip. "So we're going to the newest club that just opened up," Richie says around bites. "It's going to be lit. I got our names on the list because one chick I hooked up with…" his voice fades into the background. Slowly, regret starts to form in the deepest part of my gut, spreading like wildfire.

I shouldn't have said yes to going out.

All I want to do is go over to Lexi's place, crawl on my hands and knees, and beg her to forgive me. I want to scoop her up in my arms, stealing her breath, and feel her lithe body against mine. The swell of her breasts pressing up against me until I can feel her nipples pebble into hard peaks. I want to

see her luminescent, soft skin and watch it flush bright red as
I turn her on, leaving her wanton. A panting, soaking mess. I
want to bury my face in her neck, her hair, and whisper just
how I feel about her. Tell her I love her.

But I can't.

Not until I figure out who this asshole is.

And until then, I need to let her go.

Until then, I need to live my life as well.

Or at least pretend to.

CHAPTER
FORTY-TWO

LIAM

It feels a little silly going out to a club when I'm almost thirty, but more specifically because I've broken my own heart. I'd rather be curled up at home in bed, legs tangled and bodies sweaty with Lexi.

As Kane, Gavin, Richie, and I walk into the club, I slide my phone out of my inside jacket pocket and type out a quick message.

Liam: *Any updates on the IP address or who the fuck it is?*

Three dots appear immediately and bounce on my screen.

Jessie: *Nope. But they were active on the feed about twenty minutes ago on the bedroom camera. I tried to trace it, but they were only on it for a few minutes. Not long enough to trace the bouncing IP.*

Motherfucker.

My hands coil around my phone and squeeze. It's been two months, and Jessie can't fucking figure this out. She's supposed to be the best, so what's taking her so long? As if she could read my mind, I get another incoming message from her.

Jessie: *Don't worry. They haven't been really active since you broke up with Lexi. So, presumably, she's safe for now.*

The tension drains from my jaw at her message, although I didn't even realize I was clenching my teeth. At least she's been safe. If anything, that's what makes this worth it. I couldn't live if something happened to Lexi.

I slide my phone back into my pocket as we approach the entrance to the bar. There's a line-up of at least forty people waiting to get in, swaying in the line to the music that's funnelling out of the building, but the four of us stroll to the front of the line. Richie reaches out his arm to the bouncer with four hundred-dollar bills in hand. As he shakes the bouncer's hand, they lean in and bump shoulders in a bro hug.

"Thought you got us in through one of your conquests," Kane quips. Richie turns to look at Kane and scowls.

"Yeah. She hooked me up with the bouncer's info so I could get us in." Even in the darkened entrance of the club, I can still see the glow of the blush burning his skin. "Fuck you, man. We got in."

Kane and Gavin snort. "Sure, if you call greasing palms getting us in," Kane shoots back. Richie shakes his head and stomps ahead of us as Gavin and Kane chuckle. Rolling my eyes, I follow the three of them when a pretty brunette waitress greets Richie with a small peck on the cheek. His hand snakes down her waist until he's groping her ass. Her cheeks redden as her hand holds his wrist, nodding her head towards the VIP seating.

As we settle into the booth, the waitress disappears momentarily and reappears with a bottle of Macallan. The thumping of the base from the DJ swallows the sound of crushing ice as the bottle is being set in the pail. The waitress places four thick crystal tumblers on the low table. She bends low from the waist, her ass sticking out and her cleavage on full display, with a seductive smile playing on her lips. Her eyes twinkle as her eyes settle on Richie. Her hips sway to some popular remix of Calvin Harris blasting through the club as she straightens up and saunters away back to the bar. Richie's eyes follow her every movement, turning around in the booth to watch her walk away, licking his lips.

"Sorry fellas. I'll be right back," Richie shouts, pushing himself to his feet, and follows the waitress, loosening his tie as he goes. I roll my eyes, irritated, when an alert goes off on my phone. Hurriedly, I dig through my jacket and grab my phone. The calendar reminder pops up, and my heart cracks, forcing me to lose my breath. *Lexi's birthday.* How the fuck did I forget about her birthday? Admittedly, there's been a lot going on lately, but I feel like I should have sent her a gift or done something for her. Then again, it might have only made things harder or more confusing. For both of us.

A flash of blonde catches the corner of my eye, and my heart stutters in my chest. Knocking loudly on my ribs, my heart pleads my eyes to follow. Holding my breath, my eyes wander to where the streak of blonde went. Familiar long blonde waves cascade down a creamy, exposed back. The scoop-back dress dives low, almost exposing the top of her magnificent ass. The black shimmery material rounds her ass and tucks underneath, nice and short, boasting beautifully toned, smooth legs. A singular freckle dotting the back of her thigh makes my groin grow intolerably tight. I'd know those legs, that back, that freckle *anywhere.*

I know I should tear my eyes away, but I can't. Clenching my jaw, I grab a tumbler of amber off the table that Gavin just poured and down the glass in one gulp. It's like swallowing a burning baseball. I hold out my glass and flick my fingers with my other hand to signal to Gavin to refill my glass. I toss back the contents again, barely letting the rich, expensive scotch hit my lips. The burning behind my eyes and in my throat, I'd like to blame on the alcohol, but it's the blonde bombshell that's about eight feet away that's giving me this reaction. I hold out my glass for more.

"Dude, that's an eight hundred-dollar bottle of scotch. Take 'er easy and save some for the rest of us," Gavin chortles. Finally able to break my stare, I turn my glare on Gavin, my jaw pulsing.

"Fucking fill the glass, asshole."

Gavin's brows pinch as he glances at Kane, who just shrugs uninterested. Gavin tips the long neck of the bottle to the rim of my glass and fills my tumbler once more. I snap my eyes back to Lexi, who is surrounded by her friends. She doesn't know it, but she has my undivided attention.

I watch her every movement, every laugh, every breath, and drink it in like a deprived alcoholic tasting every last drop. I'm captivated by her presence, and it leaves me breathless. Her hair flicks and falls across her shoulders gracefully as she dances with her friends. I curl my hand into a fist while the other grasps my glass firmly. It takes every ounce of willpower to stay where I am. The need— no, the urge—to go over there and wrap my arms around her waist and tug her into me closely is overwhelming. To sink my tongue deep into her hot mouth and taste every corner is enticing. It's a craving I need to avoid because I don't know if I'd be able to stop again once I start.

· · ·

I spend the next two torturous hours watching Lexi from afar, wishing like fucking hell I could go over there and talk to her. Breathe her in. Have her whisper my name. Instead, I've spent the time listening to Gavin and Kane talk about work, acquisitions, and fucking random chicks. A few months ago, I would have joined in and laughed, ranted, and raved with them on these things, but now?

Now it just seems pointless. The only thing that matters to me right now is over there, and I can't do anything about it. My mind filters back to that awful night when I broke our hearts. Even in this loud club, I can still hear her sobs echoing in the corners of my brain.

Lexi is radiant tonight, and the way the lights hit her form makes her a beacon in the crowd. It's like she draws the light filtering through the club and attracts it to her. She is the sun, and everything revolves around her. Her cheeks and skin are flushed and glowing from the sheen of sweat glimmering on her body. Her hips sway her body to the beat, carefree and joyous like a nymph dancing in the forest.

I'm indulging in the view when a beefy man walks up to their group, running a hand through his dark hair. I can't see their facial expressions from here, but Lexi's body language seems to acknowledge him as friendly. He wraps his undeserving arms around Lexi, picking her up and twirling her around. I clench my jaw until it aches, and my hands curl until my knuckles crack. *Has she moved on already?* The blood pumping in my veins thickens to bubbling molten, watching her being embraced by another man. He finally releases her; a second longer and I would have been out of my seat and across the room in a flash, burying my fist into his stomach. Just as my anger rolls to a simmer, the fucker grabs her waist and starts dancing with her.

"Jade and Moores have been in meetings with lawyers constantly lately since you've quit," Gavin says, prompting me to look away from Lexi.

"So what?"

"They're worried you're going to take clients with you once you open your own firm," Kane says flatly. A small puff of air bursts from me.

"They should've thought of that before they declined making me partner then. Besides, there's nothing they can do. They were idiots and never made me sign a non-compete clause. Honestly, after all the contracts we make clients sign, you'd think they'd be more careful with their employees. Also, fuck them. It's not like I'm stealing clients if they willingly come, and I haven't spoken to any of the clients anyway."

Another waitress stops by, depositing another bottle of Macallan on the table with fresh glasses. I catch a glimpse of Lexi and the bastard grinding on the dance floor, and as possessive and angry as I feel, I can't bring myself to stop her from having fun. She looks radiant tonight, despite what I put her through, and I don't know if I have the heart to do that to her. To interrupt her fun.

"For what it's worth," I say through clenched teeth, turning my attention back to Gavin and Kane, "they should be worried about me hiring you three over stealing clients."

As the song ends, I see a flash of blonde walk by our table, and my eyes trail after it. Knowing it's Lexi instantly and watching her weave her way through the crowd towards the washrooms, my restraint snaps. *She's alone.* I excuse myself from the boys and follow Lexi through the throng of sweaty bodies. Lexi disappears into a long, dark hallway, and I slip into it behind her, tasting the strawberry scent that trails behind her.

CHAPTER FORTY-THREE

Finally, I'm able to pull myself away from Erick and my friends to use the washroom. I'm a little tipsy from the drinks they kept passing to me. I need a slight break from all their attention. I swear they've been treating me like I'm a fragile doll about to break. Not to mention the unease I feel as though someone's been watching me all night. As I step into the narrow, dark hallway towards the washrooms, my heels click audibly now as the bass and music dampen from the walls.

There's another pair of shoes that smack the ground behind me, and electricity crackles along my skin. The tiny hairs on the back of my neck prickle as I slowly turn around and stifle the urge to scream. But my heart slows, and even in the dim lighting of this hallway, I still see his beautiful stormy eyes. Our eyes lock, and the air in my lungs whoosh out of me.

"Liam?" My voice wobbles the whisper. I feel like I'm dreaming. I've imagined a thousand different ways I'd run into him, but never thought it'd happen. The thudding in my chest is almost audible with how hard my heart is ramming against my ribs. I'm scared to blink because he might disappear. That I might actually be dreaming...

"*Dove.*" His velvety voice seeps into my skin, penetrating to my heart, jolting it. With a hard kick, my heart starts again. *I can't believe he's in front of me.* My eyes flutter shut as I regain the control of my faculties and breathe deeply. Steeling myself, because I might crumble if he says the right things, I chance looking into his eyes again.

"Wha-what are you doing here?" The confidence in my voice shakes. I fold my arms across my chest, a power pose to make myself seem stronger. But I'm weak, oh-so-weak for this man. He steps forward, and I match his step back. Liam hesitates for a fraction of a second before moving closer again. He's the picture of calm, cool, and collected. Like whatever happened between us didn't faze him. I feel my heart breaking all over again.

"Who was that?" His dark voice is laced with poison as it rumbles into the hallway. Goosebumps pepper my skin, and my breathing stutters.

"Who was what?" I breathe, my brows pinch together as I narrow my eyes. *What is he talking about?*

"The guy that had his hands on you…dancing," he growls. My mouth pops open, and I'm at a loss for words. I close my eyes, shaking my head, finally finding words.

"That's what you have to say to me? After all this time? Not 'Hi, how are you? How's it been going since I broke your fucking heart?' No, it's 'Who were you dancing with?'" My voice raises a few octaves as I rant. "Well, newsflash. You don't get to fucking know." I raise my chin defiantly, glaring at him as the narrow hallway drops a few degrees. His eyes ice over, jaw ticking, and the thick vein on his neck is pulsing. He takes a giant step forward, swallowing the distance between us, forcing me to retreat until my back bumps into the wall. His hand grabs my chin, his eyes pinning me in place.

"You're *mine*," he snarls. A lump forms in my throat, and I swallow it down, brewing some confidence inside me.

"I'm not *yours*," I spit. "You lost me the moment you broke up with me."

His eyes darken, a vicious hurricane swirling behind them before a grimacing smirk tugs at his lips.

"Dove," he chuckles. "You'll always be mine." He steps closer, barely leaving an inch between our bodies. He towers over me, keeping my gaze on his, and my knees grow weak. My chest heaves as his other hand trails up my bare leg, sending shivers dancing up my spine. My skin burns from his touch, leaving a trail of scorched, wanting nerves. As his fingers trail to my inner thigh, it gradually creeps closer to the apex of my centre. My breath hitches as I feel the heat pooling in my core, and he smiles deviously.

"Just the way your body responds to my touch…" He groans, clenching his teeth. He lowers his head, trailing his nose along my cheek, inhaling deeply. "I can fucking smell your arousal, dove. *Fuck,* I've missed that smell."

My head lolls against the wall as my eyes roll back; my breathing grows ragged, making my head spin. His fingers dance across my skin, stopping as he reaches my lacy panties. Holding my breath, a strangled moan escapes me. Liam chuckles darkly, clicking his tongue. "So responsive."

I'm writhing against the wall, rolling my body to feel his fingers on me. He obliges, cupping his hand over me, his finger lightly running along the outside of my panties. "*Please,*" I whisper, keeping my eyes closed because I'm too scared to open them.

"Please what, dove?" He's toying with me. Liam keeps his fingers from touching me the way I want him to, the way I know he wants to touch me. Tracing and circling around my clothed clit, he brings his lips closer to mine, gently brushing them against mine. "Tell me what you want." I release a breath I've been holding.

"Touch me, please."

His teeth nibble my lip, and I feel the smile that's touching his as I beg.

"That wasn't so hard, was it?"

His fingers deftly push aside my panties, dipping one finger in, swirling it around. Gasping, I grip onto his shoulders to keep myself from falling. Liam groans, dropping his forehead on mine. "Fuck, you're so wet." His words come out strangled. He withdraws his finger and circles my clit once, twice, three times before diving back into my entrance. This time with two fingers.

"Liam," I moan. He mumbles under his breath, and before I know it, his lips are crushing against mine. He takes my mouth with harsh lips, and something inside me breaks and I kiss him back, devouring him. With a hunger I've never known before. His tongue flicks across my lips, seeking entry. When I part my lips, his tongue dives into my mouth, our tongues tangling together, wrestling for dominance.

As our kisses heat up, his hand matches the pace, thrusting his fingers in and out and curving them until he hits the right spot. *Oh God.* My knees tremble, and I pull Liam closer, seeking more friction. I rock my body, matching his thrusts.

"That's it, dove. Ride my hand. Take your pleasure," he purrs. I break our kiss, my head falling back against the wall with a thump. My mouth drops open, but nothing comes out. The pleasure coursing through my body strangles my voice. Liam's hips press against me and his hard cock throbs against my stomach. My hand releases his shoulder and skates down his chest and taut stomach, finding the bulge in his jeans. My hand wraps around it, grabbing his thick shaft over his pants, rubbing it. His hips jut forward, pressing harder into my palm. Liam's lips break away from mine, his arm and head thump against the wall behind me, supporting his heaving body. His ministrations on me don't stop even as my hand feverishly pumps him over his pants.

"Fucking hell, Lexi," he groans. The pulse in his neck ticks, and I sense his restraint snapping like twigs. His hand rips away from me, and I instantly whine from the loss of his fingers. Wrapping his fingers around my wrist, he pulls me away from his clothed cock, pulling my arm over my head and securing my wrist within his other hand. He holds me securely as his hand delves down under my dress again, picking up where he left off. "I need you to come for me, dove."

He presses his thumb against my clit while sinking his fingers inside me once more, curving them until he's rubbing the spot that makes my eyes roll back into my head. His fingers are rough as they thrust inside me. Tingles erupt in my body, starting from my toes, quickly washing over the rest of me, and fireworks burst behind my eyes. My pussy clenches, sucking his long, thick fingers in deeper.

"Yes. Good girl," he coos. His fingers slow into a gentle, relaxing motion as I come down from the high. "That's my girl," he whispers. His hand releases my wrist, and it flops down beside me as I catch my breath. I open my eyes, and I find his grey ones locked onto me. It feels like forever as we sit there, panting and gazing into each other's eyes. My heart aches being so close to him. My hand slides up his neck, and my fingers tangle into his hair. Liam's head leans forward and taps gently on mine. Forehead to forehead, nose to nose, I feel his hot breath seeping over my skin. His lips are millimetres away from mine, and the pull to press my lips against his is so strong. He brings his fingers to his mouth and sucks them clean.

"Delicious…" he moans.

• • •

"Ahem." Someone clears their throat. Liam's head snaps to the entrance of the hallway, and I jump, scrambling beneath Liam's heavy body, trying to straighten my dress.

"What the fuck are you doing here?" Liam growls. Footsteps grow closer, and the tension builds in Liam's muscles. He pushes himself off the wall, rolling his shoulders back and pops his neck. Heat burns through my body. I'm so embarrassed that we've got caught doing something in public. That I gave into Liam, that I let him drive me wild.

"Thought you two broke up," a familiar, but dark and dangerous, voice grumbles. My eyes flick over to see Andy, his body rigid and squared up, as if he's ready to fight.

"Andy?" I push myself off the wall and press my hands into Liam's chest, pushing some distance between us. "What are you doing here?"

Andy's eyes are unobstructed by his usual glasses, and his dark irises shift from Liam to me. A downpour of freezing rain crashes over my body as Andy's gaze locks onto mine, a sinister smile tugging at his lips.

"I'm here for a...*friend's*...birthday."

My eyes shift away from Andy, and I catch Liam's eyes narrow and I can practically hear the gears turning in his head.

CHAPTER FORTY-FOUR

Lexi's curious gaze is on me, and I feel the worry coming off her in waves. I resist the urge to comfort her, or show any signs of weakness in front of Andy.

I'm here for a friend's *birthday.*

Andy's words rattle around in my head. Something doesn't sit right. It's too coincidental that he has another friend with the same birthday as Lexi. Something dark glimmers in his eyes as he stares at Lexi. An unnerving feeling settles over me, but my hubris pushes the warning away, laughing inwardly at the thought that this nerd would do anything.

"Not that it's any of your business," I snarl at Andy. "But we were just catching up."

Andy's eyes narrow, emotions flickering in them as he shifts his focus between Lexi and me. I bare my teeth down until they almost crack from the pressure. My jaw aches from the tension. Andy stares at me for a beat longer before his face falls and any trace of malice washes away. His body deflates, shoulders hunch in, and the nervous nerd appears. The shift in his demeanour is effortless and almost terrifying. *Something isn't right with him.*

"Well, uh, sorry for barging in," he rambles. "I'll just… go to the washroom now. Sorry again." He sounds like a bumbling idiot as he ducks his head, lowering his eyes to the floor, and slips into the door a few feet in front of us.

The tension in my shoulders releases as the door snicks shut, but the nagging feeling that something isn't what it seems doesn't quite leave me. I make a mental note to have Ivan follow up and do a background search on Andy. One minute the man looked menacing and deranged, the next he's a completely different person…and I don't think Lexi noticed.

"Liam?" Lexi's sweet, angelic voice breaks me from the fog I'm swimming in. Facing her, her eyes waver as she sucks in her cheek and bites down. Her hopeful voice breaks my heart, and I know just how much I've fucked up this time. I shouldn't have followed her down this hallway. I shouldn't have kissed her or touched her. The moment I saw her in the club, I should've made an excuse to the guys and left. *Fuck.*

"Lexi, don't," I say carefully, watching her heart break in front of me…again. Pain flashes across her face, and tears spring to her eyes. "Happy birthday, dove." I lean forward, pressing my lips to her hairline, breathing in her deeply. Mustering all the courage and strength I can, I turn and walk down the dim hallway, forcing myself to take a step at a time and not look back. I love this woman with all of my being, so why can't I stop breaking her heart?

• • •

A couple of hours later, I'm pacing the length of my living room, waiting for my phone to ring.

"Fuck!" I tug at my hair until I feel a sharp pull. Stewing in misery, guilt, and all the other negative emotions I've had since I left Lexi back at the club. *When the fuck is Ivan going to call?* I'm desperately waiting for his call. I need to know everything about Andy and his interest in Lexi. He always seems to show up where Lexi is. As if I didn't have enough shit on my plate with the person fucking with me, I now have to worry about Andy too. I scrub my face, and the sweet, musky smell of Lexi still lingers on my fingers. What I wouldn't give to smell her again. To hold her in a crushing embrace and never let her go.

My phone screams into the silence of the room, breaking my inner turmoil from bubbling over. Ivan's name flashes on the screen, and I'm frantic to answer it.

"Well?" I bark.

"I also have Jessie on the line," his brute voice grumbles.

"Hiya boss," Jessie says cheerfully. I feel my eyes twitch at her pleasant disposition while I'm here, losing my mind. The deafening silence from me causes Jessie to speak again.

"Uh, you still there?" Thankfully, they can't see my eye roll, but I'm almost certain Ivan can hear it because of the telltale huff of a smug laugh.

"You were right," Ivan says. Ice freezes over my body.

"Right about what?" The words come out like hostile missiles.

"All of it. I don't know how you knew, but you were right. It was Andy. All of it," Jessie replies. "When Ivan gave me his info, it was like the magic answer. It was the key I needed to unlock the door. Before, it was like shooting a target in the dark, but once I had a definitive place to look, well, I found it. Everything. The issues with the hacking at your old place of work, the roadblocks for you opening up your own firm, the break-in at Lexi's place, the cameras…It was all Andy. And, creepily enough, he's only ever missed two of her classes since he's joined, and it's been almost a year. Either he's fucking obsessed with her or he's really fitness oriented."

Everything around me falls away, and I barely register Ivan's and Jessie's voices on the phone. I drop my hand from my ear, my fist curling around my phone until I hear it crack. The echo of, "Boss?" coming from the phone from both Ivan and Jessie are lost to the pounding blood rushing into my ears. I end the call, and my phone pings immediately.

Jessie: *The camera feed just alerted me. She's home and Andy is with her…*

Fuck.

CHAPTER
FORTY-FIVE

I watch Liam walk away, but I refuse to cry, no matter how much it hurts. No matter how desperate I am to fall apart. I will not be railroaded by heartbreak again. If he doesn't want me, fine. There are plenty of men out there who do. Even if I may never find a connection like ours again, I'll be okay. At least, this is what I tell myself to keep the tears at bay.

I close my eyes and take a deep cleansing breath, trying to visualize myself expelling all the negative energy out of my body when the door to the men's washroom pops open.

"Lexi?" Andy says. "You're still here? Is everything okay?"

Andy's voice breaks me out of the trance I'm in, and I give him a weak smile.

Nodding my head, I say, "Yep. Never better." Then an awkward silence falls between us.

"Want to grab a drink?" Andy asks, wincing slightly. As if he's expecting a big fat rejection. Which, on a normal day, I'd probably turn him down. But right now, the shame and rejection of Liam has my insides all twisted up, and I don't feel like making rational decisions.

"You know what? Yeah, I do."

The smile that creeps onto Andy's face is a little unnerving, but I push those thoughts away as he reaches out, extending a hand for me. I slip mine into his, and a cold shudder wracks my body, but I let him pull me down the hallway towards the bar. We weave through the throng of people dancing and pass my friends. I see Lillian and Abby give me curious glances and I shrug, waving them to follow us.

All six of us line up along the bar, and Lillian flags down the bartender. He saunters over, slinging a towel over his shoulder. "What can I get you?" he asks. Lillian glances over all of us standing there, exchanging glances with each of us.

"Six shots of tequila, please!" she yells, slapping down two crisp hundred-dollar bills onto the bar. The bartender flashes a wolfish grin, grabbing some top-shelf tequila and flips six shot glasses onto the bar top with ease. Filling the glasses, he never takes his eyes off Lillian, and doesn't overfill or miss a glass. I practically hear the purring coming from Lillian's chest, even over the pounding music.

The bartender slides a shot glass towards each of us, and we simultaneously pick them up, bringing them all to the middle and cheering. I close my eyes, shooting back my shot, and the burn is acidic on my throat. I peek an eye open and glance beside me, and Andy is staring at the shot glass. I can't tell what's going through his mind, but I feel like he's debating on actually drinking it.

"It's okay. I'll drink it if you just want a beer!" I place my hand on his forearm, lowering the hand to the bar so he can place the shot down. His eyes find mine, and he looks relieved, sliding the glass in my direction. He flags down the bartender to order a beer. Gripping the glass, I tip it back into my mouth, resisting the urge to vomit or cough from the sting. I feel Andy's eyes lingering on me, and I look over, and his eyes look eager. My lips tip into an awkward smile, and I quickly look away. I feel Andy sidle up beside me, closer, much closer than necessary, and his lips brush against my ear.

"Want to dance?" he asks. A shiver skates down my spine. I'm stunned, but not at all surprised by this question. I move my lips to turn him down, but Lillian grabs my arm.

"Let's dance, bitch!" She tugs me, and I shrug at Andy.

"Sure, why not?" I give Andy a small, encouraging smile, and the lot of us move to the floor to dance. Lillian pairs off with Erick while Abby and Henry look awfully cozy together. They haven't mentioned anything, but I know they're sleeping together. It's just a feeling I have, and I think it's awesome. Her dark hair with his vibrant green eyes for a child would be gorgeous.

With everyone paired up, that leaves me with Andy. I mentally groan, but there's just enough alcohol running through my veins to let "carefree Lexi" flow. Andy is standing, glancing around the area like he's trying to figure out what to do, and it makes me chuckle.

"Just let your body sway to the music!"

I grab his hands and pull him a little closer until my hands can reach his hips. Gripping his hip, I move his body to the beat of the song, but he's still making these jagged moves with his hips. I laugh out loud, and his face burns scarlet, and I instantly feel guilty.

"Here, follow me!" I turn around, reaching behind me and pulling him close. There's a musty saltiness to his smell as he gets closer, and it's a little insufferable, but I push through it. I press my ass into his hips and place his hands on my waist as I move us to the music. It takes a few seconds for him to relax and get into it.

I'm enjoying the dance when my head spins. My vision blurs, my limbs feeling heavy as I stumble slightly, and Andy's arms wrap around me to catch me from falling. My thoughts jumble in my head.

That's strange…I've only had a handful of drinks. I guess the tequila hits hard.

"Lexi? Are you okay?" Andy asks, but it sounds like I'm underwater. His muffled voice breaks in and out. "Do you need to sit down?"

I shake my head, but it only worsens the dizziness. Sweat beads on my forehead, and my body feels like it's burning up. "I don't feel too well," I mumble, stumbling into Andy. "Lillian!" I yell.

I know she's close when her minty vanilla scent wafts my way. "Oh my God, babe. What's wrong?" There's a thick concern in her words.

"I don't feel great," I moan, clutching my spinning head.

"Do you want to leave? I can bring you home." I start to nod my head, but Andy cuts in.

"I'll take her home so you don't have to leave. I don't mind."

"Lex? Is it okay if Andy brings you home?"

"Sure, yeah. I just—" I sway as my eyes feel heavy, and I struggle to keep them open. I fall into someone's arms.

"I've got you, Lexi. Let's go," Andy says, hauling me up and helping me leave the club.

We finally make it out of the club. It could have been seconds, but it felt like hours until the cool air hits my face.

"Let me flag a cab," Lillian says. I hear her shoes click away, and a few seconds later, a car comes to a stop. "Here's her purse and her jacket. Thank you for taking care of her, Andy." I feel silky smooth skin on my bare arms. "Okay, hon. Andy's going to take you home now. Call me if you need anything." I'm jostled around as I'm placed in the cab, and I hear the door slam. I lean against the cool glass, and my eyelids fall shut. It's getting harder and harder to stay awake...

"Don't worry, Lexi. I'll take *good* care of you." Andy's voice is dark and makes the hair on my neck stand, but I have no fight in me. His hand reaches out and rests on my thigh, squeezing it lightly. I will myself to move, to shake him off of me, but I can't. Instead, my body and mind give in, and everything goes black.

• • •

Everything is hazy, and I'm not sure what's going on. My eyes flutter as I try to regain control of my body, but every limb feels like it's filled with cement. I try to wiggle my fingers, but even they don't respond.

"Uhhh…" I moan, trying to make words come out, but my lips and tongue are uncooperative. My eyes finally slit open, and I notice a familiar room around me with happy pastel colours. *I'm home.* But how did I get here? The last thing I remember…The last thing I remember was seeing Liam at the club. *Oh my God, is Liam here?* Did I go home with him after what happened? Why can't I remember?

My head throbs, and it feels like a thousand tiny men are jack hammering holes into my brain. I crack my eyes open a bit more, and the blurry room comes into focus. I'm draped on my couch with my arm hanging off the edge. The sharp light in the room burns my eyes, so I squeeze them shut. I try to move, but my body still won't respond.

"Shhh, it's okay," a familiar voice coos. "I'll take care of you, baby."

"Li…am?" I manage to croak out. Somehow I know it's not him as I say his name. Something feels *wrong*. A clammy hand reaches out and pets my face. My body screams for me to flinch, but there's nothing I can do. It's like my body is paralyzed.

"Forget that prick." The icy tone sends shivers shooting through my body. "I'm here for you, baby. You'll be safe with me…" Someone walks in front of me, their legs in front of my face. As he crouches down, his face comes into view, and it's Andy. A small sense of security briefly washes over me that someone I know is here with me, even though I wish it was Liam. *Wait, did he just call me baby?*

"What…happened?" My tongue refuses to cooperate, but I manage to get something out. Andy's face flashes with concern.

"I think you just had too much to drink at the club. You should probably have some water. It'll make you feel better."

"Please," I croak. Andy's face relaxes and gives me a re-assuring smile.

"I'll be right back. Don't move," he says, chuckling to himself.

He walks away, and his footsteps fade as he enters the kitchen. I hear the tap running and a few seconds later, he's back in front of me, a cool glass of water in hand. I struggle to sit up, and Andy places the water on the table and loops his arms around me to help me. Once I'm resting against the arm of the couch, he passes the glass to me, and I take a sip. A faint, bitter taste touches my tongue as I drink, but I don't think too much of it. I hand the water back to Andy, but he refuses to take it.

"No, drink more. You need it."

"I just…need a minute."

Andy's glance rolls over me, his eyes narrow as he stud-ies my face. We sit in silence for a few moments, and my head feels light. I close my eyes tight, trying to shake off the spins. I don't remember drinking enough to feel like this; I must have blacked out at the club.

"Lexi, are you feeling okay?" Andy's voice doesn't feel concerned, almost curious. Something inside me prickles, trying to keep me alert. My gut is screaming at me that something is wrong.

"Andy…What's going…on?" My eyes flutter again, and I'm fighting myself for consciousness. Every second gets harder to stay focused. *There's something very wrong. I feel strange.*

"Just relax, baby. I'll take such good care of you." His hand reaches out and caresses my cheek, his finger trailing down the length of my neck to the swell of my breasts. The ick feeling creeps over me like a spider crawling all over my body. Little spindly legs pricking along my skin, warning me to run. As I realize that I may just be in the room with someone I shouldn't be, my consciousness fades and my eyes roll back, and everything goes black.

CHAPTER FORTY-SIX

Liam

"Drive faster!"

My driver presses the pedal to the floor, and the SUV roars, blasting through the traffic. Every inch of my body vibrates from the anger that's surging inside. If *anything* happens to Lexi, I'll never forgive myself. I can't believe I let her walk away from me at the club. I can't believe I let her go, thinking I was protecting her by staying away. I'm such a fucking idiot. My phone rings, breaking my self-admonishment.

"What's going on?" I growl into the phone.

"Um...I don't know how to say this, but I think he's drugged her." Jessie's voice breaks through the phone. I close my eyes and breathe, trying to keep the anger inside me at bay. I will wait until Andy is in front of me before I give into this rage. My fists will beat the living shit out of him if he harms her, any more than he's already done.

"How far away are you, Liam?" Jessie asks. "Ivan and I are about ten minutes away still. But I'm not sure if we'll make it in time."

"Fuck! I'm almost there."

"Hurry...I'm still on the stream, monitoring things, and it looks like he's trying to drug her again. She's just laying motionless on the couch and he's...petting her? He looks like he's going to kiss her."

"Jessie?"

"Yes, boss?"

"Shut up." I end the call, and two minutes later my driver pulls up to the side of the road to Lexi's apartment. I'm out of the car and running into the building before the vehicle rolls to a stop. My anger rolls through my body. My blood is boiling under my skin as I run up the ten flights of stairs because the elevator is too passive. I need to do something or I might just lose my mind.

Lexi

My mind is floating in and out of control. Every time I think I'm able to move or open my eyes, something heavy weighs my body down. I'm trapped in my body, like I'm just a passenger within a vessel. I'm trying to fight this darkness that's taken over my body, but it's like screaming and no one hears you.

Andy did something to me, drugged me or something. His hand crawls all over my body, exploring things he shouldn't. I shout, scream, kick, but nothing happens. I'm frozen in place, completely at his mercy. I don't even know when he would have drugged me. I don't remember taking anything from him…

The shot of tequila! Oh fuck. How could I have been so stupid? I mean, I never thought I'd be in danger with Andy. *Please don't let him do anything to me.*

His fingers trace every line, every curve of my face. I can feel the couch depressing as he leans forward and nuzzles his nose in my hair, breathing deeply. I want to scream. I want to run away. Why did my friends let me leave with him? My heart gallops in my chest, and I feel the shift in my breathing as Andy gravitates closer to me.

His hands run down the length of my body, taking his time palming my breast. Bile climbs up my throat. I'm struggling to stay conscious and fight the drugs in my system to stop Andy, but it's difficult, and it would just be easy to give into the lull and drift off, so that I don't have to remember anything later.

LIAM

I finally make it to her door, and I don't attempt to open the door properly. My adrenaline is surging through my body as my foot connects with the door, smashing it open, and it almost flies off the hinges. My eyes cloud red as I zero in on Andy as he jolts from hovering over Lexi. All of my blood boils as I see Andy with his hands on her.

"What the fuck?" Andy snarls.

"I should be asking you that," I snap back. I stalk over with a dark cloud hovering over me, and I feel the lightning and thunder brewing inside, and he cowers away, toppling over the coffee table.

"I-I…Didn't do anything yet!" He shouts, scrambling away on his hands and feet, not turning his back to me. *Smart, but not smart enough.*

"Yet? *Yet?* You fucking drugged her you piece of shit. You've been stalking her, plotting and planning this moment. I think you've done enough without touching her."

Andy's throat gulps, and I see the large swallow roll down his throat. Fucker's scared, as he should be.

"Oh, and what about the cameras? You're a fucking pervert. Who knows what twisted shit you did when you were watching her on camera."

Andy's eyes widen, his body vibrates with fear.

"H-h-how did you know about the cameras?"

"Because I take protecting Lexi seriously. As soon as I thought Lexi was in danger because of something I did— thanks for the shit you fucked up for me by the way—I did a sweep of her place."

I creep closer to Andy, and he backs into a wall. The moment his back touches the wall, his breath whooshes out of him, and his eyes are as wide as saucers, and his body is shaking like a leaf.

"Please…please don't h-h-hurt me," he stammers. *Fucking pathetic.*

"Don't fucking move, or I'll beat the shit out of you. The cops and my bodyguard are on the way to arrest your pathetic, creeper ass." I level him with a murderous glare before turning and racing over to Lexi's side. Fuck, fuck, fuck. *Please be okay…*

"Lexi," I say, gently shaking her shoulder. "Look at me, dove. Are you okay? C'mon baby, wake up." I gently pat her cheek and shake her body, trying to rouse her from whatever she's on. "C'mon, dove. Wake up for me, please. I'm here, you're safe."

Lexi's eyes rove under her lids, and I notice them flutter, as if she's trying to respond. I caress her cheek with the back of my hand before cupping it and tilting her head towards me. "I'm here, dove." I lean down, tapping my forehead to hers.

Please let her wake up. I pray to whatever God might be out there listening. I need her to wake. To see those beautiful hazel eyes, to know she's okay.

I shoot a glare over my shoulder at Andy when she doesn't wake up. His relaxed body sits ramrod straight, and his eyes are muddled with fear.

"What the fuck did you drug her with?"

Andy's mouth drops open, his lips flapping like a fish's, and it grates on my nerves. He's stumbling with trying to say something.

"Speak!"

"I…I didn't—"

"WHAT DID YOU DRUG HER WITH?"

"GHB!" He shouts. *Motherfucker.* "J-just two s-small doses to relax h-her." My fists curl, blanching white as I push off the side of the couch. But just as I'm about to go over and pummel him, Lexi stirs.

"Li...am?" Her sweet voice whispers hoarsely.

I spin around, rushing to her side, collapsing on my knees. I thread my hands through her hair, cupping the side of her face and turning it to face me.

"I'm here, dove."

CHAPTER
FORTY-SEVEN

There's nothing but shadows and darkness seeping into every corner of my soul. I can't find a sliver of light to focus on and bring me back until a familiar voice whispers in my ear, rousing me from the darkness. I hear his warm, deep voice, and it smooths over my body like a cozy blanket. Everything is foggy, and I'm having the hardest time concentrating. The voice sounds like Liam's, but he's not here. He can't be. He walked away from me *again*. But then his woodsy scent ignites my senses, and I swear Andy's drugs are making me hallucinate.

My heart thuds against my ribs.

Dove.

It's all I hear, whispering to me, over and over.

I'm here, dove.

I cling to those words, to the voice in my head that's soothing my petrified body. What was once cold shivers of disgust are now replaced by calming, warm vibrations. Like my imagination is cocooning me with pleasant feelings to overcome the trauma that I'm facing. My semiconscious mind grabs hold of these feelings and nurtures them. Revels in them, praying they keep me safe.

What the fuck did you drug her with?

Particles of a conversation take form in my head.

Speak!

I-I didn't…

What did you drug her with?!

Two voices. I'm not imagining it, am I? The fluttering in my chest intensifies when I realize there's someone else here. I move my lips to call out to the other person. To ask for help. It sounds like Liam.

Liam…but my lips won't move. *Liam!* But I only hear my voice in my head. I feel like I'm drowning in my own silence. My tongue and lips won't cooperate with me, and I feel like I'm dying on the inside.

I try again, and my tongue twitches in my mouth. I try to move my mouth, but my jaw feels like it's stuffed full of that dental putty they use to make a mould of your teeth.

"Li…am?"

Suddenly, a warm hand brushes against my cheek.

"I'm here, dove." Another warm hand grabs my hand and curls it around mine, tight. "I'm right here, and I'm not going anywhere." The hand moves from my cheek and strokes my hair with loving and gentle care.

The person bends and places a kiss on my forehead, and the scent of them fills me with the feeling of home. As their lips press against my head, I feel the electric zing on my skin. My heart is restless but calm at the same time.

It's Liam.

I'm safe.

I struggle to open my eyes, the heaviness being a formidable foe, but I'm finally able to crack them open to a small slit. Everything is blurry and dim, but I can just make out his strong square jaw that's sporting a rugged beard. His stormy eyes frantically searching my face with his thick groomed brows pulled together. My eyelids flutter like they're seizing, and I'm able to pry them open.

When they're fully open, they lock onto his beautiful grey eyes that are bursting with emotion. The rising tidal wave of emotions builds as my throat tightens, making it hard to breathe.

"You're...here?" I rasp. Tears bubble in my throat, stinging my eyes, and my heart pitter-patters in my chest. His lips split into a goofy smile, and his eyes are holding back the tears that shimmer in the corners.

"I am. And I'm not going anywhere ever again." He brings my hands to his lips, pressing kisses into my knuckles. "Lexi...I lo—"

A shadow hovers over us, and I gulp down air and shriek.

"Liam!"

A glint of a pocket knife reflects from the light over-head, and Liam bellows as Andy plunges the knife into his shoulder. He falters to the ground, and Andy tears the knife from Liam. Liam's hand clutches where blood is spilling out of the top of his shoulder, his face draining of all colour, and yet he's still grasping onto my hand with the other. A bloodcurdling scream echoes through the room, and I realize it's coming from me.

"Tsk, tsk," Andy clucks. "You should know better than to turn your back on your enemy." Andy's dark voice sends a plummeting feeling through my stomach. Andy boots Liam in the ribs with a hard *thunk,* and Liam goes flying backwards, smoking his back off the coffee table, grunting as he sprawls over the floor.

Fear douses my body until I run cold. My frayed nerves ramble inside me as I lie helplessly on the couch watching the scene unfold.

"Please, Andy…Don't…hurt him." My lips and tongue flounder as I try to gain all control over my faculties, but I'm still struggling against the poison running in my veins.

Andy's head snaps in my direction, and his eyes soften as his gaze settles on me. Out of the corner of my eye, his pocketknife dangles from his hand, Liam's blood dripping down the blade, soaking into my cream rug.

"Shhh, baby. I'll be with you soon, but the men are talking right now." He turns his attention back to Liam. Andy's shoulders roll back, puffing out his chest as he stalks closer to Liam. "I tried to fucking warn you," he says with a dark chuckle. "And you didn't listen. Sure, you did for a minute, but you just couldn't stay away, could you?" Andy's gritty voice bouncing off the walls ricocheted through the room. "If you just stayed away, I wouldn't have done this to her. I would have won her over. If you just *stayed* away, she would have loved me. I worked so hard, learning everything about her, going to all of her classes, watching her twenty-four seven…"

Nerves laced with vomit trickles up my throat threatening to spew. Disbelief ripples through my body and I shudder. *Watching me twenty-four seven?* I find what little strength I have and push myself to sit up a little.

"You're fucking sick in the head, Andy," Liam spits. "Breaking into her apartment, bugging it with cameras… That's fucking pathetic, dude. Just go and get laid some easier way." Liam smirks at the dig as Andy's eyes narrow, his body violently shaking.

"SHUT UP!" Andy screams. "I saw Lexi first; she's mine. *Mine*, not yours. I worked so hard to have her. To get her to notice me! But then you waltz in and steal her away from me. So I stole everything of yours, which isn't much, by the way." Andy chuckles. "Making you lose your job? The partnership? That was easy. The fact that's all that's going for you is *fucking pathetic*." Andy's last two words mocking Liam, trying to provoke a reaction from him and working as Liam's eyes narrow and jaw clenches.

Andy creeps closer with the blade directed at Liam, who's clutching his arm to his chest and his hand covering the wound, but blood is still seeping out between his fingers. A menacing smile and the deranged, wild look in Andy's eyes make my skin crawl.

"*Please*," I beg. "Please don't hurt Liam any more, Andy!"

Andy swats the air behind him, signalling me to shut up. "I'll do anything. I'll…I'll never see him again." Andy halts, turning to face me with curious eyes. Liam's body freezes, his chest stops rising like he's holding his breath. I feel Liam's eyes burning a hole in my head from how hard he's staring at me, but I refuse to look at him, not daring to give Andy any reason to act out. "Please. Just let him walk away. Let Liam walk away, and I'll go on a date with you."

Liam's gasp echoes through the room as my eyes stay focused on Andy. His eyes widen with glee and a creepy delighted smile spreads across his face, showing his canine snaggletooth.

"Lexi, don't—"

I cut Liam off, not taking my eyes off Andy, terrified if he loses my attention, the hold I have on him right now will break.

"Leave, Liam. Just go, that's what you're good at."

"Lexi…" His voice is broken. I hear his heart breaking, the guilt that drips from my name.

"Just go, Liam!" My voice cracks, overwhelmed by so much emotion. Andy takes a careful step forward. "Come here, Andy. I'm making Liam leave." The smile on Andy's face radiates triumph as he drops his hands to his side, letting his hand grow slack around the knife. I finally find some strength and push myself up on the couch higher, reaching my hand out for Andy. "Come here," I say encouragingly. As Andy's distracted and all too happy to come to me, Liam forces himself to his feet, clenching the groan between his teeth, so he stays silent.

Before Andy can reach for my hand and grab it, Liam barrels ahead, ramming into Andy's back. They fly forward, and Andy cracks his head off the coffee table, his head violently jerking, and his limp form cushions Liam's fall to the floor.

"Liam!" The scream shreds my throat as I leap forward, pulling Liam into my arms, his warm blood trickling down my back.

"Boss!" An unfamiliar voice rattles through the room. A large behemoth of a man dressed in all black comes bolting into the apartment. He stops dead in the middle of the room, looking at the scene, and his rigid body deflates in relief. "The cops and paramedics are on their way up now."

CHAPTER
FORTY-EIGHT

Lexi's body trembles in my arms as Ivan barrels into the room.

"Boss! The cops and paramedics are on their way up now."

Giving Ivan a curt nod, I wrap my arm tighter around Lexi, pulling her into my blood-soaked T-shirt, adrenaline surging through my body so that I don't feel the throbbing pain of the stab wound.

"Help us up, Ivan."

Ivan walks over to us, reaching his arms out and pulling Lexi to her feet first. He walks her over to the dining room and props her up on a chair. When he's certain she's steady, he comes back over for me. Once I'm on my feet, Ivan disappears down the hallway, and the clattering of doors against walls echoes through the apartment. I sit down in the chair next to Lexi when Ivan thumps back into the room, his arms full of linens.

He dumps the soft white linens onto the table, sifting through them until he finds a pillowcase that is acceptable to him. He rips it with his teeth down the centre. Ivan folds it over and over until it's a narrow, thick strip. He sets it down and finds another pillowcase and folds it into a thick, small square. His fingers work with precision as he temporarily bandages up my shoulder to stop the bleeding, making a sling for my arm out of a sheet. Once Ivan is satisfied, he takes a half step back, and a few seconds later, half a dozen pairs of stomping footsteps come down the hallway outside the apartment.

The four uniformed men step over the broken door carefully as they enter the apartment, the splintered wood cracking under their feet. The paramedics follow close behind, wheeling a gurney over the remains of the broken door, one of the front wheels clanging against the doorknob.

The paramedics make their way to Andy first, checking his vitals quickly before nodding to the police that he's fine. The cops sit him up, and Andy comes to, moaning. His hand clutches his forehead, hissing and wincing at the gash.

The next hour is a blur as we get emergency medical attention, and the police take statements. The whole time, Lexi stays glued to my side, hanging on for dear life, staining her dress with the transfer of blood from my shirt, reluctantly letting me go when the paramedics check out my wound.

"It's okay, dove. It's all over now," I reassure her, my hand squeezing hers as her eyes cloud with tears.

• • •

We spend the next few days holed up at my condo, lying around in bed, watching movies, and snuggling. During the nights, Lexi tosses and turns, mumbling in her sleep. The anger calls for me to search out Andy and fucking kill him for putting Lexi through this. And I would, except any time I go to leave the room, Lexi's breathing picks up and I see the struggle going on inside her as I move further away from her. It breaks my heart, and I just want to crumble and run over to her, scoop her into my arms, and make her feel safe.

It takes a few more days before she seems settled and somewhat herself again. Her face lights up when she's talking, her smiles are more frequent. It's nice to see her feeling better. So it comes as a shock when I wake up the next morning, sleep still heavy in my eyes, and she's bent over, sliding a pair of leggings onto her legs. Her blonde hair tucked behind one ear as the rest curtains around her face.

"Where are you going?"

"Oh," her body snaps upright. Her cheeks tint a lovely shade of pink. "You're awake."

"So it seems." I fold my arms behind my head. "Where are you going?" I ask again, more firmly.

"I've got to go home, Liam."

I bolt to sitting in a flash. "What do you mean? You're not going home, it's not safe."

Lexi gives me a weak smile and sighs.

"It's safe enough. Andy has a temporary restraining order, so that should keep him away for now until the trial, and you had Ivan remove all the cameras and replace the lock. I can't stay here, Liam. It's already been over a week."

"Why the hell not?" I growl. "You're staying here. I'm not letting you leave my sight again."

"Liam, nothing's changed. We're not together. You broke my heart. While I appreciate you letting me stay with you, I'm feeling better now—safer now. I need to go home."

"I only broke up with you to keep you safe, dove." My voice trembles.

"I know…" she whispers, looking away from me. "But you still broke my heart, and I don't know if it can be repaired. You lied to me. Instead of telling me the truth, you lied to me. Let me think that I was the problem. That I did something to have you walk away. Twice you lied to me, kept me at arm's length…I just don't think I can do it again. I don't know if I can trust you anymore."

"Lexi, I didn't mean it. Please know that I did it in the best interest of you. I never wanted to break your heart or your trust. I lov—"

"Don't Liam…Don't say those words." She snaps her gaze to me, tears brimming in her eyes. "Just…don't. Because I don't know if I can take my heart getting ripped from my chest again."

She crosses her arms across her stomach, protecting herself from the insecurities that wash over her body. I shuffle across the bed, the blankets rustling underneath me as I carefully inch closer to her until my feet plant firmly on the floor.

I pull her into my arms, tightening them around her lithe body until I can feel her chest raising against mine with every breath.

"No, you need to hear it. You need to hear that you're the reason I breathe in the morning, the reason I find myself smiling during the middle of the day, the reason I want to settle down and grow old with someone. I love you, Lexi Gardener. But you're not going anywhere if you're going home. Because your home is with me. I'm not letting you go ever again. I'll send Ivan now to go pack up your entire apartment and move you in today. But you're mine, and I'm yours. I love you." My hands cup her face, and I pepper her face in kisses while her hands cling to my forearms. Tears burst from her eyes, rolling down her cheeks, and I catch every one of them with my tongue. "It's okay, dove. Let it all out. I'm never leaving you again."

"I don't know if I'm ready to trust you again." Her voice is barely above a whisper.

"That's okay. I'm not going anywhere, so take your time, as long as it's beside me. I can't be without you another moment, Lexi. I won't do it. Please, just stay."

CHAPTER FORTY-NINE

Ten months later—October.

Lexi

I was hesitant at first to give Liam another chance, but Lillian and Abby convinced me he was deserving of another one. I swear Abby swooned when she heard the story because she said it was "straight out of a romance novel." But honestly, it felt like something straight out of a thriller.

As much as I put up a fight to resist Liam and falling so easily back into his arms, I wasn't really trying all that hard. I never ended up going back to my apartment, and Liam had all my stuff moved into his—sorry, *our*—place.

I've spent a lot of time in the last six months in therapy,

dealing with my trauma with everything that's happened. Dealing with how I feel about Liam. There was a lot of me to work on rebuilding that trust, and eventually, Liam joined me in a few sessions to work on things. But when it all boils down, I love Liam with my whole heart. I love his possessiveness, his playfulness, his seriousness, and everything in between.

I grab the small black leather box out of my purse and snap it open. My grandfather's wedding band proudly sits in the cushions, sparkling in the light. I pluck it out and look inside the band and find my grandparents' initials engraved, "G+A" for George and Arlene, beside the two fresh initials engraved, "L+L."

After everything that happened, I forgot I threw the ring across the room when Liam broke up with me. If I'd have lost it, I might just have lost my mind. I have little left from my parents or grandparents, but the thing I treasure most is my grandfather's ring. A symbol of my grandmother and grandfather's love. His love never wavered or failed, even after my grandmother died. Their marriage, their partnership, is something I've always wanted for myself. And I finally found what I was looking for.

"Are you ready, Luthor?" Lillian nudges me in the ribs with her pointy elbow. I place the ring back in the box, snapping it shut before handing it to Lillian. My cheeks ache from the massive smile on my face, nodding my head. "Are you sure? Because I've scoped out this place and know fifteen ways to sneak out if you need to run, and I've got a guy on standby with a getaway car."

I choke out a laugh, tears springing to my eyes.

"Oh my God, Lil. You're crazy, and I love you for it. Thank you for having my back."

"I'll always have your back. Especially when Liam goes and fucks up again, but this time I'll be kicking his ass." Our laughs peter out, and there's a small pregnant pause. I spread my shaky hands over the skirt of my dress, smoothing out the layers of tulle. "So that's a no to sneaking out then?"

I slap her arm playfully, wiping a stray tear from my eye.

"Of course. I'm marrying Liam today."

Lillian's eyes soften and, if I'm not mistaken, mist up.

"I'm so happy for you, Lexi. He's really a good guy. Your grandparents would be so proud." The tears burn my eyes as I hold them back.

"Stop, right now. If you make me cry and fuck up my makeup, I'll officially hate you forever," I say, my throat bobbing as I try to keep the emotion out of my voice.

LIAM

I've fucked up a lot in my life.

From the time when I was seven and broke my parents' living room window by throwing a baseball through it, to the time when I was thirteen and cheated on a history test and got caught, to the time when I took my dad's Corvette for a joyride when I was fifteen and crashed the car into the garage door trying to sneak it back home at 2 AM. But I'll always regret the biggest fuck up of my life when I broke Lexi's heart.

It took a lot of hard fucking work to gain her trust back. And I wasn't losing her this time without a fight, so I put everything I had into making myself trustworthy again. To be standing here, across from the best woman, the woman I love with my entire soul, is something I'll never take for granted. With her hazel eyes trained on me, glistening with unshed tears of happiness, my heart is bursting with love for her.

"Dearly beloved, we gather here today on this blessed fall day to join Lexi Gardener and Liam West in holy matrimony." As the minister starts the ceremony, I block out the fifty-something guests, the wedding party, the music—everything—until it all just fades away. The only two people in the world right now are Lexi and me. She's all I'll ever need, and I'll be damned if I fuck it up ever again.

I lose myself, and time, as I stare into her beautiful hazel eyes that shine with so much love as she looks at me. Nothing in the world could be more perfect than this moment. She's radiant in her snowy white ball gown that hugs every one of her curves perfectly. The sweetheart neckline bursts with the swell of her large breasts that make my mouth water, wanting to plant kisses all over her chest, and pull her pert nipples into my mouth and suck. I want to tear the fabric from her body and unwrap her like a gift on Christmas morning, letting my mouth and hands explore every inch of her perfect fucking body—

"You may now kiss the bride," the minister rips me from my dirty thoughts. My cock swells, throbbing against the zipper of my pants, and the heat rises from my core and rushes to my face. A small grin settles over my face, trying to mask the situation down below, but as I pull Lexi into my body, she gasps as she feels my hardened cock pressing against her.

Before she can give me a look, I wrap my hand around the back of her neck and crush my lips against hers. I swipe my tongue, parting her lips, and when she parts them, I dive into the kiss deeply. I lick every corner of her mouth and suck on her tongue. My hands run down the length of her body, cupping her ass and pulling it against me.

"Ahem," an embarrassed minister clears his throat. Lexi plants her hands on my chest, pushing me away, our lips making a suctioning noise as she separates from me. Her face is scarlet red, and something deep inside me growls, wishing this was the end of the wedding and we could skip the ceremony and just hole up in our suite for the rest of the night.

"Sorry," Lexi murmurs, her French manicured hand wiping the saliva from the corner of her lips. The minister nods his flushed face, pushing the glasses up his nose as he gathers his wits.

"Introducing the newly married Mr. and Mrs. West," he squeaks out before speeding off.

EPILOGUE

ONE

The moment we crash through the suite door, I'm ripping off the God-awful tie that's been suffocating me all night. My mouth is plastered to Lexi's as I leave a gap between us, flinging the tie across the room and tearing through the buttons on my shirt. Lexi breaks the kiss, stepping away from me, reaching behind her to undo the zipper.

"You better not be doing what I think you're doing," I mutter. A delicious shiver runs down her spine. "That's my dress to undo." A beautiful hue of pink spills on her skin, making my cock grow harder, if that's even possible. She drops her hands from the back of her dress, raising them up in a surrender. A cocky smile teases my lips. "Good girl."

I remove my shirt and make haste with my pants as I toe off my shoes and socks, leaving me standing in front of her in just my black silk boxers. Her eyes glide over me, taking me all in with a hunger in her eyes, and she looks absolutely fucking ravenous as her eyes land on my tented boxers.

I pull my boxers down, letting them fall down around my ankles, and my rock-hard cock bobs in the air. Her tongue flicks out of her lips, sucking the bottom one between her teeth. She finally looks up, her hazel eyes locking on to mine.

"I want to see your pretty little mouth wrapped around my cock while you wear your dress, *wife*." Her breath stutters as she steps closer to me and sinks down to her knees. My cock throbs in front of her face, a bead of pre-cum seeping out of the tiny hole. I sink my hands into her hair, pulling out the pins until her soft blonde hair falls in waves down her back. I run my thumb along her plump, red-stained lips, admiring her beauty.

"Perfect," I murmur. "Fucking perfect."

She leans forward, pressing her lips against the tip of my cock gently, rubbing her lips in the pre-cum like it was lip balm. Her lips part and her warm breath skates over my shaft, sending a shiver down my spine. My hand finds her hair, twirling her soft locks around my wrist and grabbing on.

"Put it in your mouth, dove," I growl. A playful smile dances on Lexi's lips as she moves her mouth around my aching cock, pressing featherlight kisses along my shaft.

Using her tongue, she trails a wet line from the base back to the tip, running it along the prominent vein on the underside. "Fucking tease."

She hums in agreement as her tongue swirls around the tip, flicking it along the ridge of the crown. My hand tightens on her hair, jerking it a little, making her take a sharp breath. The startle fades quickly, and she looks up at me through hooded eyes and with a sly smile.

Lexi leans forward, popping her mouth open into a little *O* as she wraps those fucking beautiful lips around my tip. My eye twitches as her hot, wet mouth takes me in slowly, inch by devastatingly pleasureful inch. Her tongue flattens under my shaft, and she hollows out her cheeks as she moves her head. I release the breath I'm holding when she starts sucking and licking in earnest.

Her hand wraps around the base of my cock, pumping it in rhythm with her mouth, all the while moaning, making my heart race faster.

"Fuck, dove. You look so beautiful with my cock in your mouth."

She pulls me deep into her mouth and I thrust my hips into her, hitting the back of her throat. She swallows, gagging a little, and it feels amazing, making my eyes roll back. Tingles spread rapid fire through my balls up my spine, and I rip myself out of her mouth before I come down her throat. A whine leaves her lips as I pull her to her feet and spin her around. I unzip her and push her dress down until it's pooling at her feet.

Scooping her into my arms, bridal style, I move us over to the bed and lay her down like she's the most delicate thing in the world. I crawl over top of her, crushing my lips to hers in a bruising kiss. Moving my way to her jaw, down her neck, and leaving kisses across every inch of her body. Worshiping her the way she deserves. I'll spend the rest of our lives making sure she knows I'm never leaving her again. Making sure she never doubts my love for her.

I press my fingers to her clit, swirling them around, revving her body up. She purrs while her body writhes under me.

"*Please, Liam*," she whispers.

I continue my ministrations, working her until her breathing is shallow, ragged. I dip a finger in, testing her, seeing just how wet she is, and she's divine. So close, almost ready for me. But first, I need to taste her.

I trail my lips down her stomach, into the dips of her hips, sucking and nipping as I go. My hand palms her breast, gently massaging it and rolling the nipple between my fingers while my mouth makes its way back up to pay attention to her other nipple. I trail my hand down the side of her body, and goosebumps pebble her skin from the gentle touch. Sliding my hand beneath her, I grab her ass and lift it off the mattress slightly.

With my flattened tongue, I slowly lick her slit from bottom to top, dipping my tongue in a little at her entrance, tasting her musky honey juices, and she shudders, moaning. Her hands dive into my hair, gripping the strands tight.

"Oh, Liam," she breathes. I swirl my tongue around in a couple of circles before sucking her throbbing clit into my mouth, her salty-sweet skin on my tastebuds. I flick my tongue on the swollen bud as I slide two fingers into her wet channel, pumping them slowly. Her pussy flutters around my fingers as I curl them, pressing against the spot that makes her scream. I continue to pump my fingers in and out, faster and faster. As she moans louder and her pussy weeps, I rub that spot faster as my mouth sucks her clit harder.

"I'm close." She barely gets the words across her lips because of all her moaning.

"Come for me, dove." I suck a little harder, move my fingers a little faster, press a little harder into her G-spot, and soon she's screaming my name, bursting around my fingers. I lazily lick her as she comes down, and after a few seconds, I withdraw my fingers and position myself between her legs.

I rub the tip of my cock along her soaked entrance, teasing her just a little more. A wolfish smile spreads across my face as I see her flushed skin and heaving chest from being thoroughly fucked with my mouth and fingers. A thrill vibrates through me as I push into her pussy, giddy to watch her face as she comes all over my cock.

"My beautiful wife," I say, sliding into her all the way to the hilt. "You feel so fucking good. I could die right now." And if I died right now, I'd die the happiest man on the earth. "You take my cock so well. You were made for me."

I roll my hips, thrusting into her in long, slow strokes. My abs strain from the controlled rhythm, and my restraint from ramming into her like a wild beast is slowly snapping one strand at a time. Her hands roam my body as her lips kiss down my neck, paying special attention to the scar on my shoulder. I shudder as her lips brush the painful reminder of that night. Her hands trail down my body, grabbing my ass and heaving it closer to her body.

"Fuck me, Liam," she begs, wrapping her legs around my waist, locking her ankles together. Every shred of restraint diminishes, and I rut into her, punishing thrust after punishing thrust. Her pussy sucks me in deeper, and she throws her head back on the pillow, her mouth falling open. She moans my name as her nails dig into my ass, trying to pull me in deeper as if she can't get enough.

I reach between us and press my thumb against her clit, giving her the extra little stimulation she needs, and she shatters around my cock with a scream. Her pussy sucks me hard until I'm sputtering streams of hot cum into her, my cock throbbing inside her. I rest my forehead on hers, our lips millimetres apart and our breaths mingling together.

"I love you, Liam," she whispers against my lips.

"I love you more, dove."

EPILOGUE TWO

The only thing I hate more than incompetent people is how the brunette across the room has been skillfully avoiding me all night. I should be happy my friend got married and focus on celebrating with him and his wonderful wife. But my mind and attention seem to only acknowledge the nerdy, curvy bombshell that fucked me, then fucked me over almost a year ago, and I've never been the same ever since.

Jessie Sinclair will be the death of me.

Since I laid eyes on her again, back in Liam's office months ago, and finally got a name for her, I've been obsessed. There's nothing about her online anywhere. It's like she's a ghost. The only thing known about her is from people that know of her and the whispers of the talented coder, Jessie Sinclair. She slipped through my fingers once, and I won't let it happen again.

She weaves herself through the small crowd on the dance floor at Lexi and Liam's wedding. Her usual brown mess of curls falls in lush, sleek lines down her back, swaying as she walks. Her thick round ass sways a little more when she's wearing those black fuck-me heels compared to her regular broken-in Chucks.

Desire and rage pulse through my veins as I watch her approach the bar. She flags down the bartender, but he's too busy paying attention to the maid of honour to notice her. Seething at his ignorance, I make my way to the bar as sweaty, drunken guests bump into me. I shoulder my way around them, rolling my eyes in annoyance.

As I near her, the pulsing in my blood turns to a boil, igniting my whole body. Her smooth coconut scent wraps around me, and I breathe her into every ounce of capacity my lungs can hold. I sidle up behind her, pressing my body into hers lightly. She responds, shivering deliciously against me, making my cock jump.

"It's a shame a pretty woman like you is being ignored." My lips brush against her ear, and she gasps as my voice rumbles in her ear. She swallows hard before answering, but doesn't dare to look at me.

"It's only a shame that the only person giving me attention right now is you," she quips. She reaches over the bar grabbing a bottle of whisky. The sight of her long fingers wrapping around the neck of the bottle sends flashes of dirty thoughts of what her hand would look like wrapped around my thick cock.

Her hand is steady as she pours the amber liquid to the brim before placing the bottle back on the bar top. She brings the tumbler to her lips, and all sorts of other dirty images cross my mind, and I wonder just what that smart mouth of hers can do.

Fuck, I'm so hard.

"Do you mind?" she asks, sliding a napkin across the bar to me. "At least wipe the drool from your mouth before it drips all over the bar." A smirk tugs at my lips.

"How about I remind you how this mouth makes your pussy drool?"

Red splashes across her face, and her breath lodges in her throat. Her teeth sink into her bottom lip, and I can hear the gears turning in her head to think of a witty comeback, but she shakes her head.

"You're fucking gross." She snorts a laugh. "Go find some other woman tonight who's desperate enough to fall into your bed, because your tricks won't work on me a second time." She swirls the booze around in the tumbler before slamming the rest of it back in one gulp. "Been there, done that. Time to move on."

Something dark shifts inside me. Clenching my jaw, my lips tighten into a thin line. My heart flickers with irritation? Anger? Desire? A nagging little voice inside me taunts me, begging me to have Jessie again. One taste a year ago wasn't enough, and I'll do anything for another. I see through her smart-ass comments and false bravado. She doesn't know it yet, but one day she'll be begging for me to fuck her again, and when that day comes, I'll happily oblige.

"Why are you smiling like that?" she asks, her eyebrows pulling together in confusion. Her chest rising and plummeting. Torn from my thoughts, I reach out and place my fingers underneath her chin, forcing her to look at me. My eyes catch her deep oceanic-blue ones.

"You'll see, *Jessie*. You're not done with me yet, and I'm nowhere near done with you." Stepping closer to her, I bury my nose in her hair and breathe in deeply. I can practically hear her heart thudding in her chest and feel the flutter of her pulse. As I straighten, I adjust my suit jacket before walking away, feeling her burning gaze on my back, smirking as I leave the wedding. I always get what I want. And what I want is another night with Jessie. To fuck her out of my system and return to my peaceful life.

ACKNOWLEDGEMENTS

A big, heartfelt thank you to all my readers. None of this could be possible without you. Thank you for continuously being part of my journey and reading my novels. It's been a lifelong dream, and to say that my FIRST series is FINISHED is unreal! I have lots of series planned that I think you're going to love. Obviously, epilogue two gave us a sneak peek into the next series…Kings of Finance.

To my amazing team of beta readers: Kim, Jenna, Maricella, Bree, Calista, Selene, and Claire. Thank you for all your time and feedback and making this story what it is today. I hope you loved Liam and Lexi as much as I did. I appreciate each and every comment, edit, and thought you put into your feedback. You are truly amazing. Words cannot express how lucky I am to have you in my corner rooting for me.

To Laura, my cover designer. You killed it again. What can I say? You're spectacular. Thank you for being you and being able to make exactly what I'm thinking in my head and seeing my vision with me.

To my editors, Kay & Danielle, thank you for all the hard work you put into making this the best version. I appreciate all your concerns, feedback, and attention to detail. You ladies are amazing and very talented at what you do. Thank you so much.

And lastly, to my friends and family. Thank you for your unwavering support whether you read my novels or just bought them to support me. I don't think I would have made it this far without you. Thank you for helping me believe in myself and helping me to gain the confidence to actually call myself an author (because for those of you that know, imposter syndrome is real).

xx,
Kate

ABOUT THE AUTHOR

Kate Smoak lives with her husband, daughter, and fur babies in a small town in Ontario, Canada. When she's not writing, she can be found curling up with a good book, playing video games, or camping at the trailer with her family.

Instagram: @katesmoakwrites
Twitter: @katesmoakwrites
Website: www.katesmoak.ca

If you enjoyed this book, it would mean
the world to me if you would leave a review.
Reviews are like tips for authors.

For more goodies and exclusive content,
please sign up for my newsletter!